The Laura Black Scottsdale Mystery Series

Books by
B A Trimmer

~~~~

The Laura Black
Scottsdale Mystery Series

Scottsdale Heat

Scottsdale Squeeze

Scottsdale Sizzle

Scottsdale Scorcher

Scottsdale Sting

Scottsdale Shuffle

Scottsdale Shadow

Scottsdale Secret

Scottsdale Silence

Scottsdale Scandal

Scottsdale Sleuth

Scottsdale Spy

~~~~

The Aloha Lagoon
Mystery Series

Hula Homicide

Homicide Honeymoon

Scottsdale Sting

Scottsdale Sting

B A TRIMMER

Editors: 'Andi' Anderson and Kimberly Mathews
Composite cover art and cover design by Janet Holmes using images under license from Shutterstock.com and Depositphotos.com.

ISBN-13: 978-1-951052-06-5

Saguaro Sky Media Co.

060125pb

E-mail the author at LauraBlackScottsdale@gmail.com
Follow at www.facebook.com/ScottsdaleSeries/

To Tammy,
for always being there with
soft words of encouragement

*Thanks to Andi, Kimberly Mathews,
Barbara Hackel, Jeanette Ellmer, and
Bonnie Costilow for their help
and encouragement.*

Scottsdale Sting

Introduction

If you've never read a Laura Black Scottsdale mystery, you can start with *Scottsdale Heat*, the first book in the series. If you'd rather start with this book, here are a few of the people you'll need to know:

Laura Black – Laura grew up in Arizona and currently works as an investigator in a Scottsdale law firm. She'd love to make the world a better place, but she also has bills to pay.

Jackson Reno – Reno is a detective for the Scottsdale Police Department and Laura's boyfriend. Reno's frustrated with Laura's constant need to involve herself with shady people and dangerous situations.

Sophia Rodriguez – Laura's best friend who works in the law office as the receptionist and paralegal. She sometimes gets to help Laura in her investigations. Sophie is a former California surfer chick and a free spirit who enjoys dating multiple men simultaneously.

Gina Rondinelli – Laura's other best friend. She's a former Scottsdale police detective and the law firm's senior investigator. She has a strict moral code and prefers to play by the rules.

Leonard Shapiro – Lenny is head of the law firm. He has no people skills but with the help of Laura, Sophie, and Gina, he usually wins his cases.

Anthony "Tough Tony" DiCenzo – Head of the local crime family. Through events over the last few months, he now owes Laura several favors. She's saved his life more than once, and he's grown very fond and protective of her.

Maximilien – The number-two man in the local crime family. He's attracted to Laura and would like to take the relationship further. Laura feels the same way, but she can't go beyond a close, flirtatious friendship while she's still with Reno.

Gabriella – A former government operative from somewhere in Eastern Europe. She currently works as a bodyguard for Tough Tony. She takes pleasure in hurting men.

Grandma Peckham – Laura's longtime neighbor who's recently decided it's time to start dating men again. Lately, she's been dating a man called Grandpa Bob.

The Cougars – A group of wealthy, sexy, and fashionable women who like to troll the clubs of Scottsdale looking for athletic younger men for hook-up relationships. Through a series of adventures, Laura, Sophie, and Gina have become unofficial members of their group.

Chapter One

"I have a problem."

I saw him mouthing the words, but my mind was racing, and nothing registered.

"Hello," he said, waving a hand in front of my face. "I have a problem. Can you help me?"

"Ah, okay, sure," I heard myself say.

I looked over at Sophie. She looked up from her desk with a glazed look in her eyes. I'm sure I looked much the same.

I glanced back at the beautiful man standing in the office reception area, and my heart started pounding again. However, my brain still hadn't caught up with what my eyes were seeing.

The man had a look of frustrated acceptance on his face. Apparently, he'd been through this scenario many times before.

"You're Stig Stevens," Sophie said with a dreamy and distant tone to her voice. "You're *The Hammer*. I've seen all of your movies. You're amazing."

The man sighed and took a deep breath. "Yes," he said in his unique Eastern European accent. "I'm Stig Stevens, but I still need your help. I need to speak with Leonard Shapiro right away. It's very urgent."

"Um, unfortunately, he's in court this morning," I said. "He won't be back until later this afternoon. Maybe we can help."

Stig Stevens looked down at Sophie and then over at me. I could tell he was having his doubts.

"Could there be two attorneys in Scottsdale named Leonard Shapiro?" he asked. "I've probably got the wrong one."

"Nope," Sophie said. "There's only one, and you're in his office."

Stig sighed with acceptance. "Fine. I need to discuss an important legal issue with Leonard. He was recommended as being the best attorney in Scottsdale. It's something very confidential, and I need to talk with him as soon as possible."

"Well," I ventured. "If you're looking to hire Lenny, we could set you up as a client of the firm. Then, we'd also be covered by the attorney-client privilege. I'm one of the investigators here, and Sophie's the paralegal. You could tell us what you need, and we could get a start on it."

"I'm not sure attorney-client privilege works that way," Stig said, but Sophie had already pulled out a standard contract and started filling in the blank spaces.

"Here," she said as she finished the first page and handed it to him to sign while filling in the second page. "I loved you in *Hammer Fall*. I think that was my favorite."

Stig hesitated a moment, picked up a pen from Sophie's desk, and signed the document. He then signed the next three pages and initialed several more.

Sophie already had her stamp out and was notarizing even

as Stig was signing. She then pulled her register from her desk and opened it.

"Um, it's not like I don't know who you are," Sophie said. "But I'll need some ID for the notary book. Almost anything official with your picture on it will work."

Stig reached into his pocket and came up empty. He then patted himself down, searching his pockets in vain.

"Shit, I didn't bring my wallet. Hold on, I've got my passport in the Hummer."

He went out the front door, and the office became very quiet. Sophie and I looked at each other and started laughing.

"Gina's not going to believe we had Stig Stevens in the office," Sophie said. "She's going to shit kittens when she finds out she missed him."

Stig returned and handed Sophie his passport. Her hands shook slightly as she took it and jotted down the information in the notary book. She looked down at the passport, then reluctantly handed it back.

"Okay, you're now a client of the firm," I said. "How can we help you?"

Stig frowned. "It's something you need to see in person to get the full impact. Come with me if you want to see what's going on. As soon as Leonard comes in, we'll need to work with him on an appropriate response."

"Okay," I said. "Show us."

"It's over at my house. If you're the investigator, I'll drive you."

I heard Sophie making a noise and looked over to see her pleading with her eyes.

"That's a good idea," I said. "But we should probably take

Sophie too. She often spots things I miss."

"Fine," he said. "Bring whoever you need, but I need to have this taken care of right away."

He looked down at Sophie. "My vehicle is big, but it only has two seats. Take your car and follow us. Do you know where I live? It's off of Yucca Road and Cameldale Way."

Sophie nodded her head. Even in a city full of luxury homes, Stig Stevens had one of the biggest and most famous.

I went back to my office, gathered up my things, and returned to reception. I followed Stig out the front door to the street.

Sophie locked the door behind us, then headed out the back to her yellow Volkswagen convertible in the alley behind the office.

Stig and I walked half a block down the street to a huge army-style Hummer, painted in desert camouflage, which was taking up two parking spaces. I looked at the license plate and wasn't surprised it read *HAMMER*.

We climbed in, and he started it up. The vehicle throbbed with power as he backed out of the parking spaces. Sophie came around the corner, and we all headed to Stig Stevens' house.

~~~

My name is Laura Black. I'm a Scottsdale native and grew up in the Granite Reef section of what is now unofficially called South Scottsdale.

I got both a degree and a husband at Arizona State University, which is in Tempe, about five miles to the south. Until three years ago, I'd been married and working as a bartender at a place called Greasewood Flat.

When the marriage ended, I decided I needed to do

something different. Sophie suggested I apply for the open investigator position at Halftown, Oeding, Shapiro, & Hopkins, the downtown Scottsdale law firm where she worked as the admin and paralegal.

I got the job and have worked there ever since. So far, I've managed to stumble my way through it without getting fired.

It pays the bills, but I don't think I'll make a career out of it. The hours are worse than bartending, and I've been threatened with bodily harm more than once.

The only thing that makes it worthwhile is sometimes I can really help someone who's in a tight spot. That alone seems to make the rest of it feel worthwhile.

~~~~

Stig drove the big Hummer north on Scottsdale Road to McDonald Drive. He then turned west, and three minutes later, we came to Cameldale Way.

Here, he turned south toward the high-dollar mega mansions nestled against the northeast side of Camelback Mountain. I'd only been in this neighborhood a couple of times over the years, but each time I'd been impressed.

Even though this is the part of the city where property values are the absolute highest, each of the houses sits on several acres. I guess when you're living in a house like this, you don't want to know you even have neighbors.

As we neared his estate, Stig pushed a button on the dashboard, and a black gate in a high-security fence swung open. We turned onto a narrow driveway that wound up to the base of Camelback Mountain.

We drove through a beautiful park-like setting for almost two hundred yards before coming to a stop at a paved courtyard in front of a huge house. A red Ferrari, a purple Maserati, and an orange McLaren were parked in front of a detached garage that had six sets of double doors. As Stig parked the Hummer between the sports cars, Sophie's Volkswagen came to a stop behind us.

The house was as big as Muffy Sternwood's, maybe bigger, and was beautiful. Its colors were artfully designed to complement the surrounding mountains and desert, and the landscaping was equal to anything found at the golf resorts.

"Holy shit," Sophie said as she got out of the car and looked up at the mansion. "It's huge."

"Come on," Stig said. "This won't take long."

He led us over to the set of double entrance doors. Each was at least nine feet high and five feet across. He punched a string of numbers into a control pad next to the door, and a light on the panel switched from red to green.

From inside the door came a metallic snapping sound as the internal locking mechanism released. Stig opened the massive door, and we went inside.

"Holy shit," Sophie said again as we stepped into the foyer.

A set of curved marble stairs wound up on either side of the massive space to an upper-floor balcony. The walls were covered in dark wood paneling, and thick marble columns supported the ceiling.

A sparkling chandelier, probably ten feet across, hung down from the high ceiling. The marble floor was so shiny it acted sort of like a mirror, making the space look even bigger and making me glad I wasn't wearing a skirt.

Whenever I'm in a home this big, it always seems more like a hotel than a house. I couldn't imagine actually living in something this large.

Stig led us through a central archway, then down a hallway that opened onto an interior atrium. This led down to a lava rock wall and tropical foliage display set next to a hotel-sized indoor-outdoor pool.

The far wall of the atrium had a large glass panel with a water passage separating the inside part of the pool from the outside. The way the space was designed reminded me a little of the lobby of the Tropical Paradise.

Thinking of that reminded me of Max, and I felt a brief pang of sadness.

As we got closer to the pool, Stig looked down at the water and hesitated. He seemed to be searching for something, and when he didn't find it, he went through an ornate wooden door with a large stained-glass panel that connected to the outside patio.

Sophie looked at me and shrugged her shoulders. We followed him through the door.

The patio and the areas surrounding the outside portion of the pool were immaculate. The terrace appeared to have been professionally landscaped in a desert oasis theme with pigmy date palms, sago palms, and trimmed bougainvillea scattered around it. A cabana sat next to the pool with an outdoor kitchen, a stainless-steel barbeque grill, and a large TV mounted to the wall.

The pool itself was blue and inviting. It had a negative-edge feature, bordered on each side by a huge queen palm, and looked out over a magnificent view of north Scottsdale and the McDowell Mountains beyond.

Stig walked over to the edge of the pool and again stared down into it. He looked up at us with a trace of panic in his eyes.

"What's wrong?" I asked.

"An hour and a half ago, there was a body in the pool. A dead body. Now it's gone."

Sophie looked up, and her eyes were big. "A dead body? Are you serious? Holy shit!"

~~~~

Ten minutes later, we returned to the courtyard in front of the house. Stig was shaken by the events of the last couple of hours, and he looked a little lost.

"Look," I said. "You aren't a doctor. We'll need to check with Lenny, but legally, I don't think you can be expected to determine if it was a dead body in your pool or not. It could have been someone alive floating in your pool, and they only looked dead, or it could have been a dummy someone threw in as a joke."

"That would be a pretty sick fucking joke if someone did that," Sophie said.

"I might not be a doctor," Stig said. "But it looked pretty dead to me."

"Tell me about the body," I said. "Was it a man or a woman?"

"It was a man," Stig said. "He was face down, but he appeared to be about my size, somewhere in his forties or fifties."

"White, black, Hispanic?"

"White, I think. The body was floating inside the house next to the glass that separates the inside part of the pool from the outside. I didn't get too close, but from where I was standing, he was sort of purple and a little blotchy."

Sophie started making a sound like Marlowe coughing up a hairball. "Excuse me," she said and disappeared back into the house.

"The deck area around the pool looked pretty wet," I said. "Was it like that when you saw the person in the pool?"

"I don't remember. Once I saw the body, it's all I focused on."

"Tell me about your movements last night and this morning. How did you find the body, and what were you doing before then?"

"I came downstairs about nine. Before that, I'd been asleep. I woke up at about eight, took a shower, and got dressed. I was coming downstairs to make myself some breakfast."

"What about last night?" I asked.

"I had a party here. There were maybe twenty-five or thirty people. A dozen people came over early to watch the Cardinals game. By six o'clock, most of the people were here for cocktails. By ten, everyone was either dancing or in the pool. They'd mostly cleared out by one or one-thirty, and that's when the rest of my staff went home. I left a few of the stragglers down here to keep going, and I went up to bed."

"Were any of your staff here before you got up? Perhaps they saw something?"

"No, I always give everyone Mondays off. It's sort of a tradition from back when things were more active here on the weekends. I'll have people here again starting tomorrow."

"Do you have any security cameras? Either inside or outside?"

"No. When I had the house built, it was before you could have cameras broadcast to your computer or phone. Everything back then ran on videotape. It seemed like more of a headache than it was worth, and I've never gotten around to putting in a new system."

"Alright," I said. "Let's go back and talk with Lenny. Then he can figure out the best way to handle this."

~~~~

Sophie took off in her car while Stig and I drove back into Old Town Scottsdale together. We looked for two adjoining parking spaces, but when we only found one open space in front of an art gallery, Stig parked there anyway, the Hummer halfway up on the sidewalk.

"Won't you get a ticket for doing that?" I asked.

"Before today, would you have known who this Hummer belongs to?"

"Well, sure. There aren't many original Army Hummers painted like this with a license plate that says *HAMMER*."

"The Scottsdale police also know who it belongs to. I love driving it, but it's so big I usually end up parking like this. I do a lot of charity events around Scottsdale – many of them for the police. I've never gotten a ticket."

We got out and walked down the block to the office. Sophie had already unlocked the front door and was holding it open for us. We walked into reception in time to hear Lenny yelling out from his office.

"Sophie, you can't take off and leave the office unattended. What if a new client had showed up and wanted to hire us?"

"Um, Lenny," I said. "Could you come out here for a moment?"

"What?" he shouted.

"We did get a new client today," Sophie said.

"Oh, really? Who is it?" Lenny stuck his head out of his office and saw Stig Stevens standing next to us. It took a few seconds for his brain to process who he was seeing.

The look on his face was easy to read. First, it was confusion, then recognition at seeing a famous movie star, and finally, a look that was uniquely Lenny.

12

It was the look of a man calculating how much to charge a wealthy client per hour. Lenny quickly composed himself and walked up to Stig, his hand outstretched, his smooth lawyer persona going.

"Stig Stevens," Lenny said without a trace of being starstruck. "Leonard Shapiro. It's a real pleasure to meet you. I'm a big fan. *Hammer Down* is one of my all-time favorites. How can we help you today?"

"Mr. Stevens is a new client of the firm," I said.

I saw the questioning look Lenny gave me.

"A *signed* new client of the firm," I said. "We were over at his house this morning, and we'd like to talk to you about some issues that arose."

"Very well," Lenny said. "Let's go into my office and discuss this in more detail."

Stig, Sophie, and I followed Lenny into his office. With a glance from Lenny, Sophie went to the wet bar on the far wall, pulled out two glasses, and started dropping ice cubes in each.

"Stig," Lenny asked. "What will you have to drink?"

"After everything that's happened today, a Jack Daniel's would be great," he said. "You might want to make it a double."

Sophie poured a double Jack for Stig and a Beam on the rocks for Lenny. Then she handed out the drinks. We all sat while Stig took a couple of long sips, then Lenny started the meeting.

"Alright, Stig," he said. "How can we help you?"

"As I've already discussed with Laura and Sophie, this morning, when I came downstairs in my house, there was a dead body floating in my pool. When we went there to look at it about an hour ago, it was gone."

Lenny put up a hand to stop him. "How do you know what you saw was a dead body? You aren't a medical doctor, and I assume you have no formal medical training. Did you perform any sort of hands-on examination? You may have seen something floating in your pool, but from a strictly legal standpoint, it doesn't necessarily mean it was a dead body."

Sophie glanced at me and smiled. I caught the mental high-five.

"I didn't examine him at all," Stig said. "But from the edge of the pool, he appeared to be a male in his forties or fifties, and he looked to be dead. He was floating face down, so I didn't get a good look at him. I knew a dead body in my pool would be serious trouble, both from a legal and a PR standpoint, so I called a friend of mine and asked who the best criminal attorney in Scottsdale was. She said it was you, and I drove straight over."

Lenny nodded with a look I'm sure he's practiced in the mirror. It was a look of concern mixed with sympathy. Two emotions I knew Lenny didn't possess. "If I could ask, who did you call?"

"It was Margaret Sternwood," Stig said. "We serve together on several charity boards. She says you're the best."

"Of course," Lenny said. "We helped her out with an issue earlier this year. Yes, we'll be glad to look into it. We'll need to track down the body – who it was, the circumstances of the death, if there was a death that is, and most importantly, who killed him and who removed him from your pool. If we find evidence that a crime occurred at your house, we'll represent you when we notify the police. We'll also need to review your security arrangements. If it's possible someone could commit a murder in your home while you were asleep, we can assume you aren't safe. We'll need to take steps to ensure you're protected."

"It's not the first break-in I've had recently. Last week, when I was at a charity event, someone broke a window and went through the house. The staff apparently scared him away before he could take anything."

"Did you report the break-in to the police?"

"No. Nothing was missing, and until now, I thought it was probably a fan. Now, I'm not sure. As you may know, public image is critical for me. If TMZ finds out my house was broken into, it'll rate a two-minute news story. If they find out a dead body was floating in my pool, it could quickly turn into a public relations nightmare. I've already called my manager, Jerry Phifer. I'll also need to call my publicist and let her know what happened. She's responsible for my image."

"Who is that?" Lenny asked.

"Jeanette Simmons," Stig said. "She's a partner at *JBC-RDS*. They're based out of Los Angeles, and they handle a lot of Hollywood A-list clients. I'll make an introduction."

Lenny got a strange look on his face, but whatever was bothering him quickly passed. "Alright," he said. "I'd like to get started on this right away. Let me ask you a few questions. Before this morning, when was the last time you looked at your pool and verified there was no one floating in it, either alive or dead?"

"It was last night. I had a party at the house for about twenty-five or thirty people. We spent the last couple of hours on the patio and in the pool. Most of the people had left by one or one-thirty. At about one-thirty, I went to bed."

"And where were you from one-thirty this morning until you found whatever it was in the pool?"

"In my bedroom, asleep."

"Can anyone verify that? Were you alone, or was someone with you?"

"I was alone. A few people carried on downstairs after I went to bed, but they were gone when I woke up. The staff took off about one. They won't be back until tomorrow."

"Alright, I'll need the names of everyone at the party, and I'll especially need to know who stayed after you went to bed." Lenny paused to take a sip of his bourbon.

"Now then, for the moment, let's assume the thing you saw in the pool was indeed a person. Tell me what you observed. You said it looked to be a man in his forties or fifties, and he was floating face down."

"The age is only a guess based on the size and shape of the body."

"What else could you tell about him?"

"He appeared to be white and maybe six feet two or three."

"Skinny, fat?"

"I would say athletic, but again, from the back, it was hard to tell."

"How was he dressed?"

"He had on a navy sports coat and tan pants. I don't remember seeing any shoes. He had short brown hair."

"Did he look like anyone who was at the party last night?"

Stig thought about it for a moment. "No, none of the men looked like that. This guy was as big as I am, plus I was the only one at the party who was wearing a jacket. Everyone else was dressed in short sleeves."

"Okay," Lenny said. "Last question. Any rings, watches, or other jewelry you can remember seeing on the body?"

Stig shook his head. "No. I guess I'm not going to be very helpful with that."

"It doesn't matter at this stage," Lenny said. "Laura will

look into it. I might have another investigator assist her. Her name is Gina Rondinelli and she spent several years as a detective with the Scottsdale Police Department. With their help, we'll get this sorted out. We'll start digging on our end right away. If you'll be available later this afternoon, Laura will probably need to talk to you to get some more information."

"I should be home most of the afternoon," Stig said.

The meeting ended with handshakes. We then went out to reception, where Stig confirmed his contact information, including his personal phone number and email. He then left through the front door.

"Damn," Sophie said. "It's not every day a famous movie star comes in and drags us over to his house to show us a dead body. Kinda disappointing when it wasn't there."

She looked at me. "How come you're the only one who gets to find the dead bodies? It's like you attract them or something. I'd like to find one, too."

"I don't attract them, and trust me, finding them isn't as much fun as it sounds. We'd still be filling out forms for the police."

Lenny seemed pleased but not as excited as I expected him to be.

"Give him a couple of hours to calm down and then re-interview him," he said. "See if he's been able to keep his story straight. Keep me up-to-date on what you find out. Although, I'll be surprised if you come up with anything at all. There's something wrong with this."

"I don't know," Sophie said. "He seemed pretty sincere when he showed up this morning."

"Of course, he sounded sincere," Lenny said. "He's an actor. That's what they do. But dead bodies don't suddenly show up in a pool in a wealthy man's house and then disappear again all by themselves."

"Why would he do this if it wasn't true?" I asked.

"I'm not sure," Lenny said. "But keep in mind it's been a few years since he had a big hit. He's an action hero, and it's getting harder to hide the fact that he's almost sixty. It wouldn't shock me if he's using us to stir up some publicity for his next picture. Isn't a new one coming out in a couple of weeks?"

"How would he use us?" I asked.

"I don't know yet," Lenny said. "Sophie, take a look in the tabloids. See if there're reports in any of them that Stig Stevens is fearful for his life or getting death threats, anything like that. Maybe something about police being called in to investigate a break-in or that Stig has a crazed female stalker; it could be anything. If so, don't be surprised if it also says there's a Scottsdale law firm checking into it. There'd need to be something like that to give the story an air of credibility."

"Not a problem," Sophie agreed. "I'll round up all I can find."

Lenny thought for a moment, then looked at me. "On the off chance you do find something, get Gina involved. Running a homicide investigation is what she's trained to do. She can be our liaison with the police if it gets that far. If we find anything, we'll also need to coordinate with Stig's agent and publicist. They'll get pissy if we don't."

"If the story's bogus, wouldn't the agent and publicist be in on it?" I asked. "Besides, if you didn't believe his story, why did you agree to keep him as a client?"

"There didn't seem to be a downside for us, and you said he'd already signed the client agreement." Lenny looked at Sophie. "What discount off the standard rate did you give him?"

"Nothing," Sophie said. "He was in a hurry."

"Full rate?" The corners of Lenny's mouth curled up in a smirky smile. "Nice. I haven't been able to charge the full hourly rate since Margaret Sternwood came in here, and that must have been nine or ten months ago."

"You could have gotten the full rate from Suzi Lu," I said. "She wouldn't have thought twice about it."

Lenny got a look of shock on his face. "What? Are you nuts? I'd been hearing about *Mistress McNasty* for ten years. I wasn't going to scare her out of the office before the case even started."

He looked at Sophie. "While you're at it, run a report on the publicist. Let's see if this is as bad as I think it is."

Lenny went back into his office just as Sophie's phone rang with Danielle's ringtone. Hearing it made my stomach clench.

I'd met her a month and a half ago while working on an assignment. Since then, she'd become friends with both Sophie and Gina.

She'd started out as my friend too, but then I found out she was the daughter of Escobar Salazar, worldwide head of a vicious drug cartel called the Black Death. After the death of Carlos the Butcher, Danielle began secretly running all criminal activity in Arizona through a man named Sergio.

Unfortunately, I'd promised to keep this knowledge to myself. I knew if I didn't keep my promise, the people I love most in the world would be hurt, or worse.

Sophie answered the phone and spent several minutes laughing and speaking to Danielle in Spanish. When she got off the phone, she looked at me. "I set up a dinner with Danielle for Friday night after work. Hopefully, Gina's free. Danielle asked if you'd be available to come along too."

"I don't know," I said. "With this new assignment, I'm not

sure what will happen."

"What gives? It's been weeks since you've gone out with us. Probably not since the day we got rid of Amber. I think Danielle's noticed it, too. She said she was going to call and invite you herself."

As if on cue, my phone rang with Danielle's ringtone, the old Eurythmics song, *Would I Lie to You?* I walked into the back offices and answered.

"Laura," Danielle said. "It's good to talk to you again. Sophie, Gina, and I are going out to dinner on Friday. I hope you'll come with us."

"Danielle," I said, keeping my voice down so no one could overhear. "I'm keeping my promise, and I won't ever say anything, but you know we can't be friends."

"I hope you'll change your mind. You were the one who introduced me to Sophie and Gina. They'll start to wonder what's wrong if you keep avoiding me. There are all sorts of ways to break a promise other than openly talking about it."

"Fine, I'll go to dinner with you, but I'm not sure how happy I'll be able to act."

"Good, that's a start. I honestly like you, Laura. You were the first real friend I made in Arizona, and I'm genuinely sorry that work has come between us. Oh, I'm restarting negotiations with Max in a few days. I'll want you to let me know Max's reactions to what we propose."

"I don't know how I can do that. I haven't talked with him in a month. Now that he's taken over the group, he won't even see me."

"Of course, he'll see you. My informants report he's not romantically involved with anyone else."

At that, my heart sped up a bit. "Alright, let me know when

you start the negotiations. I'll try to get together with him and ask him about the talks. Of course, he might not even want to meet with me. He seemed pretty definite about it the last time I talked to him."

"He'll see you," Danielle said. "I can almost guarantee it."

~~~~

I hung up with Danielle and went up front. Gina had come in while I was on the phone, and Sophie was in the middle of telling her all about our day with Stig Stevens.

"You should have seen it," Sophie said. "I've never been in a house that nice. It was almost as big as Elizabeth's. I could get used to living somewhere like that. Of course, I'd need plenty of servants. One to cook and a couple to clean. I'd want my house to be spotless for when all my rich friends dropped by. Maybe I'd need a full-time pool boy who'd spend all day bringing me drinks and giving me massages."

"You said there was a dead body?" Gina asked.

"I said we went over there to *look* at a dead body," Sophie said. "It was supposed to be floating in the pool, but when we got there, it was gone."

Gina raised an eyebrow and looked at me.

"That's what he said. He woke up, went downstairs, and there was a dead guy floating in his pool. He knows Margaret Sternwood, and he called her to see which lawyer she would recommend. Muffy told him about Lenny. Stig came down to the office, and we signed him up as a client. When we went to his house to look at the dead body, it was gone."

"Well?" Gina asked, looking at me. "What do you think?"

"Lenny doesn't think there was ever a dead body," I said. "He thinks we're being set up as part of a publicity scheme to get some buzz going about Stig's new movie. I'm not sure I agree with him. It seems strange that Stig Stevens would drive over to a lawyer to show him a dead body if there wasn't a dead body. I don't think you could make something like that up."

"Yeah," Sophie said. "But who would kill someone in the middle of the night, then come back the next day to move the body? Why wouldn't you move him right away if you didn't want a dead body to be found floating in the pool?"

"I don't know, but it did seem kind of wet on the deck around the pool. I don't know if it was wet from the party the night before or from the body coming out."

"What?" Sophie asked. "Are you saying the dead guy came back to life and crawled out of the pool? Sorta like the Walking Dead?"

"No, what I'm saying is, none of this makes sense."

~~~~

I spent the next hour in my cubicle finishing up the paperwork on a cheating spouse assignment I'd been working on for the last two weeks. I walked up and gave Sophie the folder.

She took it and put it on top of a stack of folders waiting to be filed. I looked around and noticed there were several other stacks of file folders on the tables and even a stack on one of the chairs.

"You aren't ever going to file those, are you?" I asked.

"Nope. If I file them, Lenny won't have a reason to hire a new admin. If he sees the stacks of files, maybe hiring someone will rise to the top of his list."

I glanced at the clock and saw it was already three o'clock. I went back to my cubicle and called Stig at the number he'd given Sophie. He answered right away.

I was still amazed and sort of in shock that I could pick up

22

the phone and actually call Stig Stevens. I asked if we could get together, and he said he'd be at his house for the next two hours or so. I let him know I'd be over in twenty minutes.

I grabbed my purse and went out the rear security door to the covered parking in the back alley. As I walked to my car, I broke out in a smile. For the past month, I'd been smiling whenever I drove.

After nine years of driving a reliable but uninspiring vehicle, I now had a new car. Well, it's not exactly new, but it's close enough for me.

I pushed the button on my key fob, and the lights blinked on a silver Mercedes SL convertible. I opened the door and settled myself into the comfortable leather seat.

I turned the key and felt the deep-throated hum as the huge engine fired up. I backed out into the alleyway and hit the button to open the power roof, then sat there for fifteen or twenty seconds, taking in the fact that I now owned such an amazing car.

I looked through a pile of old CDs I'd tossed on the passenger seat, opened one by Tori Amos, and shoved it in the CD player. It was a beautiful day in Arizona, and driving through Scottsdale in my new car couldn't help but put me in a good mood.

Chapter Two

I got to Stig's house and made it as far as the driveway. There was a camera intercom unit and a keypad on a post in front of the gate.

I pushed the buzzer. When no one answered, I pressed it again. After waiting about a minute, I called Stig on my phone.

"Hi, Stig, it's Laura Black. I'm at your front gate. I buzzed, but no one answered."

"Sorry, the staff has Monday off, and I'm in the back. The code to the gate is eleven, fifteen, ninety-two. I'll head to the front and meet you at the door."

I punched in the code. The indicator light switched from red to green, and the big gate silently swung open.

I drove up the drive and parked in the courtyard next to the purple Maserati convertible. There was a Tesla Model S I hadn't seen earlier.

The license plate read *Agent-1*. By the time I walked to the double front doors, Stig had them open and let me in.

~~~~

I walked in, and the house was still as grand as it seemed

the first time. Stig asked me if I wanted a drink.

I declined, and he led me down some stairs, then along a very long white hallway that ended in a formal library and music room.

The large rectangular room had a high ceiling, thick carpet, and dark wood molding. Floor-to-ceiling bookshelves lined the walls on both sides of the room, and against the front wall was a slightly raised stage.

The walls were lined with signed tour posters of Metallica, Guns & Roses, and AC/DC. The stage held a rack of keyboards and several music stands.

An electric guitar and bass were racked next to two amplifiers. Scattered in front of the stage sat a grouping of several black leather love seats and couches.

It looked like a place where people regularly got together to play. A man stood next to one of the bookshelves and turned as we approached.

"Laura, I'd like you to meet my manager, Jerry Phifer," Stig said. "Jerry and I go way back to my days as a martial arts instructor. He walked me through the process of coming to America and got me my first movie deal."

Jerry switched the drink he was holding from his right hand to his left. When we shook hands, his hands felt cold and slimy. He was a nervous-looking man, about sixty years old, with slightly bloodshot eyes and long black hair slicked back in a hoodlum style.

As I looked at him, I couldn't help but notice one of his eyes didn't focus on one place but instead seemed to move around at random. I knew I was being rude, but it was so strange I couldn't help but stare.

"Oh," Stig said with a laugh. "Jerry's nickname is Crazy-Eye. I guess you can see why."

"I wasn't always like this," Jerry said, pointing to his eye. "About ten years ago, I got into a fight with a jealous husband and got smacked in the head pretty good. I know it looks creepy as shit. I tried wearing a pirate's eyepatch but lost my depth perception. The weird thing is, my brain shuts out any extraneous information, and I can still see in three dimensions."

"Don't worry," Stig said. "You get used to looking at it. I figured you'd be working with Jerry, so it was best you meet him right away."

"Thanks," I said. "I have a few questions about last night, but before I get started, do you have the list of everyone who was at the party and who stayed after you went to bed?"

"Yeah," Jerry said, handing me three pages stapled together. "Stig and I have been putting it together. We might have missed one or two, but I think we got them all. We also included their phone numbers, so please don't lose the list. Some of the people would freak out if their numbers became public."

"It seems sort of strange you'd let people party at your house without supervision," I said.

"It's an old habit," Stig said. "Back a few years ago, the party would have started with cocktails on Saturday and gone on until Sunday night. I halfway expected to find one or two people asleep somewhere when I came downstairs this morning. Instead, I found a dead guy floating in the pool."

I glanced at the list and counted twenty-eight people. Some of the names were familiar, including Jackie Wade.

"Jackie Wade was here? The owner of the Saguaro Sky Resort?"

"Yes, I met her a few months ago when we had a charity event at the Saguaro Sky. She went all-out for the event, and she seemed to be a nice person. She was a pleasant change from some of the resort managers I sometimes work with. I don't think she stayed after dinner, or at least I don't remember seeing her dancing or in the pool."

I held up the list. "Who stayed after you went to bed?"

"It was Jerry, Luther, Vicky, Christine, and her new boyfriend," Stig said.

I gave him a look that must have shown what I was thinking.

"No, I trust them all. We've all known each other forever. Well, except for Christine's new boyfriend, but I knew she'd keep an eye on him. I have no problem with any of them hanging out at the house when I'm not here."

I looked down the list, and my eyes grew wide. "The Christine who stayed is the singer Christine Johns?"

"That's right," Stig said. "She has a house east of Camelback Mountain about a mile from here. She's in between projects, and I always invite her over. I don't know much about her boyfriend. He plays in a band, I think."

Stig's phone rang, and he looked at the number. "It's Jeanette," he said to Jerry. "After I get off the phone with her, I'll probably need to call Sterling. You two get acquainted, and I'll be right back."

He then headed out into the hallway, and we heard his low voice as he talked on the phone.

"Sterling and Jeanette?" I asked Jerry, trying not to stare at his eye. It was hard not to since it seemed to have a mind of its own, staying steady for a few seconds, then going haywire and randomly darting around the room.

"Jeanette does publicity, and Sterling's the studio handler. You'll probably get to meet them both."

"You stayed at the party after Stig went up to bed?"

"Yeah," Jerry said. "It was Me, Luther Wilcox, Vicky, Christine Johns, and her latest boyfriend, Nails. It sounds like you already know about Christine. She's the singer for Paradise Park."

"Sure, I know Christine Johns. Paradise Park's a great band. I went to see them in Phoenix a few years ago when they were on a reunion tour. But, Nails?"

"Yeah, he's the bass player for One Dimension. He's probably twenty years younger than Christine, but what the hell. He's from London, and the guy's funny as shit."

"Who's Vicky?"

"Vicky Vaughn, Stig's ex-sister-in-law. In case you don't know, Stig used to be married to Vivian Vaughn."

"The actress?"

"Yeah. Stig and Vivian got divorced five or six years ago, but he's still close to Vicky. Go figure. Anyway, we were all hanging out by the pool until two or maybe two-thirty. It was a beautiful night, and nobody wanted to leave. Temperatures last night started out in the nineties, but by midnight, they must have been down in the seventies. Don't get me wrong, I love Scottsdale, but it's been a freaking hot summer. It's been months since you could sit outside like that."

"Did anything happen while you were all sitting outside?"

"Like, did a dead body fall in the pool? Nah, nothing like that. We sat around and had a couple of drinks, then everyone went home."

"Did everyone leave at once?"

"Um, I guess, pretty much at once. Vicky said she had a dance class in the morning and needed to go. That seemed to break up the party, and everyone got up and started organizing to go home. We'd been sitting around in our bathing suits, so everyone gathered up their things and went in to get dressed. I'd changed in one of the downstairs guest bedrooms, and I'd left my clothes in there, so I went back to the same bedroom and got dressed. I guess everyone else did the same. There're four or five bedrooms in that wing."

"Did you see who left last?"

"No, I wasn't looking to see who'd stayed. I got dressed and took off."

"Did you notice whose cars were still in the courtyard?"

"Not really. Stig always keeps three or four cars out there, and I wasn't paying attention to the other cars. I think Christine's Aston Martin and Vicky's BMW were still there, but I couldn't swear it. To tell the truth, I'd had one more drink than I should have, and I was mainly thinking about the side streets I needed to take to get home."

"I'd like to talk to Luther Wilcox. Does he work in Scottsdale?"

"Sure, his office is off Hayden Road and Indian Bend. The number's on the list. Christine's and Vicky's numbers are also there in case you want to talk with them."

"I'll probably need to talk with everyone. You're his manager, what's going on with Stig's career?"

"Oh, it's as strong as ever. He's still at the top of the A-list. *Hammer's Revenge* wrapped shooting two weeks ago. *Obscura 2* is due to be released in three weeks, and he'll start filming *Time Vortex* in about a month. We'll have the final reading of the script in a couple of days. It's scheduled to be released on Memorial Day weekend next year. There are five different visual effects studios already working on the project. It'll be the studio's summer tent pole, and everyone should make a shitload of money."

"The new ones both sound like science fiction. If the new Hammer movie does well, will they continue the series?"

Jerry winced, and his eye started moving rapidly back and forth. Apparently, my question struck some kind of nerve. "Well," he said, "it's still early. We typically do a Hammer movie every other year. They've floated a couple of scripts, and we're getting closer to a final story, but nothing's nailed down yet. Stig's eager to continue the Hammer series, of course. He feels there's still a lot he can explore and bring out with the character, but he also feels it needs to be the right script."

"What's he looking for?"

"Well, it needs to be more than a great story and nonstop action, it also needs to be shot in some exciting new locations and have a believable love interest. We filmed part of *Hammer's Revenge* in Shanghai. Once we got past the bureaucracy, everyone was great. They hosted a location wrap party, and everyone got a present. I got a pair of carved jade bookends. We're thinking we could shoot part of the next project in Hong Kong and maybe also near Beijing. Stig wants to have the climactic fight scene take place on the Great Wall. It would be a first. Of course, the red tape involved with actually filming on the Great Wall is turning out to be both expensive and a real pain in the ass. You might know the Hammer movies are famous for never using computer-generated images. Everything you see on screen is performed on location by actual actors and stuntmen. It gives the series a sense of realism, but the costs involved are sometimes through the roof."

"And the love interest?"

"We've pretty much settled on using an Australian as an undercover agent who partners up with Stig. In a couple of months, they'll start a casting call among some of the up-and-coming Australian actresses and fashion models. We're looking for an Abbie Cornish or Emily Jane Browning type. We'll shoot the initial meeting scenes in Sydney and maybe have a battle with the terrorists around the Opera House, well, if we can clear up the red tape for shooting there."

"Why Australian?"

"We've wanted to cast an Australian love interest for a while. We've never shot in Australia, and it's a beautiful country. Plus, no red-blooded American male can resist a woman with an Australian accent. I know if my ex-wife had sounded like Olivia Newton-John, I never would have left her."

Stig came back into the room. I'd run out of questions for him, so I let him know I'd talk with everyone who stayed after he went to bed, and I'd keep him informed of what I found. He reminded me again, not to mention the fact that he'd found a dead body floating in the pool. I shook hands with both Stig and Jerry, then took off.

~~~~

I drove down the long winding driveway, waited while the big iron gate swung open, and then found myself back on Cameldale Way heading north to McDonald Drive. My stomach growled, and I started thinking about both dinner and Reno. I called him, and he answered right away.

"Hey," I said. "It's last minute, but are you free for dinner?"

"I am, and dinner sounds great. It's been a long day, and I could use the company."

"Frankie's?" I asked. "It's been a couple of weeks since we've been there. I can be there in twenty minutes."

"Perfect, I'll see you there."

~~~~

I pulled into Frankie's and parked in the back of the lot next to Reno's Jeep. I was gathering up my things to go in when my phone started playing the theme from *The Love Boat*, Max's ringtone.

I jumped, dropping my purse on the seat and spilling things everywhere. I looked down at Max's name on the screen and listened to it ring.

I had an inner debate about if I should answer it or not. Right before it was about to flip into voicemail, I hit the Accept button.

"Hello?"

"Laura, I'm glad I caught you. Is this a bad time?" Max's voice was as I remembered it, deep and strong but with a sense of sexy playfulness.

"I can't talk long, but I have a minute," I said. "How have you been?"

"Well, as you can imagine, I've been busy the last six weeks, but things are going well."

"How's Tony? The last time I saw him was in the hospital."

"He's home and making a steady recovery. The man is tough. He's been doing physical therapy, and it looks like he'll be walking again relatively soon. He's even back at the office a couple of days a week."

"I'm glad. I've been worried about him."

"Laura, I'd like to see you."

My heart started racing, and my mind went in several directions at once. "You'd like to see me?"

"Yes, if you have a free half-hour sometime in the next few days, I'd like to get together and discuss something you might be perfect for."

It doesn't sound like he's talking about a date.

"Oh, um, sure. I could probably break away sometime this week. Maybe tomorrow or Wednesday?"

"Alright, let's plan on tomorrow morning. Say, eleven-thirty? Let's meet at the Headhunter Lounge at the Tropical Paradise."

"Okay. I'll be there. I've missed you."

Shit why did I say that out loud?

There was a pause on the other end of the phone. The pause went on for too long, and my heart started to sink.

I shouldn't have said I missed him. That was so stupid.

Then Max's confident voice spoke. "Laura, I've missed you too. I'm actually surprised at how much I've missed you. It'll be wonderful seeing you again."

Max disconnected, and I spent a few minutes looking at the cars in the parking lot. Then, with a sense of relief and happiness that was hard to describe, I gathered up my things and hurried into the restaurant.

~~~~~

Frankie Z's is a small, family-run Italian restaurant off Hayden and Via Linda. Reno and I had been coming here every week or two ever since we started going out together. It's always been 'our restaurant,' and I can't drive by the place without thinking of him.

As I walked in, the aromas of oregano, olive oil, and garlic wrapped around me. The great smell of walking into the restaurant was probably my favorite part, next to the actual food.

Frankie was at her usual place at the hostess stand. Her bright eyes gave me the once-over, and she greeted me with a motherly smile.

"Laura, where you been?" she asked. "I haven't seen you all week. You're still so skinny. You need to come here more often. I'll feed you. Your cute boyfriend is already waiting for you. It's nice outside again, and I opened up the patio. I put you at a good table, very romantic."

She looked around and spotted one of her grandsons. She yelled at him from across the room with a surprisingly loud voice, "Angelo, show our guest to table forty-two."

I followed close behind the teenager as we wound through the lounge. Frankie's oldest son, Little Zappy, was working at his usual station behind the bar, drawing a tall beer from one of the taps.

He had a bar towel draped over his shoulder, and a white apron was wrapped around his massive body. He raised his hand and called out, "Hey, Laura," as we walked through. Angelo led me out to the patio to a table in the corner where Reno waited.

As always, it was great to see him. He's tall, strong, and confident, with a rare combination of intelligence and charisma that makes him a natural leader. When he looked at me and smiled, I knew I was safe and everything was right with the world.

Reno stood, and I gave him a hug and a quick kiss. As I sat, Dominic, the waiter, brought out two glasses of scotch and a basket of breadsticks.

He recited our usual dinner orders, and we nodded in agreement. He took off for the kitchen, and we both picked up our drinks and took a long sip.

"How was your day," I asked, munching on a breadstick. "Still stuck at your desk doing paperwork?"

"Yes, and it looks like I'll be there most of the week. Since they made me head of the district's drug intervention task force, I spend less time in the field and more time at my desk. I first write a proposal outlining a new operation. Then, I need to hold a meeting to get department buy-in. That always seems to take two or three days. Then, when we actually do have a successful field action, it takes me another three or four days to write up what we did and present it to the review board. It sometimes makes me wish I'd turned down the promotion and stayed a field commander."

As Reno talked, my mind kept going back to Max and how he'd said he missed me. I turned it over in my mind until I'd convinced myself he really meant it and wasn't merely repeating my words back to me to be polite. It was an exciting thought.

Dominic brought out our dinners and another round of scotch. As always, the food at Frankie's was the best. Neither of us talked as we dug in and made a respectable dent in our dinners.

"What are you up to this week?" Reno asked during a pause. "More backyard surveillance on cheating husbands?"

"It's not only the husbands," I said. "Half the time, it's the wives who are fed up with the men and find other partners. But this week, it looks like I'll be dealing with Hollywood actors. I was over at Stig Stevens' house a couple of times today. It's right up against Camelback Mountain and has the most gorgeous view of the city. You should see the inside. It's like something out of a Hollywood movie set."

"You're moving up in the world. I've driven by that house. You can't see much of it from the road, but I've heard it's beautiful. If I remember it right, Stig Stevens isn't married, so I'm assuming there's no cheating spouse involved with this one."

"I'm not sure what I'm dealing with yet, but it'll probably

be more interesting than sitting outside a bedroom window waiting for the clothes to come off."

As Reno described his latest drug bust, thoughts of Max missing me triggered a cascade of emotions. My body was starting to respond to some long pent-up desires.

As I halfway listened to Reno talk, I started to squirm in my seat. All I could think about were my building feelings of lust and desire.

I hoped Reno was going to be in the mood for an evening of passion. I definitely had some shameless urges that would need to be acted out.

Dominic brought out the after-dinner coffees, and Reno slowly poured the cream into both of our cups. "It's still early," he said. "Why don't you come over tonight? It's been a while, and I could use the company. I'm sure you could find an outfit in the closet for tomorrow."

I thought about having sex with Reno and how exciting it would be – then my mind flashed to Max and our conversation earlier in the evening. Knowing I would see him again in the morning was causing my heart to beat faster.

I spent several seconds thinking about both men and realized I would probably fantasize about Max the entire time I was making love with Reno. The thought surprised me at first, but then I felt a fresh flush of heat.

Yum. How hot is this going to be?

I suddenly became racked with guilt. What was I thinking? I couldn't make love to Reno while pretending I was with Max. What a terrible thing to do. I couldn't do that to either Reno or myself.

Reno looked at me. "Are you okay? You have that weird look."

"Um," I said, "would it be alright if we waited until next time? It's been a really long day, and tomorrow isn't going to be any better. Let's actually plan something for later in the week."

Reno's face fell, and I knew I'd disappointed him. "Sure," he said, "whenever you'd like. Pick a day, and we can plan on dinner and a night of sex. But don't wait too long. I'm a man, and I have needs."

"You aren't the only one with needs," I said.

Dinner ended rather awkwardly, and Reno walked me out to my car. Before I left, he kissed me and again tried to spark some interest in passion for the evening.

My body still desperately wanted to be in Reno's bed, and kissing him in the parking lot was only making it worse. I felt mixed emotions and almost said yes, but I couldn't be intimate with Reno while I spent the entire time wanting to be with Max.

Reno got into his Jeep, and I got into my convertible. It was a surprisingly lonely feeling driving back to my apartment alone.

When I pulled into the parking lot, I received a small bit of bad news. With summer now officially over, the first RV had arrived and was parked in the back corner of the lot.

I knew there'd be a slow trickle of tourists arriving from now until Thanksgiving. Then, the floodgates would open, and the annual snowbird season would officially begin. By Christmas, the apartment building parking lot would look like a used RV dealership.

~~~~~

I paid some bills, spent an hour flipping channels, and turned in around ten thirty. I tossed and turned but couldn't fall asleep.

After I'd rolled over for about the fifth time, Marlowe got annoyed and went out to the fire escape. A few seconds later, I heard the creaking sound of Grandma Peckham's cat door swinging shut.

I couldn't stop thinking about my conversation with Max and how he'd said he missed me. I was also having serious regrets about turning Reno down for the night.

My body was in desperate need of a release, or more likely, several releases. I doubted the shower massager would satisfy my pent-up desires.

For this level of need, I required an actual man. I knew Reno could do it effectively. Unfortunately, I suspected Max would also be very effective. I tossed and turned, thinking how effective he likely would be.

How do I keep getting myself into these situations?

It must have been about one-thirty or two before I finally fell asleep.

~~~~

When the alarm went off, I had a hard time getting up. I hit the snooze button three or four times before crawling out of bed.

I started a pot of coffee, then stumbled into the shower, where I stood under the water for twenty minutes and slowly came to life. After blow-drying my hair, I went to the closet and stared at my clothes.

I hoped to meet with Christine Johns and wanted to look nice without going overboard and looking like I was trying to impress her. Fortunately, it was almost the end of September, and the daytime highs had fallen back into the nineties.

It was paradise weather, considering how hot it had been over the summer. I could pretty much wear whatever looked good without having to worry about heatstroke.

After several false tries, I settled on a cream-colored sleeveless silk blouse and a mid-length navy pleated skirt. For color, I went into the box in the closet and pulled out the ruby ring Elizabeth had given me.

Of my three pieces of nice jewelry, I didn't worry so much about someone trying to steal the ring. The ruby was so big and clear it appeared to be fake.

I then settled on some flats. I would have liked to wear heels, but when I do, I inevitably end up chasing after someone.

Marlowe had come back from Grandma's and was winding around my ankles, howling to be fed. I wasn't all that hungry, so I grabbed a couple of granola bars and tossed them in my purse.

I poured the rest of the pot of coffee into *The Big Pig,* my oversized travel mug, fed my poor starving cat, and headed out the door.

~~~~

After dropping my things off at my cubicle, I walked up to reception and plopped down in one of the red leather wingback chairs next to Sophie's desk. She was reading through a stack of tabloids, and when she looked up, I could tell she hadn't gotten a lot of sleep.

Of course, I knew I looked pretty much the same. I was still holding *The Big Pig* and lifted it to take a long gulp of coffee.

Sophie had her *I'd Rather Be Surfing* mug in front of her, and she lifted it to have a long drink. We looked at each other and started laughing.

"You look beat," I said. "How late were you up last night?"

"I didn't get to bed until about two-thirty. Monday's the

only night of the week Snake has off. Did you watch the Cardinals play on Sunday?"

"No, sorry. Did he get a chance to play?"

"Yes, and that's why we were out late last night, to celebrate. He was in for three plays. On the third play, he was sacked and fumbled the ball."

"Was he upset?"

"Well, a little, but he got over it pretty quickly. He didn't expect to play at all this year. Playing in a game makes him a real NFL quarterback with actual statistics, not to mention he got ten thousand dollars in bonuses for each play."

"Nice. What about Milo? I didn't get a chance to ask you yesterday. Weren't you going to get together with him over the weekend? Did you two ever straighten things out?"

"You mean about that lame rumor you started that I was pregnant?"

"I was only trying to help."

"Well, it didn't. It's taken me a month, but I've finally convinced him I'm not carrying his child. We went out to the clubs on Saturday. It took a night of drinking and cowgirl sex, but I think he's finally good with it. Funny thing, he was kind of disappointed. I think he was looking forward to having a baby with me. Go figure."

Sophie looked closer at me. "Are you okay? You seem more moody than usual today."

"I know. I guess the assignment with Stig is bugging me."

"It's not Stig. You do know that, don't you? It's Max. You've been moping ever since you decided you weren't going to see him anymore."

"You know it wasn't only my decision. Max said he couldn't see me, at least not like that. He didn't want me to be known as the gangster's girlfriend."

Sophie made a sound with her lips that was both rude and dismissive.

"Hey," I said. "What was that for?"

"Since when has following the rules ever stopped you from doing what you needed or wanted to do? You're telling me you can't figure out a way to be with Max so the rest of the world doesn't find out about it?"

"It's not only Max, it's Reno. He can sense something's up with me. It's been sort of tense between us the last couple of weeks. It wouldn't be right for me to go out with Max, even as friends. I need to pick a guy and stick with him."

"But you picked Max. I heard you say that last month."

"Yes, but things changed. After Tony was shot, Max had to take over, and he pushed me away."

"Nope."

"What do you mean, nope?"

"Max was only being polite, and you know it. You're settling with Reno. You two went to Rocky Point last month for a weekend, and now you're back to seeing him only once or twice a week. That's why he's tense and you're grumpy. Don't tell me it's due to scheduling conflicts. The man lives less than twenty minutes from here, and you could sleep in his bed every night if that's what you really wanted."

"I'm not settling with Reno. He's a good man, and I know he loves me. The problem is Max is a good man, too, and I can't be honestly devoted to one while I want to be with the other. It's not fair to anyone. I've never figured out how you can juggle so many men at once. I feel guilty even kissing another man while I'm dating someone else. You always seem to have two or three going at once, not to mention the strays you pick up at the clubs."

"It's not the same with me. I tell the guy up front I won't be exclusive, and I'm not looking for anything permanent. I tell them we can have sex, and they can fall in love with me all they want, but I'm not getting serious or moving in with anyone. I let 'em know I already did the marriage thing, and it didn't work out so good. You'd think it would scare the men away, but it seems to attract them. They seem to think of me as a challenge. The only one who's had a problem with it is Milo. He keeps asking me to move in with him. Whenever he does, we get into an argument, and I refuse to see him or even talk to him on the phone for at least a week. You'd think he'd learn by now."

"Weren't you saying last month you were starting to think about settling down and picking only one guy to be with? What happened?"

"I go through these weird emotional swings sometimes. Fortunately, most of the time, I don't want to be with anyone for the long term. So far, I've been pretty happy with that decision."

"For me," I said, "it's not only a matter of dropping Reno and taking up with Max. Gina's right when she lectures me about him. Max is a professional criminal. I'm sure the police and probably the FBI are investigating him. His group does its best to keep a low profile, but it's still a criminal organization."

"Well, don't take Gina's lectures too seriously. She's still a little bitter about Rodger."

"Who's Rodger?"

"Haven't I ever told you about Rodger? That was Gina's ex-husband. They'd been married for four or five years when he started working for one of the crime families over in Phoenix. She found out about it and said she couldn't have a criminal as a husband, not with her being with the police. She gave him the ultimatum: stop being a crook, or I'm leaving. Long story short, he liked being a criminal, so Gina dumped him. I think she lectures you about Max so she'll feel better about her decision with Rodger. Hey, speaking of Max, why doesn't his group have a cool name like the Black Death? I never even know what to call it."

"It's part of the low-profile thing. If Max refers to it at all, he calls it the Company. He said his title is Operations Director for Scottsdale Land & Resort Management, Incorporated. Like it's some sort of regular job."

"Well, if I were you, I'd call him and see if he'll meet with you. At least you could find out if he still wants you or not. Although I'd suggest you see him somewhere in public unless you want to see him naked. The last time you made plans for a date, it was going to end with champagne and sweaty sex at his place."

"Um, he called me last night. It was right before I had dinner with Reno."

"No shit? So, are you two going out now or what?"

"It wasn't like that. He wants to meet with me, but I think it's more of a business thing. There's probably a side project they want me to work on."

Sophie blew raspberries again. "That's only an excuse. There are lots of people he could get for a business thing. He wants you involved because it's you. When are you going to see him?"

"Later this morning, over at the Tropical Paradise."

"Going to meet him in one of the hotel suites? I'd go for a room with the full honeymoon package. Champagne and strawberries always put me in the mood."

"No, I'm meeting him in the bar."

"Good thinking. Put a few drinks in him first, then take him upstairs."

Now, that sounds like a perfect idea.

I gave Sophie my best *Are you kidding me?* stare.

"Don't look at me like that. We both know it's what you want."

"Hey," I said, changing the subject. "Did I tell you one of the people at the house after Stig went to bed was Christine Johns?"

"Christine Johns?" Sophie asked. "Holy crap. Seriously? I've always loved her."

"I've seen Paradise Park in concert twice. Once when I was in high school and once three years ago during their big reunion tour."

"I remember that Paradise Park concert," Sophie said, laughing. "That's the day we met. They played outside at the Ak-Chin Pavilion. Of course, wasn't it called Blockbuster Desert Sky or maybe Cricket Wireless Pavilion back then? I don't remember. The name of the place changes a lot, and depending on who you talk to in Scottsdale, they have a different name for it. Maybe it was called the Ashley Furniture Home Store Pavilion then?"

"I won't forget that concert," I said. "I had a lawn seat. It was one of the few days with rain that summer, and I was covered in mud. I was standing in line to get a scotch to warm up, and you started laughing at me for looking so bad."

"I know," Sophie said, "I didn't even know you, and I called you the mud-woman. I still feel a little bad about that, but hey, I made up for it."

"Yes, you did, and I appreciated it. I'm glad you had an extra ticket. It was under the covered section in, like, the fifth row. Those were great seats."

"Yeah, well, I bought the tickets when I was married, but I went to the concert when I was divorced. I had the extra seat, and you looked like you could use one that wasn't in the mud. I've always loved Paradise Park. I have four or five of their CDs in a box somewhere and still have ten or fifteen of their songs in my phone."

Gina walked up to reception carrying a stack of folders. She plopped them down on Sophie's desk.

"I'm finally done with the reports," Gina said.

"Perfect," Sophie said. "I'll add them to the stacks to be filed."

"Is Lenny ever going to hire another admin?" I asked Gina.

"He says he is," Gina said, "but we may need to do it for him."

"Yeah," Sophie said. "Lenny's last pick didn't work out so well. This time, we'll need to find one that doesn't smell like a peed-on pile of burning garbage. I still miss having Annie work here. It's a shame she went back to school. She really kept the place organized."

"How'd your date go?" I asked Gina. "Weren't you going to have dinner last night with that personal trainer from your gym? What was his name? Brandon?"

"Well, I had dinner with him. Unfortunately, the man's as dumb as he is handsome. All he wanted to talk about was how good he was at baseball back in college and how he could have gone pro. It's a shame. He has a great body and a gorgeous smile. I'm thinking I still might be able to use him for a weekend, as long as he doesn't talk too much, but I don't see much of a future with him."

"Maybe we should go out with the Cougars sometime

soon," Sophie said. "If you're looking for a weekend hookup, you could probably pick up something better than a guy from the gym. At least most of the guys we meet at the clubs have money."

"How's the investigation into the missing body going?" Gina asked me.

"So far, there's nothing," I said. "No body and no evidence there ever was a body."

"I talked to Lenny about it yesterday afternoon," Gina said. "As I understand it, there was a party at Stig Stevens' house on Sunday night with around twenty-five or thirty people. Most everyone went home around one o'clock. Stig went to bed around one-thirty, and a small group stayed for some period of time. I'd concentrate my initial efforts on the people who stayed. If something happened, it's likely one of them has some knowledge of it."

"My thinking, too. There were five who stayed. I'm planning on talking with all of them, hopefully today."

"One of the people who stayed was Christine Johns from Paradise Park," Sophie said. "Maybe we'll get a chance to meet her."

"Christine Johns grew up in Scottsdale and went to Coronado High School, ten or fifteen years before I did," Gina said. "She still has a house around here somewhere, I think. I've always loved Paradise Park. It'd be cool to get to meet her."

Gina looked down at the stack of newspapers on Sophie's desk. "Lenny thinks it's all part of a publicity stunt to help out Stig's new movie. Did you find anything in the papers yet?"

"Plenty. You'd be surprised who's having affairs with who. I've counted seven or eight famous people having affairs so far this week. They have pictures and everything. My favorite one is the actor walking out of the hotel room with his mistress. The look of guilt on the woman's face is priceless. Looks like it'll be a good year to be a Hollywood divorce lawyer. Lenny should open a branch out there."

"Anything else?" Gina asked.

"Loads more," Sophie said. "Turns out space aliens have visited Washington, D.C., hundreds of times over the past two centuries. They have pictures and eyewitnesses to prove it. They even found an old diary with detailed records of alien encounters with Abraham Lincoln."

"Anything about Stig?" Gina asked.

"Nope, he seems to be pretty much off the radar. These papers seem to focus on the younger and sexier stars. I guess Stig doesn't count as tabloid material anymore."

"Has the report come back on the publicist?" Gina asked. "You know how our luck goes."

"Actually, it's coming through now," Sophie said.

The picture came out of the printer. Sophie looked at it, groaned, and shook her head. She showed it to Gina, who sighed and shook her head as well. "It figures," she said as she hit the intercom to Lenny's office. "Boss, you'd better come out here. We've got some news on Jeanette Simmons."

When Lenny walked out, Sophie handed him the picture.

"Shit," Lenny said. "It's her. I was afraid of that. When I heard Stig say Jeanette Simmons was his publicist, I *hoped* it was someone else named Jeanette Simmons."

"The name sounds familiar," I said. "Who's Jeanette Simmons?"

"Oh, you missed out on that one," Sophie said. "This all happened a few months before you were hired. When I started working here, the senior partner, Jeff Halftown, had already moved down to Pensacola, but Paul Oeding and Mark Hopkins were still here as two of the original partners. Paul got himself killed when he hit a tree while skiing in Colorado. Mark then decided to take on a law student intern to help out with the increased workload."

"Yeah," Lenny said. "He hired Jeanette, but that didn't work out so well. He started nailing her, and within a month, he was missing a lot of work. They'd be gone two or three afternoons a week so they could go to various hotels together. One night, I went home around eight o'clock, and Jeanette and Mark stayed to 'work late.' About ten-thirty, I got a call that the paramedics had been called to the office. Apparently, they'd been banging away on the office couch when Hopkins had a heart attack and fell over dead. Jeanette came to the funeral and cried, a lot. It was embarrassing for Mark's wife and family since they didn't know the girl. It was the last time I ever saw Jeanette. I assumed she got her law license and was practicing somewhere. I guess she decided to go into publicity."

"How's she to work with?" I asked.

"Well, she has a lawyer's personality," Gina said.

"Yeah, she was kind of bitchy," Sophie said.

"Hey, I'm standing right here," Lenny said.

"A little snotty, too," Sophie said. "But in between being bitchy and snotty, she was alright."

"Hopefully, she's gotten better," I said.

"I doubt it," Sophie said. "Freaking lawyers, they're all pretty much the same. Not one of them is worth anything."

"Still here," Lenny said. He then turned and walked back to his office.

Chapter Three

I went back to my cubicle and mapped out my day. I needed to talk with Stig's accountant, Luther Wilcox, Stig's ex-sister-in-law, Vicky Vaughn, Christine Johns, and possibly her boyfriend, Nails.

They'd all stayed at the party after Stig went to bed and would likely be my best shot at finding out what happened. Depending on what I got from them, I might also need to go down the list of people who'd left the party early.

I knew Stig wanted to keep his discovery in the pool a secret, so I'd need to be careful how I went about this. I decided to get the easiest one out of the way first.

I called Luther Wilcox at the office number I'd gotten from Jerry. A woman answered the phone, and I explained who I was and what I wanted. She said Mr. Wilcox was in a meeting but would be free in half an hour.

I told her I'd be right over.

~~~~

I pulled into a parking lot at Hayden and Indian Bend. Luther Wilcox had an office in a nice but nondescript building in an office park with several identical single-story buildings.

Each building had an orange roof and rock wall accents. In front of each building were a couple of mesquite and palo verde trees, along with some rosemary bushes and prickly pear cacti.

The office park was neat and orderly but not particularly memorable. It seemed like the perfect location for an accountant.

I found a group of fan palms and parked under their shade. I then found the right building and walked in.

The receptionist said to have a seat while she called Mr. Wilcox. After about two minutes, a large man in his fifties came out and greeted me.

He must have been six four with dark skin and short black hair with tinges of grey at the temples. When he talked, his deep voice reminded me a little of James Earl Jones.

"Stig said you wanted to talk about the other night," Luther said. "There isn't much to tell, but I'll do my best."

We went into his office, and I had a seat. While Luther organized some files on his desk, I took a moment to look around the office.

One entire wall was lined with floor-to-ceiling bookshelves, about half of which were filled with accounting books. Instead of standard bookends, the books were held up by various golfing trophies and small pieces of artwork.

One of the pieces was a fat gold cat that looked a little like Grumpy Cat. Several pictures on the walls showed Luther posing with other golfers at various tournaments.

I could only assume the other golfers in the pictures were famous, but the only ones I recognized were Stig Stevens and Tiger Woods.

"You've been with Stig a long time?" I asked when he finished with his files and looked at me.

"That's right. I first met Stig back in the eighties when I was starting my accounting practice in Hollywood. I had several actors who were either at the end of their careers or just starting out. Stig and I were introduced at a party, and we liked each other from the start. No one had heard of him at the time, but I saw the potential. Currently, I have only a few clients, and Stig is by far my largest account. I moved out to Scottsdale about fifteen years ago to be closer to him."

"Tell me about what happened the other night after Stig went to bed."

"There's not much to tell. Everyone sat outside by the pool, and I enjoyed some of his excellent bourbon. It was a gorgeous night. We'd arranged our chairs to look out at the lights of Scottsdale."

"Who stayed?"

"There was Jerry, Christine, and her latest boyfriend; I never did catch his name, and of course, Vicky. She always comes to Stig's parties, and she's always one of the last to leave."

"Vicky Vaughn, Stig's ex-sister-in-law? Isn't that sort of unusual?"

"Not really. She had a thing for Stig even before he got married to Vivian."

"She never acted on it?"

"Well, she tried a few times. I think they even had a brief fling a few years ago, but it's pretty obvious Stig has her firmly in the friend zone. Stig still gets along well with Vivian. I don't think he wants to muddy up the relationship by getting together with her sister."

"What about Christine Johns and her boyfriend? His name is Nails."

"Nails? It figures. The last half-hour, they were in the pool. She was giving him a crotch massage through his Speedo."

"Didn't that cause a stir?"

"Gods, no. We were all a little *hammered* by then, if you'll excuse my joke. We noticed it, but Christine's always doing things like that, and we go with it. That woman changes boyfriends like I change socks. When Vicky said she was leaving, we all scattered to the bedrooms to put our street clothes back on. Christine and her boyfriend made a beeline for the nearest bedroom. Strike me down if it wasn't more than two or three minutes before Christine started moaning and yelling. She's incredibly loud, and her boyfriend must be some sort of endurance athlete or something. Once Christine started moaning, she never paused for more than fifteen or twenty seconds before it started up again. It was rather fascinating, in a car wreck sense. Between the moaning and Christine yelling out detailed instructions, it left little to the imagination. They were still going at it when I left."

"Do you know what time that was?"

"Um, not really. Two or two-thirty. I suppose it could have been later. I wasn't keeping track."

"There were another twenty or so people at the party. Could you make me a list of their names and email it to me?"

"No problem. Keep in mind I'll miss a few since I didn't know some of the people."

"Did anything unusual happen at the party? Any problems?"

"No, it was a typical party at Stig's. Dinner was a casual buffet, then everyone found a bedroom to change into their bathing suits, and the party moved outside to the pool. Everybody spent the next three or four hours dancing or in the water. Stig had a DJ until about twelve-thirty or one. That's when almost everyone took off."

"You're Stig's accountant. How's he doing financially?"

"Stig said to be open with you. He's still bringing in a substantial income, but it's not what it once was. Each of his last three science fiction movies has grossed, on average, six-point-two percent worse than the one before it. He's done a few oddball movies, like the one with the kids, and those always do well, but, honestly, those opportunities are also closing. He's getting too old for action movies, he never was a romantic lead, and he's still too young to play the wise Army general or grandfather type."

"What about the Hammer movies? How are those doing?"

"The fall-off for the Hammer series is even worse than the science fiction projects. The last two have averaged a twelve-point-six percent domestic drop-off. The one Stig just finished shooting, *Hammer's Revenge,* likely won't break even in the domestic gross. We're counting on strong overseas revenue to keep the studio from pulling the plug on the series. Of course, it also explains why Stig co-starred with a Chinese fashion model in the latest Hammer movie and why some of the scenes were shot in Shanghai. The dialogue was purposefully kept simple so it could be easily overdubbed in both Mandarin and Cantonese. We're now basically making Hammer movies for the Chinese market."

"Are you saying Stig's going broke?"

Luther looked like I'd slapped him, and then he started laughing. "Gods, no, not at all. Are you calling me irresponsible, girl? No, Stig's personal wealth continues to rise. His debt is basically zero, and he's had a solid eight-figure income each of the last seventeen years. We've invested prudently, and he's set for life and beyond. What I'm saying is that his days of receiving leading roles in action and science fiction movies are likely drawing to a close. If *Obscura 2, Time*

Vortex, and *Hammer's Revenge* don't exceed projections, they may be his last until he starts doing tough guy reunion movies."

"That's not what Jerry Phifer says. He says Stig's career has never looked better."

"Jerry's job is to make everyone feel good about Stig's career. My job's to keep it based in reality."

~~~~~

I went down to the parking lot and sat in my car under the shade of the fan palms. It was a lovely morning with temperatures somewhere in the eighties, and having the roof down was a treat. I had about half an hour before my meeting with Max, so I thought I'd try to arrange the rest of the day.

I first called Stig's ex-sister-in-law Vicky Vaughn and let her know who I was and what I needed. She said she was heading home from shopping and anytime in the afternoon would be good to meet. She gave me the address, and I saw it was in north Scottsdale, not too far from Jackie Wade's house.

I then took a deep breath and called Christine Johns. I tried to remember to breathe as I spoke.

When Christine answered, I calmly introduced myself and asked if I could arrange a meeting. She said Stig had already called, and she'd be at home later in the afternoon and available until about seven o'clock.

I told her I'd stop by around four-thirty. After disconnecting, I let out a big breath. I was glad I'd made it through the conversation without my voice shaking.

~~~~~

I drove the short ten-minute drive to the Tropical Paradise. I was a little early, so I parked in visitor's parking and walked up the hill to the main building. I've always loved the resort's tropical theme, and walking through the lobby is probably as close as I'll ever get to Hawaii.

I walked down the main hallway to the Headhunter Lounge. I didn't think it opened until later in the day, so I wasn't surprised to see a red velvet rope stretched across the entrance.

I was also wasn't surprised to see a beefy-looking guy in a black polo standing there to open the rope and let me through. For some reason, I've come to expect these things when dealing with Max.

I walked into the lounge and passed another couple of large guys in black polos stationed near the entrance. They seemed to know who I was and didn't say a word as I passed.

As I walked into the empty bar, I saw Tony DiCenzo sitting at a table, watching me come in. He was in a wheelchair but otherwise looked good. Johnny Scarpazzi was standing near Tony's table, and a woman in a waitress uniform was standing behind the bar cleaning glasses.

Coming into the otherwise empty and silent lounge felt a little creepy. Still, I bent down and gave Tony a hug.

"You look good," I said, happy to see he looked strong and appeared to be mentally sharp. "I hear the rehab is going well."

"The doctors tell me that with a few months of physical therapy, I should be able to walk with the assistance of a cane," Tony said in his gruff voice. "That I can do. It will be good not to be wheeled around like a child."

I took a seat next to Tony at one of the tables. The woman tending the bar walked over and placed a glass in front of each of us.

I wasn't surprised that both held three fingers of scotch along with a single ice cube. I held up my glass in a salute to Tony, and he did the same. We clinked them together, and each took a sip.

As I've come to expect with the good stuff, the scotch evaporated in my mouth, then dissipated in a sensation of flavors. I closed my eyes and felt a wave of pleasure wash over me.

"Oh, yum," I said. "Tony, this is amazing."

"I'm glad you like it. Knowing your leanings toward the drink has given me a chance to explore a little with our local spirit distributor. The one we're drinking is a twenty-five-year-old single malt from Bowmore. When my distributor told me about it, I thought of you."

"You got this just to share with me?" I said, truly moved. "Thank you, Tony. It's delicious. It sort of reminds me of a bottle of Balvenie I once shared with Muffy Sternwood."

"It's good for me to learn new things and discover new pleasures, even at my age. Speaking of new things, how's my old car working out for you?"

"It's perfect," I said. "It's great driving something so beautiful. It's been a while since I've had a car where everything works, and I'm still getting used to it. I couldn't have asked for anything nicer."

Tony made a small waving gesture of dismissal. "I wanted to give you something you needed. I've always enjoyed driving the car, and I felt it could be useful in your line of work. It's the kind of well-made but non-descript car you see all over Scottsdale. I know when I've parked at the Scottsdale Fashion Square, I've sometimes had a difficult time identifying it amongst all the others."

I took another sip of the wonderful scotch. As with the first sip, the drink seemed to evaporate in my mouth.

"It's a big improvement over my last car," I said. "With the duct tape, the bungee cord, and the bullet hole, it was getting harder to blend in. Thank you."

Tony held up his glass, and we clinked them together again. We both took a sip and paused to enjoy it.

"How are you doing?" I asked. "You look surprisingly healthy for someone who took a bullet to the chest a month ago."

"I feel good, especially considering I should be dead. I never did properly thank you for alerting me when the traitor attacked. It was your actions that saved my life as much as anything the doctors did."

I gave Tony back his small hand wave of dismissal. "I saw Sal raising his gun to attack you. I was the only one who could do anything about it, so I did. You'd do the same for me. How's Max doing with filling in for you? If you'll be walking again soon, how much longer will he need to be in charge?"

"It's not the walking. I'm very functional in the chair. Honestly, it's more the loss of energy. Since I was released from the hospital, I can only work for two or three hours before I lose focus and need to stop. It's as if my body is devoting all its energies toward healing. The demands of the job are full-time, so I'll need to completely regain my strength before I can take over again."

"Can't you share the job with Max?"

"It's best not to have two people in charge. Not only for this business but for any business. I've tried it before, and the results were poor. I ended up spending the majority of my time coordinating leadership with the other person, and even then, a certain amount of overlap occurred. It led to confusion and inefficiency. Max is doing a fine job, as I knew he would. For the time being, I'm content being his senior advisor."

We both took another sip, and I started to feel relaxed from the warm glow I got when drinking a really good scotch.

"Will Max still be joining us?"

"He had a phone call he needed to take," Tony said. "I didn't want you to wait by yourself, so I came down first." He held up his glass. "Fortunately, we were able to put our time together to good use. Ah, here he comes now."

I stood up and turned toward the entrance where Max was winding his way towards us through the empty lounge.

Between the effects of the scotch and my anticipation of seeing Max, I couldn't control myself. I went forward a couple of steps and hugged him as he walked up to our table.

Holding him against me filled me with a sense of happiness I hadn't felt in weeks. I congratulated myself on outwardly keeping it to a brief and friendly hug, even though I desperately wanted to jump up, wrap my legs around his waist, and cover his face with kisses.

"Laura," Max said in his deep but soft and smooth voice. "It's good to see you again. Thank you for agreeing to meet with us."

"No problem," I said. "Tony and I were catching up and drinking a wonderful scotch he discovered."

"You've turned Tony on to scotch over the past few months," Max said. "It's become one of his passions. I've heard more about Highlands and Lowlands and peat and water than I ever knew existed."

"It's wonderful," I said. "You should try some."

"Unfortunately, I can't right now. I never realized the number of meetings involved with leading the company. I'll be completely tied up until later tonight."

We both sat at the table next to Tony. Gabriella had also come into the lounge and had positioned herself off to the side, her black leather bag slung casually over her shoulder.

She seemed to be fully healed from her broken ribs and

was again wearing a tight black leather jumpsuit. It was trimmed in red and was very low cut.

She still looked like a dangerous jungle predator, but I again noticed that she was also a shockingly beautiful woman. Seeing her come in with Max caused a small twinge of jealousy.

Stop it. You know men aren't her passion, unless she's shooting at them.

As I thought about it, what exactly did I know about Gabriella? She had originally met Max somewhere in Eastern Europe about ten years ago while she was on some sort of secret mission.

Knowing Gabriella, it likely involved shooting someone whom her government considered a bad guy. At the time, Max was on his own secret mission for Uncle Sam, and the two of them met.

Max somehow convinced Gabriella to work for our side, and they spent a few years doing secret government missions together. When Max left the government and began working for Tony, he asked to bring Gabriella on as well.

Within a few years, she'd risen to become Tony's personal bodyguard. Now that Tony was sidelined and out of the chain of command, she had become Max's guardian angel.

The only other solid thing I knew about Gabriella was she got sexually turned on by shooting people, men in particular. I'd been with her twice when a gunfight was about to occur, and I knew she found it to be an erotic experience. Her face would flush, and her breathing would quicken.

I'm pretty sure she achieved multiple orgasms while she was shooting her Uzi at Smith and Jones, the brothers from the Consortium. I'm also pretty sure she did the same thing when she emptied her clip into Carlos the Butcher.

But even if shooting men was her preferred form of release, did it mean she was opposed to being with a man in the normal way? Was it possible she had her eyes on Max? They were certainly together enough, alone and working long into the night.

"Laura?" Max asked. "Are you alright?"

"Sorry," I said. "I was spacing out a little. It's really nice to see you again."

"Now that we're all together," Tony said, "I'll get right to it. I know how precious time is to Max as of late. Since the death of Carlos Valentino, the Black Death in Arizona is now led by a man named Sergio Torres. You may have seen him last month during the conference. He was the large man seated to the right of Carlos with a long facial scar and a full black mustache."

"I remember him," I said. "He looked like an older version of Carlos." A shudder ran through my body as I remembered what had happened that terrible day.

"As a result of the last meeting," Tony said, "both sides are a little leery of another direct conference. Sergio has suggested negotiations be carried out through intermediaries, and we think it's a good idea, at least, to start."

"That seems reasonable," I said. "How do they propose to begin?"

"They have an office manager at the Scottsdale branch of Southwest Desert Transport, which, as you now know, is run by the Black Death. Max tells me you've had some dealings with the business, and according to Sergio, you've already met her. We did some investigating and found out this office manager apparently used to work in Guadalajara directly for Escobar Salazar, the head of the entire cartel. Sergio trusts her to relay messages between the two groups."

"Sergio's right," I said. "I've met her. Her name is Danielle."

"Do you think she's someone you can work with?" Max asked.

"Someone I can work with?"

"She suggested that you be the intermediary on our side."

Shit, I should have seen that coming.

"Tony, I don't know. Helping out from the background is more in line with what I do. Direct involvement's something I've never been comfortable with."

"I realize this, and you're free to decline," Tony said. "It would, however, be a great personal service to myself, to Max, and to the entire organization. You're the ideal person. We'd trust you to relay the messages accurately, along with any hidden meaning you might notice behind the words. Plus, from what we understand, this Danielle considers you to be a friend. Perhaps you can get her to reveal more information than her bosses might otherwise want her to tell."

Damn. I don't think I can get out of this.

I looked between Tony and Max. "Alright, I'll be the go-between. Hopefully, we can get this over with quickly."

~~~~

I left the Tropical Paradise and drove up Scottsdale Road to Thompson Peak Parkway, then turned east until I got to Greyhawk. Vicky Vaughn's house was located along one of the fairways on Tailfeather Drive, two or three blocks from Jackie's and about a quarter of a mile from the clubhouse.

Greyhawk is a beautiful desert-style golf course. The houses surrounding it all have desert landscaping, some with small round patches of grass in the front lawns.

I've played at Greyhawk once before, and it's great, as long as you can keep your ball on the manicured fairway. If you're off the grass, you'll find yourself on desert hard pack, hitting your ball from underneath a cactus or creosote bush.

Vicky lived in a neat two-story tract home along a street of similar-looking houses. All the houses had similar multi-toned orange tile roofs. Most of the landscaping looked professional, and the few cars on the street were all newer and expensive.

I parked in the driveway and rang the doorbell. Vicky opened the door, and I introduced myself.

She was a tall, athletic woman in her late forties with long, auburn hair styled in loose curls. This gave her a fun and playful look. She had a beautiful smile, and I liked her right away.

She invited me in, and we walked through the house. She stopped in each room to show off some of the pieces of art she had picked up over the years.

Vicky seemed to like original oil landscapes, travel curios, and small marble figurines of horses. Each room we walked through had at least one shelf filled with small animal carvings.

I noticed everyone collects something. In college, the guys collected beer bottles, while the girls collected earrings and stuffed animals.

When I first got married, I ended up with a kitchen full of pig figurines, pig towels, pig spoon holders, and pig salt and pepper shakers. I've noticed that women over twenty-five tend to gravitate toward shoes and jewelry, but as they get older, they'll branch out to dolls, commemorative plates, or something unique like replica lighthouses.

When we stopped by her kitchen, Vicky opened the fridge and offered me a bottle of San Pellegrino. I gladly accepted, and we went out to a covered patio and sat at a small round table next to her pool.

"The weather's been so beautiful the past few days," Vicky said, "I've been spending as much time as I can outside. I've lived here for almost fifteen years, and I'm still surprised at how hot the summers are."

My mind flashed back over the past few months and the times the heat had almost killed me. First was when I was locked in the trunk of my car and had already passed out with heatstroke before my friend Chugger McIntyre rescued me.

The second time had been even worse. I'd been trapped in a semi-trailer in the middle of the desert. I'd needed to use a military rifle and about three hundred bullets to shoot my way out, only to find myself stranded on an exposed hill, slowly baking to death in the unforgiving Arizona desert sun.

"Are you alright?" Vicky asked. "You were staring at the pool."

"Sorry," I said. "Let's start at the beginning. I assume you met Stig through your sister?"

"That's right. I was living in Denver, and Vivian invited me out to California to meet Stig. They'd been going out for three or four months by then. We all got along great and often traveled together or went on double dates."

"You've stayed friends with Stig over the years. Weren't you upset when he divorced your sister?"

"Well, sure. I was pissed at the time, but after a few months, I was able to see the bigger picture. When Vivian first met Stig, she was a beautiful but struggling actress whose biggest role had been in *Slaughter Sorority 3: The Naked Terror*. She had about a dozen lines, flashed her boobs a couple of times, and then was murdered by the psycho killer. She met Stig when they were filming *Hammer On*. She had a small part as the bimbo girlfriend of the lead terrorist. They were married about a year and a half later, and she became a Hollywood A-list actress. Viv and Stig did three movies together, and it's because of Stig she now has everything she could ever want – money, fame, even respect. She bought this house for me, and I've lived here ever since. Stig and I have always gotten along, and we're good friends. He invites me over whenever he has a party, and I always go if I'm in town."

"How often does he have a party?"

"Um, maybe three or four times a year. It used to be more often, but that was when Vivian was there to organize everything. I think Stig still has the parties mainly as a way to keep in touch with all the people he knows in Scottsdale."

"I heard there was a DJ until about twelve-thirty or so, and then most of the guests left."

"That's right. Most everyone took off, but I stayed. The night was beautiful, and I love the view overlooking Scottsdale from the pool. Luther and Jerry also stayed and worked their way through Stig's liquor cabinet. Christine was there with her latest boy-toy. She was calling him Nails. I have no idea what his real name is. They spent their time in the pool warming each other up for sex. I was happy they waited to go into a bedroom before they started. I was afraid they'd start going at it in the water. I swim in that pool, and I'm not sure how well the filters would clean out a load of jizz."

"When did you take off?"

"It must have been two or two thirty. I had a class the next morning, and I wanted to be awake for it."

"Who else was there when you left?"

"I don't know for sure. Christine was in the bedroom across the hall having loud sex with Nails. It was echoing in my room, and I could pretty much hear everything. Nails is a good-looking kid, and to be honest, it was kind of turning me on. I took my time getting dressed, so Jerry and Luther had probably already left by the time I took off."

"Did you notice whose cars were still in the courtyard?"

"No, sorry. Stig likes to show off his latest acquisitions, and the courtyard always looks like an auto showroom."

"What about the party? Could you email me a list of everyone who was there?"

"I could try, but I'll miss a bunch."

"No problem. Did anything unusual happen at the party?"

"Not really. It was a pretty normal party. Well, except for the guy who got into an argument."

"What guy?"

"I was on the other side of the room, so I didn't see most of it. The party had just started, maybe halfway through cocktails, and some drunk guy came in and wanted to talk to Stig. I guess the people at the door told him to go away. There was an argument for about a minute, and then he left."

"Do you know who he was?"

"No, never saw him before."

"What did he look like?"

"I only saw him for a second. He was just a guy—tall, white, with dark hair."

"Long hair or short?"

"It looked short, but it could have been pulled back."

"What was he wearing?"

"Um, I really didn't see. A white or yellow shirt, maybe?"

"Who did he argue with? Stig?"

"No, I think Stig was out on the patio by the pool when it

happened."

"Did you see who he was arguing with?"

"Not really. It might have been Jerry. Maybe Luther was over there, too. Like I said, it didn't last long, and he left. The main gate to the street was open all night, so anyone could have wandered in."

I talked to Vicky for another ten or fifteen minutes without finding out a lot of information. From the way she spoke about Stig, I suspected Luther was right, and she still had a serious crush on him.

I wondered what it would be like to spend ten or fifteen years wanting to be with someone who didn't want you. I hoped I would never have to find out.

~~~~

I went out to my car and punched Christine Johns' address into the navigation system. When the directions came up, I thought the street looked familiar.

I cruised down Scottsdale Road to Jackrabbit, turned west, and drove to Monte Vista Drive. From there, I drove south into an immaculate neighborhood of larger custom homes, mostly with desert landscaping.

As I got to the address, I realized I had been here before. Directly across from Christine's was the house where Terry Lennox lived.

The change in Terry's house was amazing. The last time I'd been here, the place had looked like an abandoned garbage dump.

Piles of trash and beer cans had been heaped against the side of the house. The landscaping had been neglected for months if not years.

There'd even been an old toilet on the porch near the front

door. I remembered how someone long ago had set a plastic flowerpot in the toilet bowl. The cracked toilet with its pot of dead flowers had pretty much summed up my feelings toward the property.

Now, the landscaping was shaped, trimmed, and clean. A beautiful mesquite tree had been added, the house repainted, and the toilet was gone.

It had been transformed from being the neighborhood eyesore to the nicest house on the block. I wondered if Terry still lived there.

With my heart pounding, I walked up and rang Christine's bell. A few seconds later, a voice came from a camera-intercom unit next to the door.

"Yes, who is it?"

"Christine, it's Laura Black. I called you earlier. I'm here to talk about the party at Stig's the other night."

The door opened, and Christine Johns was standing in front of me. She was dressed in sequined blue jeans and a pink polo shirt. Her blonde hair was still halfway down her back, with her trademark big bangs.

My mind flashed back to when I was a teenager, and I'd first seen Paradise Park when they played America West Arena. The rest of the band wore the typical black leather and silk outfits popular at the time, but Christine came out in a flowing blue dress.

What I remembered most about the dress was that it had side flaps attached to her wrists, which turned into angel wings whenever she lifted her arms. At the time, she was thought to be one of the sexiest women in music.

Several men in the crowd were wearing T-shirts describing the sexual acts they wanted Christine to perform on them. I remembered sitting in the crowd and pretending I was

Christine Johns – on stage, dressed in beautiful clothes, and singing rock ballads to fifteen thousand screaming fans.

"Yes?" Christine said. "You wanted to talk with me?"

"Oh, sorry," I said. "I've always been a fan, and it's sort of a shock to talk with you in person."

"It's alright. I get that all the time. It's nice that people still recognize me. I haven't released a new album in ten years, and I haven't been on tour for the last three years."

She led me into her house, and although it wasn't huge compared to Stig's or Muffy Sternwood's, it probably had six or seven bedrooms and was immaculately decorated.

"It's almost cocktail time," Christine said. "Would you like a glass of wine? I could show you around."

I briefly lost my mind at the thought of having one of my rock idols show me around her house.

"Wow," I said. "Yes, please. That would be great."

We went into her spotless kitchen, where she pulled down two oversized red wine glasses from an overhead rack and set them on the counter. From a built-in wine rack, she pulled out a bottle and quickly trimmed the foil with a smooth and practiced motion. A cork puller was mounted to her cabinet, and with one smooth motion, the bottle was open.

"I don't often drink," she said, "it's too easy to fall into a habit. But when I do have a glass of wine, I want it to be memorable. I should have probably opened this bottle earlier to let it breathe, but I think it will be okay."

She then turned the bottle around to show me the label. "This is a 2007 Jordan Cabernet Sauvignon from the Alexander Valley in California. I've always loved John Jordan's wines, and the 2007 is said to be his best vintage of the decade. I bought several cases last week to age in the basement, and I've been looking for an excuse to open one."

She poured three fingers into each of the oversized glasses and handed one to me. She then spent several seconds swirling the wine, smelling it, and looking at the sides of the glass.

She did the swirling, the smelling, and the looking thing three times. Not wanting to seem like an idiot, I did the same. But honestly, all I smelled and saw was the wine.

Christine took a long sip, and I did the same. It took several seconds for me to process what was happening. Like Muffy's scotch, I didn't so much swallow the drink; instead, it seemed to disappear in my mouth.

What followed was the delicate and delicious flavor of the wine. It was hard for me to describe how I felt about it.

It wasn't so much that I was drinking the wine; it was more as if I was experiencing it. I'd never had a wine that acted like a good scotch. Maybe I should find out more about the stuff.

I noticed Christine was looking at me with some concern. "Are you okay?" She asked.

"This is wonderful," I said. "I've never had a wine like this. Most of the wine I drink is either out of a box or is two bottles for ten dollars from the *BevMo!* on Shea Boulevard. I've only felt something like this before with some of the scotches I've had."

"It's amazing, isn't it? You can see why I limit myself to the good stuff. Let me show you around the house."

She gave me a tour of the house, which was bigger than it looked from the street. As we walked from room to room, Christine pointed out some of her favorite mementos and objets d'art.

She apparently had a lot of famous friends, and it seemed like everyone had given her something as a keepsake. My favorite piece was a small gold bear Tom Petty had given her for her fortieth birthday.

Each of the bear's eyes was a brilliant two-carat ruby. They fit perfectly with the playful look on the bear's face.

We ended up in a cavernous living room that sort of reminded me of being in a Hard Rock Café. There were several gold records, pictures, and signed guitars mounted on the walls.

All the gold and platinum records were Christine's, either with Paradise Park or from her solo career. The pictures on the wall were of Christine surrounded by other famous people.

I noticed one of the bigger ones was of Christine and Stig somewhere tropical on a cliff overlooking a turquoise-blue ocean. The largest picture was of Christine surrounded by the other members of Paradise Park.

It was a casual group portrait that must have been taken backstage on one of their earlier tours. The people in the picture all had playful and friendly expressions, nothing that foreshadowed the stormy relationships that would cause so much trouble as the years went on.

I glanced at the guitars and saw that one was autographed by The Edge from U2, one was signed by Eric Clapton, and Eddie Van Halen signed one. There was a baby grand piano in the corner, and from the stacks of sheet music, it appeared to be played often.

We both sat on a white leather couch. I knew if I thought too much about what I was going to say, I'd start to babble like a teenager. Instead of thinking, I started talking.

"Tell me about the party at Stig's the other night. What do you remember about it?"

"Well, it was nice, but there wasn't anything special about it. I was there with my boyfriend, Nails. I wanted to introduce him to everyone, but we got there kind of late and spent most of the time hanging out on the patio by the pool. If you've never been there, Stig's patio has the best view of the lights of Scottsdale. I can spend hours looking out over the city. From up on the side of Camelback Mountain, Scottsdale almost looks alive. I once wrote a song about the view from Stig's pool. It was called *Golden City*."

"I always loved that song. I had no idea it was about Scottsdale. I've been to Stig's and seen the view from his pool, but only during the day. I'll have to go back after dark sometime. About the other night, tell me about the party. Did you happen to hear or see anything unusual while you were there? Was anyone acting strange? Was everyone getting along? Did anyone get into an argument or anything like that?"

"No, not that I overheard, but we didn't get there until after the dinner. If something happened earlier, we would've missed it."

"No problem. I'm mainly interested in what happened after Stig went up to bed. You were part of the group that stayed?"

"That's right. Nails and I stayed. Jerry and Luther were there, too. Vicky Vaughn was there for a while, but she took off about an hour after Stig went to bed. She was sitting between Jerry and Luther and having a conversation with both of them, but after Stig left, I could tell she was looking for a polite excuse to leave. She's had a crush on Stig forever, and after he took off, her heart wasn't into being there."

"Does it seem strange the party went on after the host took off?"

"Oh, not at all. Stig always tells us to stay as late as we want or even stay the night if we feel like it. There are plenty of bedrooms, and everyone's known each other for years. Back when Vivian was there, we'd usually start the party on a Saturday night and wrap it up sometime on Sunday afternoon, usually after the Cardinals football game finished. Stig's a big fan."

"What'd everyone do after Stig went to bed?"

"Mostly hung around and talked. Like I said, Vicky was sitting between Luther and Jerry. They were both vying for her attention, but they were both too drunk to do much more than talk. Nails and I were in the pool."

"And after everyone got up to change out of their swimsuits?"

"Well, I guess you could say Nails and I took our time getting dressed in one of the bedrooms. By the time we left, I think everyone else had already taken off."

"Before you went home, did you happen to walk by the pool again?"

"No, the bedrooms in that wing of the house go right out to the front entrance hallway."

"Is it possible Nails heard or saw anything?" I asked.

"Maybe. I'll give you his number. I think they're playing Chicago tonight." Christine looked at me for a moment. "Stig called me yesterday and said you'd stop by, but he didn't say what was going on. Why all the questions?"

"Well, um, it appears that between the time everyone left, and the time Stig woke up, someone broke into the house."

"Oh shit. Is Stig okay? Did they take anything?"

"No, nothing like that," I said. "But I'm trying to figure out anything I can about what happened."

"This is the second time it's happened. Stig said someone broke into the house last week too. They broke a window that time."

Christine then shook her head and laughed. "You know, it

wouldn't be hard for someone to break in. I've been teasing Stig about it for years. He hasn't changed the codes to the driveway gate or for the front door in all the time I've known him, and that goes back over fifteen years. With everyone who's been in or out of the house over the years, half of Scottsdale must know how to get in."

I thanked Christine and gave her my card. I asked her to let me know if she could think of anything else. When she opened the front door, and I saw the street, I had to ask about Terry.

"By the way," I said. "The house across the street. Do you know who lives there now?"

"Oh, sure. That's Terry Lennox's house. He's the singer for Dog Farts."

She started laughing. "I know, it's a terrible name for a band, but Terry's not bad, for a kid. I sang with Dog Farts at a charity gig a few months ago at the Arizona Biltmore. It was fun, and they raised a lot of money for whatever charity it was."

"I've been to Terry's house before," I said. "It was pretty trashed at the time, but it looks beautiful now. I assumed Terry had moved out and someone new had moved in."

"Oh, I know what you mean, but Terry still lives there. He started cleaning it up a few months ago. He fixed the landscaping and had a crew over to repaint it. I always thought Terry's trashed house was an extension of his stage persona, you know, a way to keep him in character. I'm not sure what happened, but I'm glad he cleaned it up. It looked awful."

I didn't say anything, but I knew all too well what had happened to Terry Lennox. Both Terry and his dad had gone through a lot. I was glad it ultimately had a positive effect on him.

Chapter Four

I left Christine's house and started driving back to my apartment. The sun was going down, and the sky had become a bright, iridescent mixture of red, yellow, and orange. Sunset had to be my favorite time of the day in Scottsdale, and driving through the city in a convertible with the top down was an amazing experience.

On a whim, I turned west on McDonald Drive and drove to the Echo Canyon trailhead on the west side of Camelback Mountain. I found a spot with a great view of the city and the sunset.

I then sat there for around twenty or twenty-five minutes, watching the sky slowly grow dark.

~~~~

I pulled out my phone and called Nails at the number Christine had given me. When he answered, he was somewhere with a lot of echoes, people talking loudly, and women yelling out in drunken *whoops* and *wooh-hoohs*.

"Buggering hell," Nails said when he answered. His British accent was so strong I would have laughed if any of my friends had tried it, but with Nails, I knew it was genuine. It was rather charming.

"Unknown caller," he said, "I'm very glad you rang me up. I thought I'd turned my phone off. I'd have been properly chuffed if it had gone off during the show."

"Where are you?"

"Yes, let me think. Right, we're in Chicago tonight. We're playing at a venue called United Center. It's really quite nice, although, to be honest, we were originally only scheduled for two nights, but then the bleeders added a third night. Completely buggered my scheduled day off, but there it is. I suppose it's all for the best. It'll help me pay for a foolishly large house I recently purchased in Bampton. That's in Oxfordshire, rather near the famous university."

"You're playing *the* United Center? In Chicago? Doesn't that hold like twenty-thousand people?"

"Yes, I believe so. Somewhere in that range. It should be quite nice. Now then, whom am I talking to?"

"My name's Laura Black. I wanted to ask you about the party the other night at Stig Stevens' house."

"Whose house?"

"Stig Stevens."

"No, I'm afraid the name doesn't ring a bell."

"In Scottsdale… In Arizona… The party you went to with Christine Johns."

"Oh, right, *that* party. Sorry, I never really did get the host's proper name. Somebody called him Hammer, and since my name is Nails, it seemed to amuse everyone. He was an actor or some such, wasn't he? I do remember it was a lovely house. I very much liked the view from the pool. Matter of fact, Christine called a few minutes ago and said someone would be calling about that. I suppose she was referring to you. Bloody good luck, I still had my phone on. Otherwise, you might never have gotten through. I almost never have it turned on."

"Let me ask you about the other night at Stig Stevens' house. Did anything strange or unusual happen after Stig went to bed, and it was only the five of you left out by the pool?"

"Well, there were a couple of geezers trying to hit on this good-looking bird."

"Vicky?"

"Yeah, that's the one, but she wasn't having any of it, and after a while, she decided she needed to see a man about a dog. She was a bit of alright. If I'd been on the pull, I might have gone for her myself."

"Aren't you in your twenties and in a famous band?" I asked. "Why don't you go for women your own age? You must have plenty of opportunities."

"Well, you see, I have somewhat of a passion for the older ladies. Not the grannies, you understand, but rather the women who know what they're doing. These young tarts toss themselves against us all the time, but all they know how to do is lay there and giggle. I prefer a woman with some experience. You know, a woman who knows how to please a chap."

"Other than the men who were talking to Vicky, did anything unusual happen after Stig went to bed? Did anyone else come into the house? Were there any arguments or fights?"

"Well, no, not that I heard," Nails said. "Christine and I were in the pool for a bit of slap and tickle, and then we were off into one of the bedrooms. Christine is quite loud, so if there were any arguments or fights happening outside, I didn't hear them."

There was some more yelling coming through the phone. In the background, a man was speaking loudly over the rest of the voices.

"Sorry, Laura, not to be rude," Nails said. "But apparently, there's something of a riot going on out in the crowd. The thing is, we're a bit late getting out on stage tonight. I should probably go before someone starts a fire. Once there's been a fire, they tend to cancel the show."

"Okay, you'd better go."

"Right then," Nails said. "Cheers!"

The phone disconnected, and I sat for several minutes looking down at the lights coming on all over the city.

~~~~

As I drove east on McDonald to Miller Road and then on to my apartment, I reviewed my progress on the assignment. So far, I'd found out a lot about what had happened after Stig went to bed, but I wasn't any closer to finding out about the dead body floating in the pool.

The only thing that seemed out of place was an argument that had apparently happened near the beginning of the party. According to Vicky, someone had come into the house and argued with Jerry and maybe Luther.

She said it was quickly over, and then the man left. Jerry hadn't mentioned it, and neither had Luther. It would likely go nowhere, but at the moment, it was all I had.

I called Stig's manager, Jerry Phifer. When he answered, he was somewhere noisy.

"Hi, Jerry. It's Laura Black. I have a couple of questions. Would it be possible for us to get together and talk?"

"Sure," he said. "I'm at Duke's. It's a bar on McDowell at the Greenbelt. The Diamondbacks game is on. Come on over."

"I know where Duke's is," I said. "I'll be right over."

~~~~

The Indian Bend Wash is a wide, dry riverbed that cuts through the middle of Scottsdale from Shea Boulevard to the north, south to the Tempe Town Lake. Forty years ago, the Army Corps of Engineers had wanted to turn the wash into a long concrete flood control ditch, as they had done to the Los Angeles River.

Not wanting to waste so much prime real estate, the city decided instead to shape the riverbed into a manicured desert oasis, eleven miles long and two hundred yards across. They then renamed the riverbed as the Scottsdale Greenbelt.

Ninety-nine percent of the time, it's a beautiful string of golf courses, bike paths, lakes, and lush subtropical parks. The other one percent of the time, it floods due to a desert thunderstorm. Then, the Greenbelt turns back into a river.

The parks and golf courses flood out for a day or two, but nobody seems to mind. Everyone waits for the water to recede, they hose off the sidewalks, and then things return to normal.

Duke's Sports Grill sits on the Greenbelt at East McDowell Road. It's about the best place to watch sports on the south side of Scottsdale. I usually end up either there or at Zipps on Camelback whenever I want to go out and watch a game.

~~~~

I made it to Duke's, parked next to Jerry's Tesla, and went in. The place was packed, but it didn't take me long to find Jerry.

He was seated at a long table with five women. All of them were in their twenties or early thirties, and all of them were dressed for a night out.

Jerry wore an Arizona Diamondbacks jersey and was at the center of the group. From the empty glasses on the table, it was clear they'd all been there a while.

I walked up and caught Jerry's eye. He stood up and

excused himself, saying he'd be right back.

There were some mild protests, and a couple of the women gave me the once-over. Jerry flipped down a couple of twenties and told a tall blonde woman seated next to him to order another round.

We walked to the bar, and he ordered a beer and then asked me what I wanted to drink. I ordered a Chivas, then led Jerry outside to the back patio.

It was a lot quieter, and we found a table with a nice view of the Greenbelt. As we looked out, several joggers and a couple of rollerbladers drifted by on the bike path.

Jerry pulled out a pack of cigarettes and lit one up with a gold Zippo. He then took a couple of gulps of beer and looked over at me.

From the way he was slurring his words, it wasn't his first pint of the night. His good eye was locked onto my cleavage while his other eye was roaming around at random. Despite what Stig had assured me, I still found it to be a little disturbing.

"What's with all the women?" I asked.

"Hey, I'm a big-time Hollywood agent. All of those girls want to be in Stig's next picture."

"Uh-huh," I said. "And how many of them will actually get to be in one of Stig's movies?"

"Well, there were two last year and one so far this year. That's the tall blonde next to me at the table in there."

Jerry sighed, "Okay, so she's amazing. That girl has talents you wouldn't believe. I had to put her in *Obscura 2* so she'd keep seeing me. I'm not sure if she made it into the final edit or not, but being on location and shooting a few scenes seemed to be good enough for her. I've already scheduled her to be an extra in *Time Vortex*."

I looked at him with my best cynical look. "You dangle the offer of being in a movie so these girls will have sex with you?"

"Pretty much," he said as he shrugged his shoulders.

I looked at him with my best *you've got to be kidding me* look.

"Hey, I'm not proud," he said as he held up his hands. "But it's the system. Besides, I'm good with my promises. I've already talked to the *Time Vortex* casting director, and you never know. She'll get an audition, and he may even give her a speaking part."

He then leaned over and tried his drunken best to speak confidentially. "I suppose it depends on how nice she is to him."

I shook my head. Sometimes, I think I'd heard everything, but I guess not. I decided to get this over with as quickly as possible.

"Earlier, on the night of the party," I said, "did you get into an argument with someone at the front door?"

Jerry paused and thought for a minute. The question seemed to rattle him, and both eyes darted around for several seconds.

"Um, yeah, I guess," he said. "It didn't seem like a big thing. It wasn't so much an argument as a loud discussion. Frank Fender showed up as everyone was arriving."

"Who's Frank Fender?"

"He used to be Stig's stunt double but hasn't worked on a project for four or five years. He wanted to talk to Stig about working on the next film, but he was drunk and in no shape to talk with anyone. Luther and I told him to go home and sleep it off. I told him to call the office later in the week, and we'd look into putting him into the next project."

"And *are* you going to use him in the next project?"

Jerry got a weird look on his face, and his bad eye started spinning in circles. It was a little upsetting to look at.

"No," Jerry said with a shake of his head. "The studio won't touch him. Frank's had somewhat of a grudge against Stig, and he's been suing us off and on for the last three or four years. Even if he were perfect for the project, no one at the studio wants him around."

"And that's even after you told him to call you? Isn't that sort of wrong?"

Jerry lifted his arms in a sign of defeat.

"Welcome to Hollywood."

~~~~

I left Duke's and drove the two miles up Miller Road to my apartment. I didn't feel like walking up the stairs, so I took the elevator.

I was walking down the hall to my apartment when I heard *Dancing with the Stars* blasting through Grandma Peckham's door. Grandma's been my next-door neighbor since I moved in over three years ago.

She takes care of Marlowe when I'm out and is a good person to talk to whenever I have a problem. I knocked on her door, and after a moment, the TV went quiet. I then heard the shuffling sounds of Grandma coming to the door.

"Well, Laura," Grandma said as she opened the door. Her eyes were glassy, and she had a big smile on her face. "I haven't seen you in a couple of weeks. Come on in. How've you been? I'm drinking Jamaican Jerks tonight. Would you like one?"

"Sure," I said as I walked in and sat on Grandma's big couch. "A Jerk sounds great."

Marlowe was on his chair, asleep on his afghan. He opened his eyes at the sound of me talking with Grandma. He stretched his legs, rolled over, then fell asleep again.

So much for the unrestrained enthusiasm of a loyal pet greeting a beloved master. I'm still thinking about trading him in for a dog or maybe a hamster.

Grandma went into her kitchen and started making a drink she calls a Jamaican Jerk, which is Diet Pepsi with a shot of Appleton rum. Grandma discovered the Appleton Estate rum plantation while on an extended backpacking trip to Jamaica back when she was in college.

As far as I know, it's the only type of alcohol she drinks. Grandma also loves Diet Pepsi, so it was only natural that she would eventually combine the two.

I asked her about the name of the drink, and she said, "Yes, there was a story behind it," but she would be "too embarrassed to go into it." All I've ever been able to get out of her was that there were three young Jamaican men involved, and she was sore for days afterward.

While Grandma was making the drink, I looked around the room. Unlike my place, Grandma's apartment is always spotless.

I looked at the pictures of her family and thought I noticed a new one on the table. It was of a pretty blonde woman, about twenty-five or thirty, holding a smiling baby girl of Asian descent.

Grandma came back and handed me the drink. She'd also made herself a fresh one. Since I knew Grandma already had a Jerk in her, she'd be in a talkative mood.

Fortunately, it would only last until she finished the second one. After two Jerks, Grandma mumbles incoherently, and she shuffles off to bed.

"Who's this?" I asked, pointing to the new picture. "I don't think I've seen this one before."

"That's my granddaughter, Meghan. She's a lawyer out in Boulder. She adopted a baby girl from China named Xiu Mei. I got the picture a few days ago."

"She's very pretty," I said.

Grandma sighed. "It's nice Meghan has a daughter now. Of course, it's not like when I was young. Back then, if a woman wanted a family, she had to go to college, meet an up-and-coming young man, help him get through school, and then help him find his first job. They'd buy their first home and start having babies. Of course, things are always changing, but back in the seventies, a woman could usually count on having three or four children before her husband left her for a younger woman. Up until about ten or fifteen years ago, people would at least get married to have children. Not so much these days. It's more normal for people to live together and have babies."

"Is Meghan living with anyone?" I asked.

Grandma shook her head. "Meghan apparently isn't interested in having a partner of any kind. Honestly, it wouldn't surprise me to find out she's still a virgin. Rather than deal with all of the kissing and touching normally involved in the process, she skipped that part and went straight to having children."

Grandma took a long sip of her drink and kept talking. "Personally, I think she's missing out by not having a man. They can be so terribly useful. Not only for sex, you understand, but for the day-to-day things like carrying groceries and pulling things off the top shelf. Most of them are even good for killing the spiders that come into the bathroom."

"Speaking of men," I said. "What happened to Grandpa Bob and the other guy? What was his name? I haven't seen either of them around lately."

"Oh, that was Ray, and you're right. After the two of them got into an argument in the hallway last month, I dropped both of them. It's probably for the best. Bob wanted us to move in together, and he was hinting at marriage. Ray was good-looking, but he was sort of a wet blanket in the sack. Since I was mainly dating them for sex, it made sense to drop them both."

"Are you going to start looking again?"

"Well, my profile's still on the dating site, but I'm not writing anyone back. I might wait a while before I start responding again. Honestly, with all the men I've had in the last six months, I've needed this month off to catch my breath. It was getting to the point where I was mixing up their names and forgetting what we'd done together."

"That could be embarrassing," I said.

"Well, a little. But I'd tell them I was having a senior moment, and they were always good with it."

"How was it, going out with so many men?"

"Well, it was a little disorganized at first. I really hadn't dated anyone in years, and I'd pretty much forgotten how to do it. Eventually, I developed a system. The first date was usually dinner, and if he picked up the check, we'd neck a little in the parking lot. If he kissed good enough, we'd have a second date. While we were kissing on the second date, I'd reach down and find out if his penis still worked or not."

"In the parking lot?"

"Sure, I'm not going to invite a lot of strange men over to the house, at least until I get to know them. Besides, what are they going to do, arrest me for groping old men in the parking lot of the Old Town Tortilla Factory? Anyway, if they could get a stiffy after I squeezed their package a few times, we'd go out on a third date. If they bought dinner, I'd bring them home and check out how they were in bed. Even after they passed the first two tests, you'd be surprised at how many of them needed to pop into the bathroom first to take the blue pill before things could get going."

"How many of them passed the third test?"

"Maybe four or five, all together. Once I found out they were good in bed, I had to decide if I could stand being around them or not. Forget what you see on TV. If I'd been honest and said I was only looking for sex and nothing else, it would've hurt their feelings. They wanted to do other stuff, too, like movies and museums. So, the last test was to spend the entire day with them doing something or even going on an overnight trip. One man took me to Sedona, and one man took me up to the Grand Canyon."

"How'd those work out?"

"Well, to be honest, the only one I actually enjoyed being with was Grandpa Bob. He's a big movie fan, and we both like the same types of movies, more or less. Whenever we'd watch an old movie, he'd tell me what was going on in his life when the movie first came out, and I'd tell him what had been going on in mine. Turns out, we'd both gotten married right after *Ben-Hur* came out. I'm talking about the real one, not the awful remake they did with Morgan Freeman."

"That was the one with Charlton Heston, wasn't it?"

"Oh yes. That man had a presence on the screen. They don't make actors like that anymore. Cary Grant, John Wayne, Humphrey Bogart. You didn't care what the movie was. You only went to see what they were up to. I don't even know who half of the actors are anymore. They seem to come and go so fast."

I looked over, and Grandma's glass was empty. I knew the visit was about to be over.

"Well, Grandma," I said. "I know you need to get to bed soon, so I won't keep you."

"Bed?" Grandma asked, her voice already sleepy. Yes, I suppose I should probably turn in. It's been lovely chatting with you, dear. Please come back soon."

Grandma was already walking back to her bedroom, so I scooped up Marlowe. I made sure Grandma's door locked behind me, then walked to my apartment.

I did the one-handed juggling act to pull the keys out of my purse while trying not to disturb the cat. Once I made it in, I put Marlowe on my bed, where he promptly fell back asleep.

I stripped off my clothes and put on a long and comfortable T-shirt. I grabbed a caffeine-free Diet Pepsi from the fridge and settled myself on the couch. I then snatched up the remote and happily started flipping channels.

I was halfway through an episode of *Say Yes to the Dress: Atlanta* when my phone rang with Danielle's ringtone.

Damn it.

I answered, even though I already knew what she wanted.

"Hi, Danielle," I said, trying to sound upbeat.

"Laura, it's good to talk with you again. Max called me earlier tonight and said you'd be willing to act as his negotiator in the talks."

"Well, to be honest, I really didn't have much of a choice. Tony and Max sort of volunteered me. But if we're going to do this, let's get it over with."

"I was thinking the same thing. Can you meet with me tomorrow for an early lunch?"

"I should be able to," I said. "What time?"

"I was thinking eleven-thirty. What about La Playa Bonita on Scottsdale Road up by CrackerJax? Would Mexican be alright?"

"Sure," I said. "I know where it is. I'll see you tomorrow."

This is really going to suck.

~~~~

The alarm went off at seven, and I pounded on it until it shut off. I stumbled into the kitchen and put on the coffee. I then sleepwalked into the shower and stood there, nearly immobile, for fifteen minutes as feeling slowly came back to my arms and legs.

One of the nice things about September is that you start to get cold water again, and the conditioner doesn't immediately rinse out of your hair. During the summer, the water coming out of the cold-water tap was roughly the same temperature as what came out of the hot.

With the change of seasons, the water from the cold side was now starting to feel a tiny bit cooler. It was another sign that summer was ending, and paradise weather was almost ready to return.

After the shower, I went back into the kitchen and poured a cup of coffee into my *Dr. Who* mug. Seeing David Tennent and Billie Piper smiling back at me as I poured my morning coffee always made me smile.

I ignored Marlowe's desperate cries for food and went into the bedroom to stare into the closet. I knew I was going to meet with Danielle, and although I wasn't trying to impress her, I also didn't want to look like I was purposely trying to look crappy.

After a couple of false starts, I settled on some black slacks and a lavender short-sleeve top. A few minutes in front of the mirror and I was as good as I was going to get.

I went back into the kitchen and poured the rest of the coffee into *The Big Pig*. From the fridge, I tossed a strawberry Greek yogurt into my purse. I fed Marlowe and left before he had a chance to throw up.

~~~~

With my coffee mug in one hand, I locked the apartment, then took the back stairs out to the parking lot. As I got to my car, a kid stepped in front of me.

He was medium height and bone-thin, wearing a red T-shirt, beat-up jeans, and dirty white cross-trainers. He had short dark hair, a short scruffy beard, and couldn't have been more than nineteen or twenty. He had the forlorn look of someone who'd started to figure out that things in the real world wouldn't always go his way.

Looking closer, the boy had two black eyes, and the entire left side of his face was an angry purple bruise. Above his left cheekbone was a deep gash, held together with a butterfly bandage.

I'd had wounds like that before, and I was about to advise him to get stitches for the cut so it wouldn't scar. Instead, before I could say anything, he pulled his hand out from his front pocket and snapped open a switchblade.

Shit, stay calm. This doesn't feel like a Black Death thing.

"Alright," he said, "you know what I want."

"What? You want me to have sex with you because you have a knife?"

"No, not sex, although maybe later if you don't do everything I say."

"So, what do you want?"

"Don't play dumb with me, bitch."

"Language!" I said. "And I have no idea what you're talking about."

"Oh, you know exactly what I'm talking about. I want *The Child*."

"What child?"

"Don't play stupid. It was in the fancy wooden box, and you know exactly where it is. We're going to get in your car, and you're going to drive me to *The Child*. If you don't, I'm going to stab you, and I'll keep stabbing you until you tell me what I want to know."

He seemed to think about it for a few seconds. "Then I'll force you to have sex with me in your car."

Okay, so this guy is nuts.

"Look," I said, "I don't know what you're talking about, and the knife isn't going to help."

"Oh, it'll help me get exactly what I want from you, bitch."

"Fine," I said. "You've got me. I'll drive you to it, but I'll need to get out my keys."

"Okay, but I'm watching you."

I carefully set *The Big Pig* on the hood of my car. I then opened my purse, pulled out my gun, and pointed it at his chest.

I felt a pang of regret that my Baby Glock had been taken from me the month before. All I had now was my old .25 semi-automatic.

The kid saw the gun, and he jerked upright. His eyes grew big, and he took a quick step back. He then took a closer look at my tiny gun, and his eyes narrowed.

"What the hell is that?" he scoffed. "A .22? Are you serious?"

"It's a .25, and if you don't get out of here, I'll show you what it does."

Still with a look of contempt on his face, he lunged at me with the knife. I took a step back and shot him in the foot.

The gun made a pathetic popping sound rather than the satisfying roar of my Baby Glock, but it did the job. The kid yelped and dropped the knife.

He then fell to the ground and clutched at his foot. "You bitch! You shot me."

"What'd you expect me to do?" I looked at where the bullet went into his cross-trainer, and it was well off to the side. In fact, I'd almost missed his foot altogether.

"It doesn't look like anything other than a flesh wound," I said. "But if you'd like me to call the police, they'll be glad to take you to a hospital."

"Sure, you'd like that," he sneered. "If I go in again, I'm not coming out for ten years. I'll fix it myself, but then I'll be back for you, bitch."

He began to limp out of the parking lot, leaving a small dot of blood with each step. I grabbed my coffee mug and watched as he limped down the street, eventually stopping at the bus stop halfway down the next block.

I hung back and waited until the bus came and took him away. I went back to my car and found the knife lying next to the back tire.

I briefly considered saving it as evidence to show the police. Instead, I picked it up, walked over to the dumpster, and tossed it in.

Sometimes I hate my job.

~~~~

Once I arrived at the office and dropped my bag off at my

cubicle, I walked up and sat in the wingback chair next to Sophie's desk.

"What's wrong?" she asked. "You don't look so good."

"I'm having a shitty day."

"What happened this time? Did you get stuffed in the trunk of your car and almost die of heatstroke again? Or did somebody force your car off the road and then threaten to shoot you again? Or did somebody handcuff you to a bed and threaten to gut you like a fish?"

Sophie stopped and got a confused look on her face. "Was it gut you like a fish, or were they going to shoot you that time? I sometimes forget what they threatened to do to you."

"You were right the first time," I said. "It was gut me like a fish."

"Well? What happened today?"

"Some jerk pulled a knife on me in my parking lot this morning."

"You're right. That's a shitty way to start out the day. What happened?"

"He came at me, and I had to shoot him in the foot."

"Ouch. That's a shitty way for him to start his day too."

"Don't tell Gina. She'd want me to report it, and I really don't want to spend the rest of the day filling out forms and answering questions."

"My lips are sealed. What did he want? Money or sex?"

"He was asking about someone he was calling the child. Does that ring any bells?"

"What child?"

"That's what I've been asking."

"Nope," Sophie said. "Did you try Googling *child*? It's kinda generic, but you never know."

"No, but it's a good idea. Try it."

Sophie went to her computer and started typing. "Um, so this probably isn't going to help. There are one billion four hundred and seventy million results for *child*."

"Anything worthwhile?"

Sophie started flipping through computer pages. "Nope. Of course, it would help if I knew whose child I was looking for."

"If I knew that, you wouldn't need to look it up. Okay, this won't get us anywhere. Let's narrow it down. Try 'famous children' instead."

Sophie typed, then shook her head. "We're down to two hundred and thirty million results, but it's really not any better."

I tried to remember what the kid with the knife had actually said. "When he asked me about it, he was calling it *The Child*, like it was a name rather than a description. Try that."

Sophie started typing again. "Nope, still way too many results."

"Anything relevant?"

"Um, there were movies in 1977, 2005, and 2012 called *The Child*."

"Was Stig Stevens in any of them?"

"Um, no, but the last one starred Sunny Mabrey. She's good. She did *Snakes on a Plane*. That's a classic."

"What else?"

"Um, there was a Star Trek Next Generation episode called *The Child*. I watched that one a few weeks ago on Netflix. It was the first episode from season two, the one where

Commander Riker shows up with a beard. Anyway, Deanna Troi gets pregnant by a space alien and has a baby in like two days. Of course, things go to hell, and the child has to kill himself, or else everyone on the Enterprise would die from a space plague. Although I guess he really didn't die. He went all science fiction and changed into a point of energy and floated out into space."

"Anything else?"

Sophie flipped through five or six more computer pages. "Nope, you gotta give me more."

"The guy said something about the child and a fancy wooden box, but that doesn't make a lot of sense."

"Maybe he buried somebody's child in a wooden box, like a coffin?"

Sophie typed several combinations of 'the child' and 'wood box', but nothing came up. She then looked up some recent cases of children being buried alive, but there was nothing from Arizona over the last eight or ten years.

"Nope," she said. "He didn't give you enough information. Next time, you need to get accosted by a smarter class of hoodlum. How'd your meeting with Max go? Did it turn into a date?"

"No, it was like I thought. We met to discuss a side project. Tony was there too."

"Well, side project or not. I think it's Max's way of telling you he hasn't forgotten about you."

~~~~

Gina came into reception from the door to the street carrying a tray with three coffees. She handed one to Sophie and then one to me.

"I saw your car pull in, so I got you one, too," she said.

"Thanks," I said. "I can use this."

"Thanks," Sophie said as she poured the coffee into her *I'd Rather Be Surfing* mug. "I had a long night last night, and I need this. You can't have too much coffee in the morning."

I popped the top off *The Big Pig* and poured the coffee in. "That smells great," I said. "What is it?"

"Cinnamon vanilla," Gina said. "They started selling it this week at the shop across the street."

Sophie took a sip. "Nice, it's sort of like a mocha horchata."

"What's going on with your missing body?" Gina asked.

"Nothing so far. I talked with everyone who stayed at the party after Stig went to bed, but it's leading me nowhere. I found out about an argument at the party earlier in the night, but that doesn't seem like it'll go anywhere either."

"If there really was a dead body, there had to be some sort of motivation for someone to commit the murder. An argument seems like the closest thing you have to a motive so far. Don't give up until you get two or three opinions on it."

"Did you get a chance to talk with Christine Johns?" Sophie asked. "What's she like?"

"She was nice. She gave me a glass of some great-tasting wine and then showed me around her house. It wasn't as big as Stig's, but it was beautiful. It had enough rock 'n roll memorabilia on the walls to look like a Hard Rock Café."

"Damn," Sophie said. "I'm totally jealous."

"Me too," said Gina. "Hopefully, you'll have an excuse to bring her by the office sometime. I'd love to meet her."

"Yeah, bring her in," Sophie said. "We can make Lenny take a picture of the four of us. I'd love to put that on Instagram."

Chapter Five

I still had an hour before I needed to leave for my lunch meeting with Danielle. I went back to my cubicle and tried to organize the rest of my day.

I'd now talked with everyone who stayed at the party after Stig had gone to bed. Although nothing was obvious, I did have a few questions for Stig.

Next would be the household staff. If nothing came from that, I'd need to go down the list of party guests, one by one.

I silently dreaded doing all of those interviews. It would be a long and tedious process that would likely lead nowhere. Unfortunately, I didn't see another way forward.

I called Stig, and when he answered, it sounded like he was in a car.

"Hi, Stig, it's Laura Black."

"Hello, Laura. Can you hear me alright? I'm driving with the top down."

"I hear you fine. Will you have any time to talk later today?"

"I have a charity luncheon at The Boulders, but it should

be over by one or one-fifteen. I should be home by two o'clock, two-thirty at the latest. You know the gate combination. Ring the front doorbell when you get there."

"Okay. I'll see you then."

~~~~

At thirty-five minutes after eleven, I pulled into the parking lot for La Playa Bonita. They have half a dozen locations scattered throughout Phoenix and Scottsdale, but I haven't been to one in years.

I tend to think of the big chain restaurants as tourist-Mexican places where the snowbirds go when they make their annual winter pilgrimage to Arizona. The food at the chains is typically bland, the music is loud, and the decorations are usually over the top.

When I go out for Mexican food, I typically go to one of the small neighborhood places that may not even have a sign out front. The kind of place where no one is speaking English, and the only decoration is a TV on the wall blaring out a soccer game in Spanish.

There'll be a salsa bar along one wall with four or five different salsas, ranging from a mild pico de gallo to a flamethrower hot dark red. The food is always better than the chains, even if the décor is worse.

I walked into the restaurant and looked around. As its name suggested, the place was set up like a tropical beach bar.

The music playing through the overhead speakers and the decorations on the walls were festive. It was nice but not too much.

There were a lot of people, with everyone talking and having a good time. For a chain restaurant, it seemed like a nice place.

I went to the hostess stand and said I was meeting Danielle Ortega. A woman in a fluffy, brightly colored dress led me to one of the private banquet rooms in the back.

Walking past tables of sizzling fajitas made my stomach growl. I hadn't been able to eat before the meeting, and now I realized how hungry I was.

I looked around the room and saw three grim-looking men casually sitting next to the entrances and exits. I'd seen them all before, and they were starting to look familiar.

Other than the men, the large room was empty except for Danielle. She was seated alone at a small table against a back wall.

I sat across from her, and a waitress came to the table with a basket of chips and salsa, along with a pitcher of margaritas and two glasses. I poured the drinks and handed one to Danielle.

There was an uncomfortable silence as we both sat and looked down at the drinks. At last, Danielle spoke.

"Laura, thank you for agreeing to meet with me. We need to restart the negotiations. My hope is your close relationships with Max and Tony will allow us to finish this quickly. I know you've been avoiding me, and I suppose I can understand why, but it will be good to work with you on this. Maybe we can even be friends again?"

"How do you expect us to be friends or even work together after you left me alone to die?" I asked.

"Aren't you forgetting I also saved your life? I didn't ask you to come and kidnap me right before I was supposed to go to the big meeting with Tony. If you'd stayed at home, none of it would have happened. Raul wanted to spend the entire night slowly slicing off your face with his razor. I stopped him before he was able to do anything gruesome to you. He's very upset with me for doing that, by the way. He still feels he owes you a great deal of pain for what you did to his eye with that can of wasp spray."

"I came to get you because you were my friend. I'd found out there was the possibility of a shootout where you worked, and I was afraid something would happen to you. I wanted to get you as far away from it as I could."

Danielle studied her drink for a moment, then looked up at me. "You see," she said, talking low so the men couldn't overhear, "we both took a chance that day. I'm not sorry I saved your life. The only part I regret is telling you the truth about who I am. It was very foolish of me. I thought you were about to die, and I couldn't see a way of saving you, so I told you the truth. I thought you deserved to know. When I was able to save you at the end, it put me in a very delicate position. You and Sergio are the only two people in America who know who my father is. I know my secret's safe with Sergio because it's in his best interest to keep it quiet. I hope I can also trust you."

"Well, if not, you said you'd kill Sophie and Gina."

Danielle waved her hand as if it weren't anything of importance. It reminded me of Tony.

"I was upset. You need to understand that it was a very difficult day for me. I had seen Carlos gunned down, and I'd known him all of my life. My only goal in making the threat was to show how important it was for you to keep your word and not tell anyone. I like both Sophie and Gina, and I'd feel terrible if anything happened to either of them. So, what do you think? Can we still be friends?"

"Um, maybe. I don't know. You still left me to die that day. I was tied up and dangling from the end of the chain like a piñata when you walked out of the room. I had no idea if you had any intention of coming back. In fact, you'd made it pretty clear you weren't going to. I thought I was going to be tortured to death at the hands of that sick fuck Raul."

"I only left you there because I couldn't see a way to get you out of it. Don't forget, I did come back and rescue you before Raul had a chance to use his razor on you."

I got a flashback of Raul holding his straight razor, inches in front of my eyes, slowly twisting it back and forth so I could see the lights of the torture chamber flicker across the sharp, thin blade. I could smell his foul breath as he laughed and told me how badly he was going to hurt me.

I could feel the sensation of him pulling my lower lip out until my eyes watered from the pain. I remembered him taunting me that it was going to be hard for me to kiss anyone without lips, but maybe I could get a skin graft from my ass that would sort of look like lips. I then recalled the feeling of cold steel against my skin as he started to cut.

"Laura?" Danielle asked. "Are you okay?"

"Yes, and you're right," I said. "You did come back and rescue me. I probably wouldn't be alive if you hadn't. I never did thank you for doing that."

"Okay, so no more threats. If my secret gets out, then all hell will break loose, and a lot of people on both sides will be killed. Neither one of us wants that to happen. Do I still have your word? Is my secret still safe with you?"

"I won't break my word."

"Good. Alright, as far as the negotiations with Tony go, nothing's changed since talks broke down six weeks ago."

"Broke down?" I asked. "You mean when Sal Monza tried to kill Tony, and then it became a general shootout?"

"Yes. I still don't know why Sal did that. He was secretly placed high up in Tony's organization, and he was feeding us good information. I think Tony was bluffing when he said he knew who the traitor was. Sal messed up everything and was killed because his ego was bruised." She shrugged her shoulders and shook her head. "Men."

I held up my glass, and she did the same. "Men," I said. "Can't live with them. Can't legally shoot them or set them on fire."

Danielle and I clinked our glasses together, and each took a long sip of our margaritas. There was a moment of silence as we were each lost in our thoughts.

I was still uncertain how I felt about Danielle. On the one hand, she was a criminal and had casually stood by as I was about to be tortured.

On the other hand, I could see her as a woman who had been thrust into a position she didn't want to be in. Her father had sent her to Arizona to secretly watch over and control a group of vicious men.

If any of it ever came out, she could easily be arrested or killed. It must be a life that was both lonely and terrifying.

No matter how I felt about our past history together, I was going to have to work with her and probably even socialize with her. Maybe, as time went on, we could even form some sort of a friendship.

"Alright," I said. "Let's take care of the negotiations. As I understand it, you want to import heroin into the country. Tony's never wanted anything to do with that since he's morally opposed to the drug. So, there're probably no issues there. You don't want him to interfere as you consolidate your position among the numerous smaller gangs that are also currently importing heroin. Correct?"

"Yes, not to interfere and not to do anything to hinder us. Sal let us know it was Tony who alerted the authorities when we brought the shipment into Scottsdale in March. Many of our best men were arrested, and we lost the entire load. Losing the shipment was the reason Escobar asked me to come up to Scottsdale. He wanted a first-hand account of the situation from someone he could trust. Max and Tony need to understand they can't do anything like that again, or it will touch off a full-scale war."

"Okay, that makes sense, and I think Tony and Max will go for it."

"The trickier part is the arms trafficking," Danielle said. "It's most efficient for us to bring a truckload of heroin into the country and then return the truck to Mexico full of weapons. These trucks have secret compartments that make it very easy for drugs and arms to pass over the border. It's not so hard for us to get guns in America. Sometimes, your government even helps us get them. We know men in Central America and Mexico who will pay a lot for American weapons. You stumbled across one of our shipments last month as we were moving the arms down to our warehouse at the border."

Danielle paused and got a sad look on her face. "You really don't know how much destroying that shipment disrupted our organization."

"I didn't mean to do anything to the guns or the grenades. I certainly didn't mean to blow up the truck. I was locked inside and slowly baking to death. I was only trying to get out. The fire was an accident."

"I understand, and if I'd been in your position, I would've likely done the same. But now, Tony and Max need to be willing to split the arms trafficking with us. We think there's enough demand for both of us to succeed. In fact, we may be able to help each other."

"What do you mean?"

"We sometimes have requests for certain types of exotic

weapons, and we can't find the product. I know Tony has connections in the weapons business that we lack, especially with the military arms manufacturers in Texas and California. If Max and Tony are willing to work together on these special sales, it could benefit both of us."

"I'll pass on your message. I honestly have no idea how they'll feel about that."

"Thank you, Laura," Danielle said. I think, between the two of us, we'll be able to end the squabbling between our groups. I don't think either side wants a war."

At that, I held up my margarita again, and Danielle did the same.

"No more war sounds like a good goal to me," I said as we clinked the glasses together.

"Give peace a chance," Danielle said, and we each drained our glasses.

~~~~

After lunch, it was still too early to meet with Stig, so I drove back to the office. Gina was out, and Lenny had the door to his office closed. Sophie was at her desk with a bored expression.

"What's up?" I asked.

"Not a thing," she said. "What are you doing this afternoon?"

"Going back to Stig's house. I need to ask him a few questions."

"Oh, take me with you," Sophie said. "I don't know when I'll ever be able to talk to a real movie star again."

I glanced at Lenny's door. "Won't he mind?"

"Nope, he'll be in there all afternoon prepping for a

hearing. I'll lock the front door and forward the phone to my cell. He'll never even know I was gone."

"Well, come along then."

We went out to my car and got in. I pulled out of my parking space and lowered the top.

"I still can't believe Tough Tony gave you his car," Sophie said. "It's f'ing beautiful."

"I know. I'm still having a hard time believing it's mine. I've never had anything like this in my life."

"It's about time someone gave you something useful. Not that getting sparkly diamonds or huge rubies is a bad thing. I love my necklace and wouldn't trade it for anything, but this is something you can actually use. What did you end up doing with that old piece of shit car you had? Did you sell it or just abandon it somewhere?"

"I haven't done anything with it yet. It's parked at my apartment, in the last row of the lot. I pulled the plate and canceled the insurance."

"So, you abandoned it."

"Well, sort of."

"Good move. Even if you sold it, you'd probably feel guilty about dumping your problems on someone else."

~~~~

We drove to Stig's driveway, and I pulled up to the black gate. I reached out to the keypad and punched in the code Stig had given me. With a soft mechanical hum, the big gate slowly swung open.

"It's amazing you have the secret code to get into a Hollywood movie star's house," Sophie said.

"According to Christine, Stig's given out the code to half

of Scottsdale. It's one of the reasons I'm having a problem narrowing down what happened the other night."

We drove up to the courtyard and parked next to a red Jaguar F-type convertible. Stig had another three sports cars sitting out as if on display. We got out, and Sophie spent a minute walking around the vehicles.

"I could get used to being rich," she said as we walked up to the front door. "I'd have a big house and a lot of fancy cars. I'd park them like this too, like having so many expensive sports cars was no big deal, and I might have forgotten I'd left a few of them parked out on the driveway."

I rang the doorbell, and we waited. After a minute, the door opened, and a man I'd never seen before was standing in front of us.

He was about seventy years old and thin as a rail. I realized he must be part of the household staff.

"Good afternoon," he said. "I am Carter. How may I help you?"

"I'm Laura Black," I said. "We're here to see Stig. He's expecting us."

The man led us to a study off the main entrance hall, which was little more than a fancy waiting room. There was a desk without drawers, a few coffee table books, and several plain but comfortable chairs.

One thing that stood out was a full-length, life-size oil painting of Stig as Staff Sargeant Hancock from one of the early Hammer movies, maybe *Hammer Blast*. What struck me about the painting was the incredible level of detail the artist had included.

The rifle Stig was holding and the grenades hanging on his belt looked real enough to reach out and take. It was as if Sergeant Hancock was standing next to us, about to go out and battle evil.

~~~~

Stig showed up three or four minutes later and led us out to the back patio. We sat at a table next to the pool under a brightly-colored umbrella. The view of Scottsdale was as beautiful as I remembered, and I hoped we'd have a chance to be here at night when the lights of the city were shining.

A woman came out holding a tray with three tall glasses of iced tea. Each glass had an orange slice hanging off the side.

I took a sip, and it was a combination of mango and passion fruit. I'd never had anything quite like it before, but it was light and delicious.

"That's a great picture of you in your study," I said.

"It was a publicity painting they did for *Hammer Fall,*" Stig said. "That was the third movie in the series and was the one that really took off at the box office. The picture hung in the office of the studio president for about a decade. He gave it to me as a gift a few years ago."

"That movie was great," Sophie said. "I also liked your tough guy with the kids movie, *Sargent Daycare*. I thought it was hilarious when you were a drill instructor and an Army *SNAFU* had you assigned to a class of kids at the camp daycare. When the terrorists took over the post, it was up to you and the children to save the day."

"It was a trend back then. Arnold did *Kindergarten Cop,* and Vin Diesel did *The Pacifier*. Even Dwayne 'The Rock' Johnson did *The Game Plan*. Everyone had to do a movie like that."

"How was it working with a bunch of kids?" Sophie asked.

"It was interesting. Half of them were nieces and nephews of the producers and the studio bigwigs. They were clueless and had to be coached line by line what to do. We shot some scenes fifteen or twenty times and usually ended up using an ad-libbed line the kid made up on the spot when he forgot what he was supposed to say. The other half were eight and nine-year-old actors who'd been in acting school for upwards of four or five years. They were great once they got going, but their parents had convinced them they were now A-list movie stars, and they needed to be treated the same as any other A-lister. They each wanted a private trailer, a personal makeup artist, a personal script coach, and even stand-ins and doubles."

"It was still a great movie," I said.

"Oh yeah. The movie turned out well. The reviews were solid, and the studio made a ton of money. They want me to do a sequel, but I've been putting them off. Honestly, I'm getting too old for action movies. Lately I've been in a lot of Sci-Fi thrillers. The audience loves those, and I don't need to have as many fight scenes. Those start to wear me out."

"Those are wonderful movies," Sophie said. "I loved *Obscura*, where the aliens took over the earth through mind control, and only you and the swimsuit model knew what was actually going on. It was great when you gave *'The Hammer'* to one of the aliens."

"*The Hammer* is my signature move. You know, we did it as an ad-lib in the first Hammer movie, *Guts 'n Glory*. I was supposed to have a long fight scene with a terrorist. We'd spent all day shooting it, and I thought we had it, but the director wanted one more take before we wrapped for the day. Instead of doing the scene, I walked up to the terrorist, balled up my fist, and brought it down on his head, killing him instantly. I'd talked it over with the stunt actor ahead of time, and he played it perfectly, complete with a death grimace and rolling his eyes up into his skull as he fell dead. The director liked it and wrote a line for one of the other actors to say I'd 'nailed the terrorist with *The Hammer of Freedom*'. From then on, I've given *'The*

Hammer' to at least one bad guy in every movie I've ever made, even the ones that aren't official Hammer movies."

"Yeah," Sophie said, "I loved how you gave that space alien *'The Hammer'*. Then you turned and smiled at the camera, like you were letting us in on the joke."

"Yeah, I'll be eighty years old doing *The Expendables 15,* and I'll still be giving *'The Hammer'* to the bad guys."

We paused and sipped our iced tea. The pool was peaceful, and the view of Scottsdale was fascinating.

The desert air was clear, and every detail of the city was visible. I could have easily sat there all afternoon and watched the sun go down from Stig's patio.

I thought we'd better get the interview out of the way while we still had Stig's attention. "I've looked into everything that happened at the party, both before and after you went to bed," I said. "So far, nothing seems relevant to the dead guy you found in the pool."

"I assumed that was the case," Stig said. "Christine and Vicky both called and asked me what was going on. From what they said, neither one saw anything unusual."

"I'll still need to go down the list of everyone who was at the party, but I'm not sure if I'll get a lot of new information."

"What else can I do to help your investigation?" Stig asked.

Something from Monday had been stuck in my mind, and this seemed like a good time to ask. "Did you say you were wearing a jacket at the party? That seems pretty unusual. It's the middle of September in Scottsdale."

Stig laughed. Apparently, he'd been asked the question before. "Over the years, I've gotten used to the heat," he said. "I typically keep the windows open as long as I can in the summer and only use the air-conditioning when it starts to get really hot in June, and I can see the staff sweating. Even when I do run the AC, I set it at about seventy-eight or eighty. But I know my friends run their air-conditioning most of the year and keep it set much colder, like at seventy-five. Whenever I have a party, I cool down my house to make it comfortable for my friends. The night of the party, I was cold all through dinner. I didn't get warm again until the party had moved outside next to the pool."

"Okay, I know what you mean," I said. "When I go out to a restaurant, I usually bring a sweater. I know they'll keep it at sixty-eight degrees for the tourists. You can tell who the Scottsdale natives are because they're the ones who bring coats and sweatshirts into movie theaters."

"I do the same thing," Stig said. "I'll usually wear a sweater whenever I go to a movie premier since they always keep the theaters so cold. Jeanette suggested the sweater to soften my image, but honestly, I wear one to stay warm."

"Let's talk general home security," I said. "The keypad combinations on your gate and front door, how often do you change them?"

"It's been a while," he admitted. "To be honest, I lost the book that describes how to do it, and I've been too lazy to look it up on the internet."

"How many people have the combinations?"

"I'm not sure, ten or twelve, well probably more than that. But they're all trusted people, and I wouldn't have any worries about any of them."

"Okay, but give me as many people as you can remember. If someone came in after the party, it's possible they had the codes."

"Well, there's Jerry and Luther, Vivian and Vicky,

Christine, and then the women I've dated since my divorce from Viv. There are probably eight or ten of them. I guess I'd also need to include guests I've had stay here for more than a few days. I usually give them the codes too."

"So, how many people would you guess you've given the codes to over the years?"

"It's probably more than I remember. Maybe thirty or forty."

"So, it's a safe bet the number is pretty high, and most of the people who've been close to you over the last ten or fifteen years have it. It doesn't really narrow down who could have come in. I'd suggest you have one of your staff look up how to change the codes, then do it within a few days. I'd feel better if there was at least some level of protection around you."

Stig nodded. It wasn't exactly a yes, but it seemed about as good as I was going to get.

"By the way," Stig said, "Speaking of security. I still can't find my wallet. I know I had it with me the night of the party, but I haven't seen it since. It's possible whoever killed the dead guy stole it."

Or maybe one of your 'trusted friends' at the party took it?

"Okay," I said. "I'll keep an eye out for it."

~~~~

We chatted for a few minutes, then Sophie and I stood up to leave. When we did, I had another stray thought and looked at Stig.

"This may not have anything to do with the dead guy, but earlier today, I was asked about a 'child' or maybe 'the child,' possibly in a fancy wooden box. Does that ring any bells?"

"Not really," Stig said. "My daughter's going to USC and lives in Los Angeles with Vivian. There haven't been any children over here in months. I did get a nice wooden box a few weeks ago, but it had nothing to do with a child."

"Alright, tell me about the box part."

"I think you know we finished filming *Hammer's Revenge* about three weeks ago. At the wrap party in Shanghai, we did a formal exchange of gifts with the people who'd arranged for us to film in China. We gave out seven or eight gifts, and I got one directly from Mr. Zhang, the main Chinese money guy. We gave him a blast gun I'd used when I played Colonel Abrams in *Galaxy Brigade*. The studio did a nice job with it. It was mounted on a gold stand in a glass display case."

"What'd you get?"

"It was a little green stone carving, probably jade. It was pretty, but not something I'd ever keep. I did like the box, though. It was made of some sort of dark wood, and it was beautifully carved. It had mother-of-pearl inlays all over it. I have the box down in the music room if you'd like to see it."

"Sure, maybe it will help clear this up."

We walked down a flight of stairs and then down the long hallway to the music room. Sophie saw the signed AC/DC and Metallica tour posters on the far wall and walked over to look at them.

Stig went to the bookshelf and paused. He then looked at the other shelves all along the wall.

After about fifteen or twenty seconds of searching, he turned to me. From the look on his face, I knew what he was going to say.

"It's not here."

"Where's it supposed to be?" I asked.

"Right here," he said, pointing to a shelf half-full of books. I put it here two weeks ago."

"How big was it?"

"It was about the size of a shoe box, maybe a little bigger," he said as he held his hands about a foot apart.

"Do you know what kind of wood it was made out of?"

"Not really, but it was dark and nicely carved. The top of the lid had two trees facing each other. There was mother-of-pearl embedded into the wood to look like fruit hanging on the trees. It had a silver key with intricate scrollwork on it. The whole thing was really very beautiful."

"What was in the box?" I asked. "A stone carving?"

"Well, I think it was made of stone, and I'm sure it was supposed to be artistic. It was green and from China, so I assume it was jade. To be honest, it looked like the same sort of junk you get at any of the tourist shops. I'm not a big collector of travel knick-knacks, but I did like the box."

I had a sudden revelation. "When we were talking with Lenny at the office on Monday, you said your house had been broken into about a week ago. Christine mentioned it, too. You said nothing had been taken, but is it possible they took the box then?"

"No," Stig said, "I showed Jerry the box and the carving a few days before the party."

"Oh," I said, slightly disappointed. "What happened to the jade? Do you still have it somewhere, or was it in the box when they took it?"

"I asked Jerry to find someone who'd want it. My friends seem to collect things like that. I figured someone would be interested in it. Jerry said he'd put it on one of the tables in the entrance hall before the party. Maybe it's still there?"

"Jade?" Sophie said as she walked over. "Isn't that valuable?"

"Some can be, but most aren't," Stig said. "There are a lot of green rocks in China, and in the tourist shops, they're all labeled as 'jade.' Jerry got a pair of jade bookends, and I know I saw the same set in a souvenir store for thirty dollars."

"Your piece of jade," I asked. "What did it look like?"

"Well, it wasn't a figurine or an animal. It was something artistic."

"Artistic?" Sophie asked.

"Weird looking," Stig said. "I thought it looked like a bug sitting on a green ocean wave. Like I said, weird."

We went back through the house to the entrance hall, and Stig showed me the table where Jerry would have placed the little sculpture. As I expected, the carving wasn't there.

"Anyone who was at the party could have it now," Stig said. "Maybe Jerry knows who took it. Do you think it's important?"

"No idea," I said. "But someone broke into your house a week ago, your Chinese box is missing, and this week you saw a dead guy in your pool. I'm not a big believer in coincidence. All of those things could somehow be related."

~~~~~

We left Stig's house and drove back to Old Town. Sophie said she was getting hungry, so we drove to the Bottled Blonde.

It's located across from the Maya Day and Nightclub on Indian Plaza, in the nightclub district off Buckboard Trail. During the day, it's a pizza place, but at night, it's more of a club.

I parked in the public lot we normally use when we go to the Maya, and we walked to the Bottled Blonde. At night, it gets crowded, but since it was only a quarter after five, we were able to get a table relatively quickly.

We sat, and both of us started to relax. I didn't realize how tense being with Stig for the afternoon had made me. Sophie must have felt the same thing because she started laughing.

"Can you believe we spent the afternoon with Stig Stevens?" she asked. "Gina's going to be totally jealous. You know, we should have asked him to take some pictures with us. I don't know if anyone is going to believe we were over at his house. Next time, we have to do pictures. Let's do them on the patio overlooking Scottsdale. Wasn't the view amazing?"

The waitress came by, and we ordered drinks. A scotch with one ice cube for me and a gin and tonic for Sophie. I also ordered a Margherita pizza while Sophie had the Supremo, which had a little bit of everything on it.

As we sat, I asked Sophie what she thought about everything.

"Well, I can understand why Stig got upset when he found a dead body floating in his pool. Can you imagine how gross it's going to be swimming in the pool after knowing there's been a dead guy in it? I mean, who knows what sort of nastiness leaked out of his body? I don't know if shocking the pool would do enough to get dead-body residue out of it. If I were Stig, I'd drain it, sanitize it, and then completely refill it. That way, you'd know you got everything out."

"Yes, but what do you think about the situation now?"

"Hey, no body, no crime. The dead guy seems to have walked out of the house all by himself. No one knows anything about it. I think Stig should let it go. Maybe he should beef up his security system a little. You know, change the code to his driveway gate and stuff."

"That's all you'd do if you found a body in your pool?"

"What else are you going to do?" Sophie thought about it for a moment. "Well, what about the missing box? Why don't you look for that? Jerry probably told everyone the whole story of the sculpture, and maybe someone thought it would be okay to take the box once they had the jade?"

"Maybe," I said. "But that doesn't seem like it will be related to the dead guy at all."

"True, but it will make it look like you're doing something useful and keep you busy until something else comes up. Plus, it will generate billable hours for Lenny. He'll like that."

"Maybe."

The waitress brought our pizzas out, and for a while, we became too busy with eating to pay attention to the assignment.

~~~~

After dinner, I drove Sophie back to the office. Lenny's car was still parked in his spot in the back.

"Do you think he knows you were gone?" I asked.

"Oh, sure. He started texting me when we were having iced tea by the pool."

"Was he upset that you were missing?"

"I told him we were over at Stig's house, and it seemed good enough for him."

Chapter Six

I made it back to my apartment a little after eight. Grandma's apartment was quiet, so she was either still out or had decided to turn in early.

I sat for a while on my couch, flipping through channels, trying to organize my thoughts. The dead body in the pool assignment was going nowhere.

My next step would be to interview Stig's household staff and everyone at the party. I wasn't looking forward to that, and I wasn't sure how much information I'd get from it.

I thought about Sophie's suggestion about finding the box. Although not directly connected with the guy in the pool, it was an unusual coincidence. Add that to the kid who'd pulled a knife on me and asked about a box, and it almost seemed like a trend.

I called Jerry Phifer, and he answered after three rings. In the background, I heard the clinking of silverware on dishes and the low murmur of people talking.

"Jerry, it's Laura Black. Sorry, did I catch you at dinner?"

"It's no problem," he said in a voice I could tell was meant for whoever was listening to him talk. The voice reminded me of an actor on stage reciting lines. "But I'll have to keep this brief. I'm having dinner with Jessica Jensen."

"Is that the blonde you were with last night?"

"That's right," Jerry said, still in his false stage voice. "The word's starting to get out about her. She totally killed it in *Obscura 2* and is currently up for a part in *Time Vortex*."

"Look," I said. "I won't interfere with you and your protégé, but I need to ask you about the little green sculpture Stig got from China."

"Oh yes," Jerry said. "It was one of the gifts we got at the party after shooting wrapped in Shanghai. You know, everyone on the cast got along so well on the shoot. It was as if we were all a big family. What about it?"

"Did Stig ask you to do something with it?"

"Um, hold on a second," Jerry said, then muffled through the phone, I heard, "Sorry babe, it's the coast. I'll need to take this. I'll only be a minute."

Thirty seconds later, I heard traffic noises in the background and realized Jerry must have stepped out into the parking lot. I then heard the sound of a Zippo lighter opening and closing. After several more seconds of hearing Jerry puff on a cigarette, he came back on.

"Sorry about that," he said, as I heard him exhale a lung full of smoke. "Yeah, a few days ago, Stig gave me the key to the box he got in China and asked me to see if anyone at the party wanted the little figurine. I put it out on the table near the front door."

"Tell me about the carving. What did it look like? Color, shape, size?"

"Not much to tell. It was smooth and green. Maybe nine or ten inches long."

"Was it made of jade?"

"I don't know anything about jade. It was green, and it felt like a rock, so yeah, maybe it was jade. Of course, it was really smooth, and the thing was almost clear enough to see through, so maybe it was only plastic. Like I said, I'm no expert in rocks."

"What was the carving?" I asked. "Stig said it was a bug on an ocean wave."

"Stig was close," Jerry said, laughing. "But swear to God it was a cricket or maybe a grasshopper sitting on a leaf. Of all the things you could do for a carving, they chose a grasshopper on a leaf."

"Do you know who at the party took it?"

"Um, no, sorry. I told most everyone about it, so really, it could have been anyone."

Shit.

"What did you do with the key? Did you leave it in the box?"

"Um, let me think. No, I think I still have it somewhere. I should probably get it back to Stig."

"No rush," I said. "The box is missing."

"Shit, what happened?"

"I don't know yet. When was the last time you saw it?"

"It was the day of the party. Stig had given me the key the day before. I took the green thing out of the box and put it on the table by the front door."

I had a thought. "At the party, did you really tell everyone about the little green sculpture, or did you only tell the women?"

Jerry thought for a moment, and I could hear him puffing

on the cigarette. "Well, maybe you're right. Come to think of it, I did only tell the women. But there were a few of the men who knew about it, too, like Luther. You know, what I can't understand is, who the hell would want to steal an empty box? Do you think this has anything to do with the dead guy?"

"I don't know, but things aren't adding up, and that always makes me nervous."

"Alright," Jerry said. "Let me know if I can do anything else for you, but wait until tomorrow to call. After another drink or two, Jessica's going to start to get horny. If things go well, I won't be answering the phone again until morning."

~~~~

I couldn't think of anything else to do on the assignment, so I put on a T-shirt and started to wind down for the night. I had just sat back down on the couch when my phone rang with Reno's ringtone.

I mentally slapped myself for not calling him sooner. I'd promised to set up a date for later in the week, and it was already Wednesday. I smiled when I remembered I'd promised to set up not only a date but a romantic evening as well.

I'd been feeling sexually frustrated ever since I'd turned him down on Monday, and seeing Max had only made it worse. Being with Reno for a long dinner and a night at his place would do us both a world of good.

Darn, I might have to skip dinner with Danielle on Friday night after all.

"Hey, you," I said. "How's your week been? Sorry I didn't call sooner. It's been nuts around here."

"Laura, we need to talk," he said, his voice having the flat, dull tone he got when conducting official police business.

Shit, this can't be good.

"Um, sure," I said. "What's up?"

"Look, you know we're constantly running surveillance programs on persons of interest in Scottsdale. Now that Tony DiCenzo appears to be sidelined, one of his lieutenants, a man named Maximilian Bettencourt, seems to have taken over."

Bettencourt? Huh, go figure.

"We believe Bettencourt's only leading the group until Tough Tony recovers from his latest injury, but these things sometimes have a way of becoming permanent. Yesterday, Bettencourt took several meetings, mostly involving his development company, Scottsdale Land and Resort Management. However, he did have one meeting with Tony DiCenzo and a woman. That woman was you."

Oh, shit.

"Do you have some sort of explanation for why you met with the heads of the largest criminal organization in Arizona?"

Although Reno still had his emotionless cop voice going, I could tell he was upset.

"Um, wow," I said. My mind scrambled to come up with something plausible. As usual, when I couldn't think of anything that sounded better, I told the truth—well, some of it.

"Hey, you know how this works. One of the advantages of not having a badge is I can go places, do things, and talk to people you can't touch. I'm working on an investigation for Lenny and needed to talk to Max Bettencourt about part of it. I called over and set up the meeting. We talked for about twenty minutes, and then I left. I didn't know Tony DiCenzo would be there too."

"What did you talk about?"

"You mean you didn't have him wired for sound?"

"Don't get this way. A lot of people suspect that

Bettencourt and his group are responsible for the upswing in heroin coming into Arizona over the last six months. They're responsible for a lot of misery and death."

"But his group isn't involved in heroin. That's the Mexican cartel called the Black Death."

Shit, maybe I shouldn't have said that part.

"And how would you know that?" Reno asked.

Damn, I definitely shouldn't have said that part.

"Um, I thought everyone knew that. I've been hearing about them ever since Jackie Wade and I were being held by that group of kidnappers. They were from the Black Death. Do you remember when you rescued Jackie and me from that old grocery warehouse about six months ago? Didn't you say you confiscated a big shipment of heroin on that bust?"

"We've heard about the Black Death, but we believe that particular heroin shipment was one of Tough Tony's operations. I'd heard a rumor that Tony called in the tip that led us to the drugs, but I later found out it came from your boss, Lenny, who apparently called the Captain directly. When we questioned Lenny, he said his main concern was the kidnapping of Jackie Wade, and he'd only found out at the last minute that drugs were involved. I didn't exactly believe him, but the Captain didn't want us to press his personal informant too hard."

"Didn't you arrest a lot of people when you confiscated the heroin? Didn't they talk?"

Reno made a sound of disgust. "Everyone we got was an illegal. We couldn't keep them. According to policy, we spent seventy-two hours questioning them and then gave them to ICE, who promptly drove them over the border and released them. I'm sure they were all back in Scottsdale later the same day. So, what did you and Bettencourt talk about?"

"Um, I'm investigating some things that have happened to Stig Stevens. I was hoping Bettencourt might have some information."

"Stig Stevens, the movie actor? You're serious?"

"Yes, and I shouldn't have told you, so please keep it quiet. I've been dealing with Stig and his manager for the past couple of days. I can't tell you what it's about, but if any of this makes it into the press, it will be a total shit storm."

"Okay, I'm not sure what's up with this, but I trust you'll stay away from Bettencourt, and you'll let me know if anything official comes up. Right?"

"Sure," I said, suddenly pissed. "You'll be the first one I call."

I hung up and threw the phone down on the couch.

Jerk.

~~~~

I was sound asleep and in the middle of a great dream when I heard my phone ringing. I ignored it as long as I could, then rolled over, picked it up, and hit the accept button.

"Hello," I mumbled into the phone.

"Laura, it's Jerry. I know it's f'ing early, but I don't suppose you know where Stig is?"

"Why would I know where Stig is? What time is it?"

"It's six-twenty, and Stig's missing."

"Wait a minute," I said, trying to clear my head. "If it's only six-twenty, how do you know he's missing? He's probably still in bed."

"No, it's not like that. We had a six o'clock Skype meeting scheduled with the writers in London to do a final run-through on the *Time Vortex* script. I got to the house about five-thirty.

Stig has a nice video conference room, and I was there, waiting for him to come down. By a quarter to six, I began to get a little worried. Stig and I usually do a coffee before these script meetings. It helps him get into character. At six, London called in, but there was no Stig. I had Carter go up to his bedroom to tell him the meeting had started, but he wasn't there. Stig has his flaws, but I've never known him to miss a meeting."

"You've tried his cell?"

"It's not turned on. It rolls straight into voicemail."

"Isn't six kinda early for a meeting?"

"It's afternoon in London. Besides, Stig was the one who set the time to correspond with his 'peak mental energy' time in the morning."

My head had started to clear, and I was becoming concerned. "When the butler went into Stig's room, what did he find? Had the bed been slept in?"

"I don't know. All I do know is that Stig is missing, and the studio knows about it. I've already gotten a call from the head of London. LA will start calling as soon as they wake up and read their messages."

"Alright," I said. "Let me get dressed, and I'll be right over."

~~~~

I made it to Stig's at about seven-thirty. I punched the combination into the gate and drove up to the house. The only car parked out front was the Tesla I knew belonged to Jerry.

I rang the doorbell, and the same butler as the day before let me in and showed me to the back patio. Jerry was sitting at a table next to the pool.

He had his phone in one hand, a lit cigarette in the other. An ashtray with half a dozen butts sat on the table next to his pack of cigarettes. He was in an animated conversation with someone over the whereabouts of Stig.

The view of the sun, low in the sky over the McDowell Mountains, was beautiful, but I doubted Jerry was in the mood to appreciate it. After two or three minutes of Jerry making promises to whoever was on the phone, he was able to hang up. He tossed the phone down on the table in disgust.

"That was the VP of Operations at the studio in LA," he said. "He wanted me to know they're officially 'concerned'. They'll be sending someone out to help me look for Stig."

"That doesn't sound very helpful."

"Nope, but that's the studio. They always have to be seen as doing something." Jerry sighed. "I'm sure they'll send out Sterling. He's Stig's handler with the studio. The guy's a real piece of work. Knowing him, he won't actually do anything. He'll ride my ass for a few days, then tell the studio I'm not doing enough."

"Well, has there been any word on Stig?" I asked as I sat next to him.

"Not a flipping thing," Jerry said. "I gotta tell you, I'm worried as shit. It's totally unlike Stig to take off like this."

"When's the last time anyone saw him?"

"Last night. Everyone but the cook took off by six. The cook stayed until about seven. She's here now and said she talked to Stig right before she went home."

"Did you ask about the bed? Had it been slept in?"

"I went up there right after I called you. The bed is still made from yesterday, and it doesn't look like he changed out of his clothes. Stig must have taken off sometime yesterday evening."

"Are any of the cars gone from the garage?"

"I haven't looked yet. Of course, I don't know if it will help. Stig has a collection of about thirty cars. Most of them are stored in a building out by McCormick Ranch. He rotates six or seven of his current favorites out here at any given time. Maybe Carter would be able to say if one was missing."

~~~~

We went up to Stig's room, but it was as Jerry had said. The bed was still made, and nothing looked out of place. We asked Carter about the clothes, and he confirmed he didn't find Stig's outfit from the day before.

We then went down to the garages. Here, we had better luck.

Despite what Jerry had feared, we both noticed that the purple Maserati roadster wasn't there. I suggested we go back to the pool to talk it over.

Jerry walked to the pool bar in the cabana and made himself a tall bourbon on the rocks. He asked me if I'd like a drink.

I shook my head, and we sat at the table by the pool. Jerry lit up a cigarette and took a long sip of his drink.

"I was afraid something like this would eventually happen," he said. "It's a given in Hollywood. All A-listers eventually snap. I've been thrilled that Stig has stayed cool for so long. Finding that body might have pushed him over the edge."

"I'll check out the possibility of foul play, but so far, it's looking like Stig left on his own. It's a good sign. It means he could come back at any moment."

Jerry didn't say anything. Instead, he sipped on his bourbon and looked out over the city. His bad eye was darting around in some sort of random motion. I could tell he wasn't the type to handle stressful situations well.

"The last few days have been pretty stressful for Stig," I said. "Does he have somewhere he normally goes when he takes off?"

"Well, he has a place in LA. The studio's already been there, but the staff says they haven't seen Stig since he came back from China. They're under orders to let the studio know if they see him."

"Where else would he have gone? Is there somewhere he might have gone if he only wanted to get away for a day or two and relax?"

"What?" Jerry asked as he lit up another cigarette. "Like a Buddhist monastery? A cabin in the woods? Nah, Stig doesn't have anything like that."

He paused and seemed to think. "Come to think about it, he does have a cabin in the woods. Well, it's not exactly his. Christine bought a place in Jerome a couple of years ago. She'd planned on fixing it up and converting it into a high-end day spa, but she ran into a problem with zoning. Seems her building was one of the original structures from back when Jerome was a mining boomtown, and the city won't let her change anything major. Stig's used it as a weekend retreat a couple of times."

"It seems like a stretch, but I'll go up and check it out. Do you have the address?"

"I've been there, but it's been a couple of years. Give Christine a call. She'll be able to tell you where it is. I should probably stick around here in case Stig comes back but let me know what you find."

~~~~

Jerry went into the house to make some calls while I got up and walked around the pool. Between the water, the view, and the desert oasis landscaping, it was a peaceful and relaxing spot.

I would have loved to stay here all morning. Instead, I pulled out my phone.

I called Christine, apologized for calling so early, and told her about Stig. I mentioned that Jerry thought Stig might have wanted to go up to her place in Jerome.

"It's possible," she said. "He has a key, and I'm almost never there. I told him he could use it whenever he wanted."

"Could you give me the address? I'd like to go up and check it out."

"Sure," she said. "Or, if you can wait for a couple of hours, I'll go up with you. If he really is missing, I'd like to help find him. That way, we can get into the building and check it out together. I have a charity opening in an hour, but it shouldn't last more than an hour and a half. Where should I meet you?"

"Why don't you swing by the law office? It's in the Old Town Arts district, and we can drive up from there."

"That would be perfect," she said. "It takes about two hours to get to Jerome from Scottsdale, so we should be up and back before dinner."

I gave her the address for the office, and she disconnected. I then called Sophie.

"Hey, are you and Gina going to be around later this morning? Stig's missing, and I need to find him. Christine Johns will be over, then we're going up to Jerome to see if Stig's in a place she owns there. If you're both there, I'll introduce you."

"You lost the client again? You know, you have a bad habit of doing that. Does Lenny know?"

"No. I should probably tell him, but I think I'll spend the day looking for Stig first. Who knows, maybe I'll find him and won't need to tell Lenny anything."

"Well, good luck with that. Speaking of Lenny, I'd love to meet Christine Johns, but this probably isn't the best day for Lenny to meet her. He's going through another one of those phases. The man really needs to find a girlfriend or at least visit one of those Thai massage places on a regular basis."

"What's going on this time?"

"He came out a few minutes ago and asked if I had any pictures of Elle. Come to think of it, it's the second time he's asked. He spent the night with her like six months ago, and I think he's still thinking about it."

"He hasn't been like this in a couple of months," I said. "I was hoping it had stopped."

"Oh, it gets worse. I think he's going commando today, and when he came out of his office, he had a stiffy."

"Yuck!"

"It was so gross. I nearly threw up in my trashcan. It wouldn't be good to have a lot of clients or people in the office today. When Lenny goes through one of these phases, it usually takes him a day or two to calm down. He should be good by tomorrow afternoon."

"Well, Christine will be there about eleven or eleven-thirty. Hopefully, we can keep them in separate rooms. At the moment, she's concerned about Stig and eager to help. I don't want Lenny to do anything to mess that up."

~~~~

I left Stig's and slowly made my way to Old Town. I made a point of driving down most of the side streets in Stig's neighborhood.

Since he was likely driving his purple Maserati, I thought he wouldn't be all that hard to spot. I'm not sure why I thought he would abandon his car somewhere near his house, but since

I didn't find it anywhere, I guessed I was wrong.

I was feeling hungry after my early morning with Jerry, and Christine wouldn't be at the office for almost two hours, so I decided to splurge and stopped by the Morning Squeeze for breakfast. It wasn't too crowded for a Thursday morning, and I was able to get a booth. The server came over and I ordered eggs Benedict and coffee.

As I sat and munched, I went over the morning and tried to come up with an explanation for what happened to Stig. I wasn't buying Jerry's idea that Stig was overstressed or was somehow starting to lose it. Maybe it was because I still thought of Stig as Sargent Hancock, and I was pretty sure he was still in control of his emotions.

I also wasn't sure about driving up to Jerome to look for him, but at the moment, I didn't have any other ideas, and the thought of spending the afternoon with Christine Johns was appealing. If nothing else, getting to know her better would make up for the lost time in case it was a dead end.

~~~~

I got to the office about ten-fifteen and parked in my space in the back. Gina was up in reception talking to Sophie.

When they saw me, they both wanted to know what had happened to Stig. I told them what I knew, which wasn't a lot.

I also confirmed Christine would be stopping by the office before we went to Jerome. Sophie and Gina were both thrilled, and we started reminiscing about Paradise Park and the concerts we'd attended over the years.

By eleven o'clock, we were keeping our eyes on the street, looking for any sign of Christine. While we waited, we asked Gina about her weekend and if she had any plans. She blushed a little and said she was thinking about making another date with the trainer from the gym.

"Didn't you say the guy was a loser?" Sophie asked.

"Well, yes," Gina said. "But I was thinking maybe one more evening with him wouldn't be so bad. Maybe I could figure out something for us to do so I won't have to hear him talk so much."

We started laughing, and Gina blushed a deeper red.

"Well, you know my advice for booty calls," Sophie said. "Go to his place. There's nothing worse than finishing up and having him fall asleep in your bed. It's always awkward when he wakes up in the morning and realizes where he is. Then, you both have to pretend you're still attracted to each other, at least until he leaves. Or it's even worse when he wakes up in the middle of the night, and he gets dressed in the dark and crashes into stuff as he tries to escape."

"I'll keep that in mind," Gina said.

The door to the street opened, and we all turned. I had expected Christine, but the woman who walked in was definitely not Christine. Instead, she was tall, thin, and had gorgeous straight auburn hair that fell halfway down her back.

She was immaculately dressed in a tight gold skirt with matching Ferrucci shoes and handbag. I recognized them from the Ferrucci website as the new styles that had only come out the month before.

Her makeup was perfect, and her boobs were about two sizes larger than could be expected if they were real. She reminded me of one of the cougars, with the exception that she was roughly my age, maybe a few years older. She looked around the office with a knowing eye as if she'd been here before.

"Well," she said, "I never thought I'd be back here again."

Gina and Sophie walked over, and they both gave her a polite hug.

"It's good to see you again," Gina said. "With everything going on, I figured you'd probably stop by."

I caught a whiff of some light and expensive perfume, again reminding me of one of the cougars. Gina started to introduce me. Instead of listening, the woman loudly talked over her.

"Alright," she said, "we've got a lot of work to do on this. First things first. Anything said about this outside the office goes through me. No exceptions. No talking to the press, your friends, or your family. Not one word. Everyone wants to be famous, and TMZ pays in cash with no questions asked. If this does get out, expect to see people and paparazzi hanging around outside the office. Expect them to start hanging around outside of your house or apartment as well. It goes without saying that you don't talk with any of them. I'm sure I'll have tasks for everyone to complete, so please clear your schedules. Everything else can wait. I've heard you've already been investigating this body in the pool thing, and you're currently looking for Stig? I'll need a full report on what you've found so far. Where's Lenny? I need to coordinate with him."

She then strode across reception, opened Lenny's door, and marched into his office. The door closed with a loud bang, and then the room went quiet while we all took a breath.

"What was that?" I asked.

"That would be Jeanette," Gina said, a bit annoyed. "The famous Jeanette Simmons."

Sophie looked up with a grumpy look on her face. "Freaking lawyers."

The door to the street opened again, and this time, I heard Sophie give out a loud gasp. I turned to see Christine walk in. She saw me and smiled.

"Hi, Laura," she said. "It looks like I have the right place."

Both Sophie and Gina were staring at Christine. Not wanting this to get awkward, I quickly introduced them.

"I'm a big fan," Sophie said. "I've been following you ever since you joined Paradise Park. I think I have everything you've ever done."

"Thank you," Christine said. 'It's always wonderful to meet my fans, and I'm grateful so many people have stuck with me over the years."

As she said it, I could tell she meant it. It was sort of surprising that such a big star truly appreciated her fans.

"We went to the same high school," Gina said. "It's nice you still live in Scottsdale."

"Well," Christine said, "I grew up in Scottsdale, and my parents still live here. I have a house in LA, but I spend most of my time here. It's comforting to have a stable place to return to, especially after coming back from a tour."

"Pictures!" Sophie said, then she looked over at Christine. "Um, do you mind?"

"Not at all," Christine said. "Should we use your phone?"

"Hell yes," Sophie said as she pulled out her phone.

We then spent several minutes crowding together as Sophie took several selfies of the group.

"Hold on a second," Gina said, disappearing into the back room and then coming back, holding one of the big Nikons we use for surveillance.

"This has a timer," Gina said. "It should make a nice picture."

She placed it on Sophie's desk, and we gathered in front of the bookshelf on the back wall. Gina set the timer, and we smiled as the camera counted down and then took the picture.

Gina went to get the camera when Christine said. "Let's do some more. We need to put ourselves into poses."

With Christine directing, we took pictures of ourselves acting serious, goofy, angry, sexy, and sleazy. After looking at the sleazy one, Christine laughed and made us all promise it would never show up on the internet.

"It was great meeting you," Gina said. "Unfortunately, I need to take off. I'm working on an assignment and have to be in north Scottsdale in half an hour."

As Gina walked to the back, the door to Lenny's office opened, and Jeanette came out with Lenny trailing behind. Unable to stop myself, I looked and saw that Lenny still had an erection. I heard Sophie say "gross" under her breath.

Lenny took three steps into reception, and then his eyes locked onto Christine. There was an instant look of recognition. Lenny tried to compose himself, and he walked toward Christine with his hand out.

Christine's mouth had fallen open, and she was looking at the obvious problem in Lenny's pants. Lenny saw where she was staring, and he looked down at himself. He saw the issue, and his face turned bright red.

"Um, um…" Lenny stammered as he dropped his hand. He then turned and quickly walked back into his office. He closed the door, and we heard the metallic snap of the lock being engaged.

Jeanette looked at Christine, and she broke out in a warm and friendly smile. The contrast between the snarling beast she had been and this new woman standing before us was startling.

She walked up to Christine and held out her hand.

"Jeanette Simmons," she said, "partner at JBC-RDS. We met at one of Stig's parties about a year ago. Are you still with Cushman and Rodgers?"

"Yes," Christine said. "They've had me ever since I started with Paradise Park."

"They're good," Jeanette said. "We're mainly known for handling actors, but we also have several A-list bands and vocal performers. If you ever think about switching, we'll be glad to discuss managing your publicity."

"Thanks," Christine said. "I'll keep it in mind. Stig's talked about you, and he says you're the best publicist he's ever had. I assume you're here because of him?"

"Well, yes." She then stopped talking, unsure of how much to say, even to someone as famous as Christine.

"It's okay," Christine said. "I know all about Stig disappearing. In fact, Laura and I are about to head up to a place I have in Jerome and see if he's there. Why don't you come with us?"

"Um, where's Jerome?" Jeanette asked.

"It's a little mountain town about halfway between Prescott and Sedona," I said.

Sophie made a noise, and I could see her pleading with her eyes.

"Um, as long as we're all going," I said. We should probably take Sophie too. She's a bloodhound when it comes to tracking down a missing person."

I looked between Jeanette and Christine, and neither of them seemed to object.

"I have a two-seater, and Sophie does too," I said. "Do either of you have a car that will fit four?"

"I brought Gracie," Christine said. "It'll be a tight fit, but we can all make it."

We walked out to the street from the front door and walked

half a block until we came to Gracie. She turned out to be a green Mini Clubman with big black eyelashes attached to her headlights.

"What a cute car," Sophie said. "Laura, you should put some eyelashes on your convertible. I know they'd look good on my Volkswagen."

"I'll let you know where to get them," Christine said, "but then you'll have to give your car a name. You can't have a car with eyelashes unless you also name it."

"Well," Sophie said, "I already have a name for my car. But you probably can't have a car called 'Piece of Shit' once you put the eyelashes on it."

We all piled in Gracie and headed north toward the mountains. The drive up to the mountains was uneventful.

We had our usual bathroom break at the Sunset Point rest stop, a little way past Black Canyon City, about halfway to our destination. The view was beautiful, and it made a good chance to stretch our legs after sitting for an hour in the Mini.

I hadn't been to Jerome since I was a kid. All I remembered about the town was it was windy, and there was an interesting mining museum in the middle of it. As I remembered from before, we approached the village from below on a road that gradually wound up from the small city of Cottonwood.

As we got closer, Christine talked about the town. "Jerome's an old mining settlement. It's on the side of Cleopatra Hill overlooking the Verde Valley, about halfway between Prescott and Sedona. It's five thousand feet above sea level, so it doesn't get too hot in the summer or too cold in the winter. In its heyday in the 1920s, over ten thousand people lived in the town, and most of them were involved with mining, alcohol, gambling, and prostitution."

We spent several minutes driving through the streets of the

small town, looking for Stig's car. If he'd driven it up here, we couldn't find it.

Christine parked Gracie in an open space along Main Street between a wine bar and an art gallery. When we got out, the air was noticeably cooler than in Scottsdale, and there was the scent of pine trees and sage in the wind.

We walked past a hotel, several busy restaurants, and a couple of Western-style saloons. Even though it was only two in the afternoon, a band was already playing in one of the bars.

I also noticed that every third or fourth building had an art gallery. Some were obviously high-end, but many of them looked affordable. It was as if Old Town Scottsdale had been picked up and dropped into the middle of an old western mining camp.

A couple of buildings down from the Connor Hotel, Christine stopped in front of a three-story building that looked like an old hotel. She unlocked the front door and turned on the lights.

We found ourselves in a big room that looked like a living room from the nineteen twenties. The only things that looked out of place were a circular card table with six chairs around it and a Western-style bar that took up most of the back wall.

Although the bar was beautiful, there weren't any bottles of alcohol on the shelves or anything that showed it had been used recently. On the wall behind the bar was a large painting of a naked woman reclining on a bed. Seeing the antique painting reminded me of Penelope of Prescott.

We split up and quickly searched the building but didn't find Stig or see any traces of anyone having recently been there. We went back to the front parlor and flopped down on the couches and chairs.

Jeanette let out an exasperated sigh and started texting on

her phone. Christine disappeared for a moment, then came back with a bottle of chilled white wine. She split the bottle into four glasses she'd brought out from under the bar.

"There've been several businesses in here since the original bordello closed down in the nineteen thirties," Christine said as she passed out the wine. "But the layout of the place hasn't really changed. This was the receiving area, and you can almost imagine the men standing at the bar, playing cards, or getting to know the girls who would hang out here in the parlor. There are a dozen rooms in the back and upstairs. I thought the place would make a good inn and day spa, but I would have needed to make some extensive renovations that would involve gutting most of the interior and only leaving the original shell. Unfortunately, this is a designated historic building, and I'm not able to make those types of changes."

"You can't change *anything*?" Sophie asked.

"Oh, I can fix up anything I want. I can even rip out and replace the plumbing or the electricity. However, the city frowns upon altering the fundamental character of a building. I was going to flip it, and I've had several offers, but I've sort of turned it into a private getaway for myself and some of my friends. It's a nice place to come and relax for a weekend."

Jeanette started talking, half to herself. We looked and saw she was reading a sign hanging on the side wall above an old upright piano.

Oh, the lust for mountain gold dust,

brought us lusty mountain men.

Who's lust for mountin' women,

made them lose their gold again.

"Isn't that great?" Christine asked with a broad smile. "The sign was here when I bought the place, and the woman who owned the building thought it might be original from when this was a bordello."

"Doesn't knowing what went on in here make you feel a little creepy?" Sophie asked.

"It was a fact of life in Jerome back then. About half the buildings in town were parlor houses at one time or another," Christine said. "They started off here on Main Street, but as more people moved into town, the bordellos moved to the next street down the hill. To get to Prostitution Row, you went down Husband's Alley. If you had money, you could get a crib or even a room at one of the nicer places, like the Cuban Queen. The House of Joy is still standing, and it's a great place to shop."

"Why Jerome?" Jeanette asked. "I thought most of the new businesses were going into Sedona?"

"My parents had friends who ran a restaurant here, and as a kid, we'd come up every summer. Back in 1903, the New York Sun ran a story that called Jerome the 'Wickedest Town in the West'. The hippies took over in the nineteen seventies, and since then, the town has had a mellow, artsy feel. How could you not love that?"

"It's pretty, in a Wild West sort of way," Jeanette said.

"Before we head back, would anyone like a late lunch?" Christine asked. "My treat."

We thought it was a great idea. We quickly washed the glasses, and Christine locked up.

We walked a couple of blocks down Main Street to a place called the Mile High Grill & Inn. At first, I worried about how Jeanette would manage the uneven sidewalks with her heels. Still, she navigated the walkways and even the wooden sidewalks without thought, again reminding me of one of the cougars.

The Mile High Grill was a joy. Sophie had the ghost pepper hot wings, and Jeanette ordered the southwest Caesar salad with dressing on the side.

Christine got the grilled vegetable wrap, and I tried the Nacho Mama's mac 'n cheese, complete with green chilies, salsa, and crispy tortilla strips. It was quality comfort food, and I could see why Christine liked it so much.

After lunch, I knew Sophie would have liked to stay to browse the shops and art galleries. I would have liked to stay as well, but I could tell Jeanette was getting anxious to get back into Scottsdale to look for Stig, and I didn't want to keep Christine any longer than we'd planned.

Since this had been my only lead for finding Stig, I wasn't as desperate to go rushing back into town. Vowing to return to Jerome sometime soon to spend the day shopping, we climbed back into Gracie and made our way back down to Scottsdale.

Sophie sat up front with Christine, and by the time we pulled into Old Town, they were chatting away like old friends. They mostly talked about dating. Christine said that over the last several years, she'd developed a preference for younger men. Sophie started laughing, and I knew what she was thinking.

"We have a group of friends I need to introduce you to," Sophie said. "I think you'd fit right in."

Jeanette and I were in the back seat. She spent almost the entire time texting and looking unhappy.

I tried to think about my next move for finding Stig. I knew Jeanette and Lenny would both want me to do something immediately. Unfortunately, nothing jumped out as the next logical step.

Chapter Seven

Traffic wasn't bad, and we were back at the office by five. Christine had a commitment for the evening, so she dropped us off at the front door and took off.

We had the feeling it was going to be a late night for Lenny. Sophie gathered her things to escape for the night before he could give her additional things to do.

Jeanette marched to Lenny's office. She opened the door and looked back at me. I knew the look, so I followed her in.

Lenny sat at his desk with a pile of papers and folders in front of him. Sitting in one of the seats in front of his desk was a man wearing an expensive-looking suit. The man stood up, and Jeanette walked over to him.

They exchanged a weird greeting that consisted of a quick hug, with neither of them looking at each other, and then they quickly air-kissed each other's cheeks. The greeting was obviously perfunctory, with no more emotion or significance than a handshake.

"Laura," Lenny said, "this is Sterling Montgomery from Stig's studio. He handles all of Stig's activities from the studio side."

We briefly shook hands with the same emotionless formality of Jeanette's hug.

"Jeanette," Lenny said, "make yourself a drink and have a seat. I'm going over what we've found so far with Sterling. Did you two have any luck finding Stig?"

Jeanette went to the wet bar and made herself a gin and tonic. I was somewhat surprised when she asked me if I wanted one as well.

Although I would have loved one, I shook my head no. Jeanette took her drink, walked to the window, and looked out at the shoppers walking down the sidewalks.

"Jerome was a dead end," she said, sipping her drink. "At this point, I don't know if there's a problem or if our client only wants a day or two to be alone and recover his equilibrium. If the story about the dead body is true, he's had enough stress over the past couple of days to rattle anyone."

"Our concern," Sterling said, "is the studio needs to know one way or another so we can take whatever actions are necessary to limit Stig's exposure."

As he said this, I looked over at Jeanette. The look she gave him was professional but definitely not warm. If Sophie had been in the room, I knew what she would say about lawyers.

Jeanette took the chair next to Sterling, and they both looked at Lenny. He took control of the meeting and promptly dumped it in my lap.

"Laura, you've had this assignment all week," he said. "What have you found so far?"

I spent the next half-hour telling Lenny, Sterling, and Jeanette about my investigation into the supposedly dead body in the pool and what little I knew so far about Stig's disappearance. All three then cross-examined me, looking for holes and inconsistencies in my story.

Lenny and Jeanette asked mostly logical questions, while Sterling's questions were all over the place. He wanted to know about Stig's daily routine, the routine of the household staff, alarm systems in the house, and if I had the list of who was at the party. He also asked if Stig seemed excited or agitated about anything other than the dead body and if he had traveled anywhere after returning from China.

When they'd finally finished, I felt wrung out and exhausted. I didn't say anything about the boy who wanted to kidnap me, the missing box, or the child. I still had no idea if any of it was relevant, and I didn't want to muddy the waters.

There was a pause, and by mutual agreement, everyone got up and stretched their legs. Jeanette and Sterling went to the wet bar and made themselves another drink.

After a minute, we gathered again around Lenny's desk.

"Well?" Lenny asked, looking at me. "Where do we go from here?"

"We haven't seen any sign of foul play," I said. "Apparently, Stig got into his car voluntarily last night and drove away. Our next step will be to have the phone company put a trace on his phone. It's been off all day, but if he turns it on, we'll know where he is."

"Okay," Lenny said. "Call Sophie and have her get that started."

Jeanette held up her hand and shook her head. "We've already set up a trace with the cell carrier. If he's in the country, I'll get a text with Stig's location pinpointed as soon as he powers up his phone. Even if he's outside the country, I'll still be able to narrow his location to whatever city he's calling from."

"You're authorized to do that?" Lenny asked.

"His phone's managed through us," Jeanette said. "It's a

standard part of our service. To protect Stig's privacy, an internet search on his phone number will only list JBC-RDS in Los Angeles. We can also manage the changing of the number in case it becomes public or he picks up a stalker."

"If Stig took off last night," Sterling said, "he must have had a reason. Jeanette, with your access to his phone records, could you see who may have called him last night."

"Good idea," Jeanette said and started texting into her phone.

"Alright then," Lenny said. "What else can we do? I assume we'll need to keep the investigation in-house, at least at this point."

"That's right," Jeanette said. "Until we know of an actual problem, no word of this can leak out."

"Credit cards are the next obvious thing," I said. "If he uses one or goes to an ATM for cash, we'll be able to find him."

"I talked to Luther this morning, and he's already on it," Jeanette said. "Same set-up as with the phone. If Stig uses a card, I'll get a text."

Lenny looked at her, and I could tell he was impressed. "Nice work," he said. "You've covered all the bases. Okay, Laura will work full-time to locate Stig. I'll also bring Gina Rondinelli in wherever she's needed. Both of you make sure everyone has your contact information."

Sterling pulled out a silver case, and Jeanette reached into her bag. Each pulled out two business cards. They both put one on Lenny's desk and gave one to me.

"My number's on the card," Jeanette said. "I'm staying at the Carmine Hotel. Do you know where it is? It's the closest decent hotel to here."

"I know it," I said.

The Carmine was the home of Junior Baker's Blues Club. I smiled inwardly when I thought about my meetings there with Tony and Max.

"I'll get a room there as well," Sterling said. "I caught the first flight to Phoenix and didn't have time to book anything." He then looked over at me. "I'd like to help with the investigation. Stig's my responsibility, and I'd like to do everything I can to make sure he's alright. I can go out with you starting tonight and can help as long as needed."

Shit, that's all I need, someone trying to help.

I glanced at Lenny, and he knew what I was thinking. "Sterling," he said, "I do appreciate how eager you are to get word back on Stig. Laura and Gina are already working on this. Of course, we can always use help. Stick around after this meeting, and we can figure out how you can best be of assistance."

Sterling saw he was being humored and started to protest. Lenny calmed him and spent several minutes telling him how he would be able to make useful contributions to the investigation.

This seemed to pacify him to the point that he stopped protesting. I thought his offer to help was honest but more polite form than anything else. I doubted a Hollywood executive seriously wanted to do anything more than demand results a couple of times a day.

~~~~

I stayed at the office until almost seven. By then, Lenny, Jeanette, and Sterling had wrung out all the information they could from me.

Lenny then offered to take them both to dinner so they could discuss the case in further detail. Fortunately, he didn't include me in the invitation, so I was able to leave.

~~~~

I pulled into the parking lot at my apartment and looked around, but I didn't see anyone suspicious. I parked and hit the button to close the roof.

The electric motor smoothly hummed as my roof came up from its place in the trunk and then settled into its slot above the windshield. It was in the final process of locking into place when I heard a voice coming from behind me.

"Don't move, bitch. I have a gun this time. If you don't do everything I say, I'm going to shoot you. Not in the foot. I'm going to shoot you somewhere a little more important."

He paused and seemed to think about it. "And I still might force you to have sex with me."

Shit, not again.

"Where were you hiding?" I asked. "I looked but didn't see you anywhere."

"I was behind the RV. I've been back there for a couple of hours now."

I'm surprised one of my nosy neighbors didn't call the cops on him.

"What do you want this time? Are you going to ask me about the child in the box again? I still have no idea what you're talking about."

"My partner wants to have a chat with you."

"About what?"

"Guess you'll find out."

I thought about what I wanted to happen next. My engine was still running, and I could simply put my car into gear and leave.

The kid was definitely a jerk, but I didn't think he'd shoot at a fleeing car. As I thought more about it, I realized the investigation was stuck.

I had no leads and no prospects of getting a lead anytime soon. Honestly, going with the kid might be the best chance I'd have at finding out what was going on.

I hope I don't regret this.

"Alright," I said, "get in the car and tell me where you want to go."

Pointing his gun at me the entire time, he came around and opened the passenger door. He reached in and took my bag off the passenger seat before settling down. He then placed the bag at his feet, out of my reach.

"You're going to a place called the Phoenix Deluxe Motor Lodge," he said. "Do you know where that is?"

"Never heard of it."

"It's off of Seventh Street in Phoenix, near Interstate 10."

Looking at the gun he was pointing at me, I was definitely concerned, but for some reason, I also had to suppress a smile. It was a revolver, but massively oversized, likely a .45 Magnum.

It had a long, thick barrel and a huge cylinder that held six oversized bullets. Fully loaded, the gun must have weighed almost four pounds and would have been a bear to aim or even hold steady.

Of course, the thing that kept my humor down was the fact that the awkward monster of a gun was currently pointed at me.

"It will take about half an hour to get there," I said. "Try not to accidentally shoot me."

~~~~

We drove into downtown Phoenix, and the kid directed me

where to go. As we cruised down the Loop-202, the kid pulled out a phone and called to tell his partner we were on our way.

As I thought would happen, he at first kept the gun pointed at me, but after only a minute or two, he was resting it on his leg. After ten minutes, he had laid it on his lap, his hand only loosely holding it. If I had slammed on the brakes, the gun would have gone flying.

~~~~

The Phoenix Deluxe Motor Lodge turned out to be a disgusting dump. At one time, it might have been part of a budget national chain, but that was long ago. Now, it looked like the kind of place that rented rooms by the hour.

I parked in the space with the fewest oil stains and broken glass. The kid was wearing a lightweight jacket, and as he got out of the car, he managed to get the oversized gun into one of the pockets. For the sake of the investigation, I hoped the cops didn't choose this night to raid the motel.

"Hey," I said as he started to walk toward the motel. "Let me take my purse. I don't want it sitting on the floor in the open like that. It won't be here when we come back out."

The kid reached in and pulled out my purse. Unfortunately, he wasn't gullible enough to give it to me. Instead, he held it under his arm.

We climbed a cracked stairway to the rooms on the second floor of the building. The kid took a keycard from his pocket, laid it on top of the railing, and then stepped back.

"Take the keycard and go into the room in front of you."

I took the card and used it to open the flimsy metal door. The room was as horrible as I imagined.

The carpet smelled of mildew, and the ceiling had stains from a recent water leak. I looked at the bed, and my stomach twisted at the idea of sleeping in it for the night.

A man was sitting on a chair watching ESPN SportsCenter on a small TV and drinking a Four Peaks Kilt Lifter. He had an ice bucket with three more beers on the table next to him.

He was tall and athletic with short reddish-blond hair, a deep tan, and a face full of sun freckles. He might have been in his late thirties, but the lines around his eyes were that of a much older man. His only unusual physical feature was a large and jagged scar on his right forearm.

"Sorry for the abrupt invitation," he said as we walked into the room. "I have a proposition for you. After you hear me out, you're free to go. Cyril, give the lady back her bag."

As I listened to him talk, all I could think of was Steve Irwin, the Australian known as *The Crocodile Hunter*.

"She has a gun in there," Cyril whined. "It's the same fucking gun she used to shoot me."

"Cyril, be a good lad," the big Australian said. "Give her the bag and wait outside. Go smoke a couple of cigarettes."

Cyril spent several seconds staring at me with a look that was supposed to be intimidating. He then gave me back my purse and stomped out of the room. As he left, he shut the door hard.

"Go ahead," the man said. "Have a seat. There's beer in the bucket if you want one. Feel free to take out your gun if it would make you more comfortable. Although, I'd urge you not to shoot me, at least until you hear what I have to say."

I reached into my purse and took out my pistol. I didn't point it towards him, exactly, but I felt better having it in my hand. He picked up the TV remote and turned the volume down.

"Sorry about Cyril," he said in his thick Australian accent.

"I normally work alone, but as part of the arrangement allowing me into your country, Cyril was the local boy assigned to be my mate for the trip. It's partly for him to gain experience and partly so he can keep an eye on me. He's a tosser, if you want God's truth, but I'm stuck with him. And so you know, I did not authorize him to molest you the other day. That was his bright idea to gain points with his superiors."

"And who are they?"

"Let's instead talk about why you're here. Couple a weeks ago, Stig Stevens was in Shanghai and was given a present as part of a going-away party for his latest movie. The present was in an ornate wooden box. Unfortunately, there was, well, a mix-up, and he was given the wrong box. I need to get it back."

"How are you involved with this?" I asked. "Who are you working for?"

"Let's assume it's someone important, and they don't want their name casually thrown about. My profession is finder. If something's lost, I go and find it. My name's McKinsey, but my friends know me as Digga."

"Okay, I'm assuming it was you who broke into Stig's house a week ago."

"Someone broke into Stig's house? When was this?"

"It was five or six days after Stig got back from Shanghai. Are you saying it wasn't you?"

"No, but it would fit into everything that's going on."

"Was it Cyril?"

"Unlikely. I don't think he knew about this before I arrived. I've kept a pretty close eye on him, especially since he went after you. Serves him proper getting shot, if you ask me. Do us both a favor and put him in hospital for a week or two next time. Do you have any details on the break-in?"

I thought about how much to tell him. After all, there was a good chance he was lying through his teeth.

"Not a lot," I said. "Somebody broke a window and started a search but was apparently frightened away by the staff. I'm not sure if they found what they were looking for, but from what I understand, it was pretty amateurish."

"That part also makes sense. Finding this is going to take a professional."

"Are you saying they brought you here from Australia just to find Stig's box?"

"That's about the size of it. We watched the house for a couple a days, waiting for a good time to go in. The main problem with the job was there was always a half-dozen workers milling about the place during the day, and there's likely an elaborate alarm system at night. I thought it was probable the box would be somewhere in the house, but if not, I would need to question Stig directly."

"So, what did you do?" I asked.

"The party on Sunday night seemed like the perfect opportunity. The gate to the street was open, and people were coming and going all night. We waited until about two o'clock that morning. By then, nearly everyone, including the staff, had left, and we went in."

"Did you find the box?"

"Well, not at first. There was a couple a people rooting around in one of the rooms and the Sheila was moaning and screaming. It made it a little hard to concentrate. We didn't find the box straight-away, but we eventually had a bit a luck. When we got to the big room with the pool, Stig Stevens was sitting in a chair next to the water. The scene struck me as rather surreal, like something outta one of his movies. The only light in the room was coming up from the pool. It was bouncing off the walls in a rhythmic strobe-light sort of way. Now, I normally don't like to be spotted, especially by the person I'm stealing from. But in this case, I knew I'd only have one chance at finding the box, and Stig was on the piss, drunk, you'd say. He was more than halfway through a bottle of tequila and was drinking with the flies. I knew he wouldn't remember a thing, so it seemed like the perfect time for questioning him about the box."

"Drinking with the flies?"

"He was by himself."

"What happened?" I asked.

"I tried to start a friendly convo. I asked what had become of the box he received in Shanghai."

"What did he say?"

"Stig answered in a drunken slur that he didn't know what the fuck I was talking about. I repeated my statement that I needed to know the whereabouts of the box he received in Shanghai. I said it was given in error, and I would exchange it for something of greater value."

"What happened?"

"After several minutes of me asking questions and Stig not answering, Cyril became agitated and gave him a slap across the face. Now, you slap most blokes, and it usually gets a reaction. I knew Stig Stevens made a living off his face, and so his reaction to having it threatened would likely be strong. Well, maybe he was a bit too far gone from the tequila, but the slap merely seemed to wake him up to the point where he could have a lucid conversation. He said he still didn't know what the fuck I was talking about, and he didn't go to Shanghai with everyone else. As he spoke this time, I noticed the voice and face were wrong. Wrong to the point I began to doubt the man was, in fact, Stig Stevens."

"Why was that?" I asked.

"I'll admit I had several moments of confusion. I was inside Stig Stevens' house, next to Stig Stevens' pool, talking to a man who, from a distance, appeared to be Stig Stevens. I should mention we'd been discreetly watching the events on the poolside patio all evening, and the man was dressed identically to what I had seen Stig Stevens wearing at the party before he changed into his swimmers. I briefly considered that perhaps the person I knew as Stig Stevens on the movie screen might, in fact, be this bloke, only with heavy makeup. I rejected that thought and instead concluded that the man Cyril had slapped was not Stig Stevens."

"Confusing situation," I said. "What'd you do?"

"Unfortunately, at the very moment I was having my revelation, Cyril became even more aggressive. He hit the bloke hard in the forehead and started yelling at him to talk. It was a stupid thing to do. The bloke came up mad as a cut snake and threw a ripper punch directly into Cyril's face. I'll tell ya, the bloke knew how to fight. He didn't even drop his tequila bottle. Cyril went airborne and landed hard against the rock wall next to the pool."

"What happened then?"

"Cyril lunged against the man, and they began to tussle. I stood up to intervene. This wouldn't help me get what I'd come for, and I wanted to keep the situation from getting any worse. Of course, I wasn't in too much of a hurry since Cyril was a skinny little fuck, and this bloke was big and knew how to handle himself. Honestly, I was going to enjoy watching Cyril take a few shots. Figured it would keep him quiet for a couple a days."

"What happened with the fight?" I asked.

"Unfortunately, Cyril and the man were fighting next to

the pool, and the bloke fell into the water. Regrettably, he didn't go in cleanly. The back of his head made solid contact with the edge of the pool. The sound of his skull cracking was loud, even from where I was standing. The man sank like a rock, and there was a fair bit of blood."

"My God," I said. "Why didn't you jump in and get him out?"

"I would have, but it was no use. One look showed the bloke was already dead. I looked over and saw Cyril had a bloody great gash on the side of his face. We were making a dog's breakfast out of the job. I grabbed a pool towel to make sure Cyril didn't drip any blood and sent him outside to wait. Fortunately, the house was so big that even with the fighting, no one was woken up by the racket. Maybe it was because the loud sex moans from the Sheila were still echoing through the house, and it seemed to drown out any other noise. I then went through the house, room by room, until I found the box on a bookshelf in some sort of music room. I pinched the box, retrieved Cyril, and came back here."

"So why are you telling me all this?"

"Unfortunately, when I picked open the lock, what was supposed to be in the box wasn't in the box."

"And what was supposed to be in the box?"

Digga hesitated. Apparently, he hadn't decided how open he wanted to be with me.

"Look," I said. "You went to a lot of trouble to get me here. If you want my help, you're going to have to tell me what you know."

"Right. It's a piece of sculpted jade called *The Child*. It's a small carving, about twenty-five centimeters long. It's gone walkabout, and I've been hired to find it and bring it back. They showed me an old black-and-white photo of it, and it's a grasshopper sitting on a leaf. I assume it's valuable since they sent me to go after it. That's all I know about it."

Digga paused, and I took a minute to process what I'd heard.

"Okay," I said. "Let me see if I've got this. Stig got a box from Shanghai about three weeks ago, and you've been hired to get it back. You went to Stig's house the night of the party to steal it. You couldn't find the box right away and instead killed a man who was not Stig Stevens and left him floating in the pool. You eventually found and stole the box from Stig's house but later discovered it was empty. You don't care about the actual box; you're mainly looking for a jade carving called *The Child*. It's green, looks like a leaf, and is nine or ten inches long. Did I get it right?"

Digga brightened. "Every word. Good on ya. The only thing I would add is I didn't kill the bloke. That was my tosser mate, Cyril."

That seems like a fine point, but I won't argue it here.

"Okay, so why are you telling me this?"

Unfortunately, I knew exactly where this was going.

"I've recently found out you're an investigator working for Stig's solicitor. I want you to help me recover *The Child*."

"And why would I want to do that?"

"I'm being paid two hundred thousand dollars U.S. to find it. If you help me get it back, everything will be ripper, and I'll give you fifteen thousand U.S. as a finder's fee. I've seen you go in and out of the house several times. I know you were hired to find out what's going on, and Stig Stevens apparently trusts you. You can steer the investigation towards locating *The Child*. You can then recover it and return it to me."

"And you'll do what with it?"

"Disappear."

"So, why would I want to do that?"

"Everyone needs money."

"I don't need it that bad." I then asked the question that was the real reason I was willing to come here. "Do you know where Stig is? He's been missing all day."

"Well, Miss Black, I could make an educated guess, but all I know for sure is I don't have anything to do with it. There's more going on with this than you currently know or I'm able to talk about. I suggest we partner up on this. Trust me, it will be better for you and better for Stig if we can clear this up quickly. The longer this goes on, the more danger everyone will be in."

"I don't know. Partnering up with the bad guys doesn't seem like the best idea. Let me sleep on it."

He pulled a blank card from his pocket and wrote a phone number on it. "I have a disposable phone," he said. "It's untraceable, but I'll have it with me for a few more days. Call me if you wish to help. If we can find *The Child* in the next day or two, then no worries. If not, well, it's bad luck for the both of us."

I pulled a card from my bag and laid it on the table. "Next time you want to talk, call me. If you send Cyril around, he's likely to get shot again."

"Tempting," Digga said. "It would be one way to get rid of him. But alright, next time I'll call."

~~~~

I walked to my car and drove back into Scottsdale. I then pulled into the first coffee shop I saw. I grabbed a booth away from everyone and ordered a decaf and a piece of key lime pie.

After the first few bites of pie, I began to calm down and

think about what had just happened. Even though I now had an idea of what was going on, I somehow felt more confused than ever.

I did what I normally do in situations like this and called Gina. From the noises in the background, she was at the gym for her evening workout. She went somewhere quiet and listened patiently while I went over the meeting with Digga.

"Ordinarily, my first call would be to the police," she said. "The man you talked to implicated his partner in a murder, and he's an accomplice in the same crime. Of course, all you can present at this point is hearsay evidence. Plus, I doubt Sterling or Jeanette will want to get the authorities involved, at least at this point."

"I think you're right. They're both here to limit the studio's exposure to this. They won't want me to make it worse. Once I call the police, it becomes official and public record."

"Well, you've talked to this Digga. Do you think he has anything to do with Stig's disappearance?"

"I don't think so. I think he's what he says he is. A burglar who was hired to find a piece of jade and then return it to whoever's paying him. I wouldn't think he'd have any need to kidnap Stig in order to get that done."

"Well, maybe, but don't trust him too much yet. He's already broken into Stig's house and thought he was interrogating him. If the jade's still lost, he might have taken Stig to find out what he knows directly."

~~~~~

I made it to my apartment, and as I walked in from the parking lot, I saw Grandma Peckham waiting in front of the elevator. Next to her was the rolling basket she'd recently bought for bringing groceries in from her car.

"Hi, Grandma," I said as I walked up to her.

"Well, Laura, this makes twice in one week. What have you been up to?"

"Same things as always. Although, the past couple of days, I've been working with Stig Stevens."

"Stig Stevens? The movie star Stig Stevens?"

"Yup."

The elevator arrived, and we got in. It slowly crawled up to the third floor.

"Well, that must be interesting," Grandma said. "What's he like in real life?"

"He's nice. You should see his house. It's amazing."

"We never used to have famous people like that here in Arizona. Before there were jet airplanes or air-conditioning, only a few of us were crazy enough to live out here in the desert. I grew up in a house at Tenth Street and Indian School Road. That was back when there was still an active Indian school there. Now, it's more of a historical park than anything. One day, my dad said we were moving up to Northern Avenue, and I thought it was terrible. At the time, there was nothing that far north but a few houses with a lot of cactus and dirt. Now, Northern Avenue is more or less the center of the city. You need to go up another ten or fifteen miles if you want to see an undeveloped patch of desert."

As Grandma talked, we got out of the elevator and walked down to her door. She opened it, and I followed her into her apartment. She continued to talk as she pulled groceries from her basket and started loading them into her refrigerator. Without asking, she pulled a caffeine-free Diet Pepsi out and handed it to me.

"What are you doing this weekend?" I asked.

Grandma got a guilty look on her face, and I swear she

blushed a little bit. "Well, I know this sounds foolish after my speech to you the other night, but I'm going out with Bob."

"That's great. What happened?"

"After you left, I started thinking about going back onto the internet site to start looking for another man. I know this sounds a little bad, but after having a man in my bedroom for so many months, I was already starting to miss the intimacy."

"Nothing wrong with that. What about Grandpa Bob?"

"Well, I went on the site and flipped through some of the pictures of the men out there. I saw Bob had put his profile back up, and I got a twinge of jealousy. One thing led to another, and I called him up. I said if he'd stop all of the foolish talk about us moving in together, I'd let him take me out on a date."

"Was he okay with that?"

"I'm not sure. He said yes, so we'll see. He's coming over Saturday night. I thought I'd give you some warning. You know how thin the walls in this building are, and I don't want you to think I'm being chased around by an axe murderer or anything."

~~~~

I went into my apartment and collapsed on the couch. Marlowe came in from the fire escape and went into the kitchen to see if there was food waiting. When he saw there wasn't, he came over to the couch and hopped up on my lap.

After ten minutes of flipping channels and listening to my cat purr, I got up. Even though it was only ten o'clock, it had been a long day, and I was beat. I put on a T-shirt and was getting ready to go to bed when my phone rang with the theme to *The Love Boat*.

My heart fluttered a bit as I answered. Max seemed to be

calling from a restaurant. It must have been somewhere nice because there was someone playing piano in the background.

"Laura, good evening," he said with his buttery-smooth voice. "I'd hoped to catch you before you went to bed. If you have the time, we'd like to talk with you tomorrow about the meeting you had with Danielle. I hope it was productive."

"It was. When and where do you want to meet?"

"If you don't mind coming back to the Tropical Paradise, let's meet tomorrow at the Dreamland Cove Bistro. With the cooler weather, we'll be able to set up a nice place to talk somewhere outside near the waterfall. Shall we say noon?"

"As of now, it works. But you need to know I'm in the middle of an assignment, and there's the possibility I may need to postpone."

"Of course. I'd understand, and I'm sure Tony would, too. Hopefully, you can make it. Let us know if you can't."

He disconnected, and I crawled into bed. Marlowe hopped up and curled into a ball at my feet.

Even though I was tired from the events of the day, I was too excited to sleep. I thought about seeing Max again and how wonderful it would be. It must have been almost midnight before I finally drifted off.

Chapter Eight

I awoke at six-fifteen the next day when Marlowe began to head-butt me softly. I rolled over and tried to ignore him.

After five minutes of head-butting and listening to him purr, I opened an eye and told him it was too early. Unfortunately, this only made him purr louder.

At six-thirty, the alarm went off. I shuffled into the kitchen with Marlowe close behind. I put on a pot of coffee, then opened a random can of cat food and plopped it into his bowl.

I turned on the local news show on the TV and went about getting ready for my day. After I got dressed, I called over to Stig's house.

The butler answered and politely told me that Mr. Stevens had not yet returned home, but he would call me straightaway upon his return. I then called Stig's phone, but it immediately rolled over to voicemail.

~~~~~

I made it to the office a little after eight. I dropped everything but *The Big Pig* off at my cubicle, then went up front and sat on the red-leather wingback chair next to Sophie's desk. We both sipped coffee while I filled her in on the events of the previous night.

"You said his name's Digga?" Sophie asked.

"Well, I'm sure it's supposed to be Digger, but with the accent, it comes out Digga."

"I loved Crocodile Dundee as a kid. My parents had it on a VHS tape, and I almost wore it out. Do you know Linda Kozlowski and Paul Hogan fell in love during the filming? They actually got married in real life. It's the accent. There's something about an Australian accent that women can't resist. What does this guy look like? Is he cute?"

"Um, he's a criminal, and his partner committed a murder."

"Yeah, but you said he didn't have anything to do with it. If you get a chance, bring him around and introduce him. Maybe we could all go out for drinks sometime."

"Sophie?"

"I'm just saying. Hey, how much of this Digga-dead-body stuff are you going to tell Jeanette and Sterling?"

"I'm not sure. I need to talk with Lenny. At this point, I don't actually have anything solid, only a lot of speculation and hearsay. Stig said there was a dead body in the pool. Digga said there was a dead body in the pool. The only problem is, there isn't actually a dead body. I don't think Sterling and Jeanette will want the police to get involved, even if I do come up with something solid. Now Stig's taken off. I don't know if he's in trouble or only hiding in a hotel somewhere."

"Well, I hope wherever he is, he decides to come back soon. He's got his entire studio riled up over this. Even though I'm sure the studio is insured against Stig not being able to finish his movies, they'll still take a big hit if Stig loses it and can't continue. By him doing crazy talk about a dead guy in the pool, then disappearing himself, they've had to send the studio executive and the publicist out here to calm things down."

"You think that's what will happen? If we don't find anything, everyone will want to hush it up?"

"I've been reading about this sort of thing for years in the tabloids. Every six months or so, a major actor will have a breakdown, and it ruins their career. It doesn't take much. It can be something as simple as they get drunk and start yelling at somebody. If it's captured on a cell phone video, they'll have it up on TMZ the next day. I bet that's why Jeanette and Sterling are really here. They may care about Stig, but his movies still gross about two-hundred and fifty million dollars each. That's a lot of incentive for making sure everything goes smoothly."

"Maybe you're right. I'd hate to stop the investigation before we find out what happened, but I can see Jeanette and that Sterling guy pulling the plug. I'm not sure where else to go with this."

"Well, Lenny's in court this morning. Unless it goes long, he should be back sometime after lunch. You can talk with him then. I'll call Danielle in a little while and confirm dinner for tonight. I hope you can make it. Maybe Gina would have some ideas. You could talk with her then. What are you doing later tonight? Weren't you supposed to go out with Reno sometime this week? If not, maybe we could all do something."

"He's sort of annoyed with me."

"What about this time?"

"When I met with Max and Tony the other day, the police were conducting surveillance. Reno thinks it's bad for his career to have me seen with them."

"Oops. Well, he's probably right about that, but I think you should keep seeing Max anyway. You know you still want him."

"Did you know Max's last name is Bettencourt?"

"Well, sure. I thought you did as well."

"No, and how'd you know? Did you run a secret search on him?"

"Of course, I did, months ago. I'm surprised you never asked me about his personal life."

"I didn't want to snoop."

Sophie rolled her eyes and made a rude sound with her lips. "Yeah, whatever. Sure, you, not wanting to snoop."

"Shut-up. Well, was there anything in it?"

"Lots, the man's had an interesting life. It was mostly about his time with the government. I couldn't really tell what agency he worked for. That part was hush-hush. He was posted all over the world, but he spent most of his time in Eastern Europe. He seemed to be some sort of problem solver, going into places where there was a 'problem', and then 'fixing the problem'. The database didn't have the details. A lot of Max's history is classified even beyond what our secret government database can access."

"Anything bad in the report?"

"Not unless you call getting a job with Tough Tony DiCenzo bad. He's never even been arrested, and his credit's eight-thirty, if that's what you mean. Are you going to see him again?"

"I'm supposed to meet with Tony and Max again today. I'm working on a project for them."

"Is that such a good idea? The police are watching him, and you know how it works out when you get involved in a project for Tony. There's usually a shootout where everyone but you has a gun."

"It's not like I volunteer for these things."

The door to the street opened, and Jeanette walked in. She still looked as fashionable as the day before, but she had toned down the Hollywood glamor.

Her heels had gone down an inch, and her jewelry was more subdued. Now, she merely looked like any of the wealthy women you always see in the Scottsdale Fashion Square. She carried a briefcase in one hand and a bakery box from Sprinkles Cupcakes in the other.

She held up the cupcakes and looked at Sophie. "Break room?"

"Wow," Sophie said. "I love Sprinkles Cupcakes. Put 'em in the conference room. We won't have to walk as far that way."

Jeanette walked into the conference room and put the box on the table. Sophie leaned over and quietly said, "Okay, maybe she's not so bad, for a lawyer."

She then followed Jeanette into the conference room and returned with a cupcake decorated with three or four types of chocolate pieces embedded in the white icing.

"Oh my God," she said after the first bite. "Laura, you gotta have one."

I took Sophie's advice and got a chocolate one with dark chocolate shavings on milk chocolate icing. When I got back to Sophie's desk, we both let Jeanette know how much we appreciated the cupcakes. "No problem," she said, then pulled a document from her briefcase.

"I took up Sterling's idea," Jeanette said. "I got a printout of all activity on Stig's phone from the night he disappeared. It turns out there was only one call in or out after five that afternoon. It was an incoming call from a local number at eight twenty-four. We've run a trace on the number and it was from a disposable phone purchased from a convenience store two days before in Glendale."

She read out the number, and I copied it down. The number looked familiar. I'd need to check the card, but I was pretty sure it was Digga's.

"Thanks," I said. "This'll give me an idea of where to go next. Have you heard anything new on Stig?"

"Not a thing. I called over to the house, and they haven't seen him. I also tried his phone several times."

"I've done the same thing," I said. "Has he ever done anything like this before?"

"No. This is something new for him. I only hope he's alright."

"We haven't heard a ransom demand from anyone," I said. "I'm assuming he wasn't kidnapped, but I'm still worried. First was the dead body, and now Stig's disappeared."

"The studio has people at his house in LA in case he shows up there. We've also let Vivian know. We should get a call if anyone sees him."

"I'll keep looking on my end. He has to be somewhere."

"Oh, there's one more thing," Jeanette said, looking at me. "Sterling will probably call you sometime this morning. He wants to help you investigate."

"What do you mean by help?"

"We had breakfast at the same time this morning, and we sat together. He told me he wants to be out with you in the field as you track down your leads."

"Um, that's not usually how I work. Half the time, I don't know where I'm going to go or what I'm going to do until it actually happens. When it does happen, it typically happens fast. I can't have a partner."

"I figured you'd say something like that. I don't blame you, but I thought I'd let you know."

"Tell me about Sterling," I said. "How does he fit in with the studio and with Stig?"

"There isn't much to tell. All A-list actors have a dedicated executive at the studio to coordinate their activities and ensure things run smoothly. Most of the work is behind the scenes, but the studio prefers to have only one point of contact when dealing directly with Stig. It's especially important right before a movie shoot when a lot of things are coming together at once."

"How's Stig with the arrangement?"

"Well, it's pretty standard. The only funny thing is Sterling and Stig can't stand each other. I've been Stig's publicist for almost three years, and I've never seen them in the same room together unless it's a planned studio event."

"What happened?"

"No idea. No one talks about it, and I've never asked."

"Stig's a big movie star," Sophie said. "Why doesn't he get someone new?"

"I asked Stig about it when I first started. He shrugged and said it was only business, and you don't have to like someone if you're only doing business with them."

"What about you?" I asked. "Do you and Sterling get along alright?"

"Oh sure, we work well together. We never socialize or anything like that, but he is efficient in coordinating schedules and events."

"If Stig doesn't like something the studio's doing, can't he make movies with someone else?" Sophie asked.

"Well, Stig isn't technically under any obligation to work exclusively with the studio, but they do hold the rights to the *Hammer* series, and they've asked that he only do projects with them. Stig's had a great career working with the studio, and everyone seems happy with the arrangement."

~~~~

I left Jeanette up front to talk with Sophie while I went back to my cubicle. I was tempted to contact Digga and ask why he'd called Stig the night he'd disappeared.

I thought about it, but was still hesitant. Digga said he'd only trade information if we partnered up. I didn't want to work that closely with a known criminal, at least until I'd exhausted every other lead.

It was becoming obvious Stig wasn't going to show up anytime soon, and it was my job to find him. I sat in the silence of the back offices and thought about what to do next. Since everything was starting to revolve around the piece of jade called *The Child*, I decided I needed to know everything I could about it.

I called the Phoenix Art Museum and asked who was in charge of the Asian collections. After being bounced around from one person to another, I finally connected with the Asian department administrator.

She provided me with some names of people who could help. Unfortunately, most of them were at a conference in Hong Kong.

I asked if anyone in the building knew anything about Chinese jade. Here, I was in luck.

The resident jade expert, Dr. Janice Lee, was in town. I then asked the admin to connect me with her, and after several minutes, she answered the phone.

I told her what I was looking for and asked when I could

come over. She said any time in the morning would be good for her. I said I was currently in Old Town Scottsdale and would be right over.

~~~~

I drove into central Phoenix and made it to the art museum. On the way, my phone rang with Sterling's number. I didn't answer it.

After I parked and went in, I tried to convince the people at the admission desk that I had an appointment with Janice Lee. They called her office to confirm, but she must have stepped away. I ended up using the company credit card to pay the eighteen-dollar entrance fee and went inside.

The museum was larger than I remembered, and it took several minutes of winding through hallways until I made it to the Asian art section. I asked one of the security guards where I could find Janice Lee, and she directed me through a doorway that led to a series of offices. Janice had one of the larger ones near the front.

I knocked on her doorframe, and Janice looked up from her desk. She was a pleasant-looking woman, maybe fifty years old, with long dark hair and oversized red glasses.

I introduced myself, and she offered to show me around the collection. I hadn't been in the Asian section since I was a kid in school, so I gladly accepted.

"We have pieces from most Asian cultures," Janice explained as we walked. That includes Tibet, Nepal, India, China, Japan, Sri Lanka, and Java. We strive to present cross-cultural comparisons between the various Asian cultures and between Asia and Europe. We attempt to tie everything together through examples of painting, religious art, and porcelain. It's a fascinating subject."

"This was great," I said after we had walked around the

collection for about fifteen minutes. "What I'm mainly interested in is Chinese jade. Have you ever heard of a piece called *The Child*? It's about ten inches long and apparently looks like some sort of bug, maybe a grasshopper, sitting on an ocean wave or maybe a leaf."

"Of course," she said. "*The Child* goes with *The Mother*."

When I looked at her with a confused look, she explained.

"*The Mother* is the popular name for an ancient jade carving in the shape of a leaf. It's maybe ten or eleven inches long, four inches wide, and about an inch thick. It's made of translucent emerald-green jade, sometimes called imperial jade. It's the rarest and most highly valued jade there is. The leaf features an intricately carved grasshopper. It was created as a present for the Emperor during the early years of the Yuan dynasty by one of the more powerful princes."

"Yuan dynasty?"

"Oh, sorry, the Yuan dynasty was the ruling dynasty of China established by Kublai Khan, the leader of the Mongolian Borjigin clan, in approximately 1271. *The Mother* was created in approximately 1273 and is a very famous piece. It's on permanent exhibit at the National Museum in Beijing."

"And *The Child*?"

"Well, *The Child* is the name of the companion piece that was supposedly carved at the same time as *The Mother*. The story has it that *The Child* was kept by the prince who had commissioned *The Mother* as a sign of his enduring friendship and fidelity to the Emperor. From pictures of *The Child* taken in the 1880s, the 1940s, and again in the early 1970s, it has a similar, but smaller, grasshopper on a similar, but slightly smaller, leaf. Unlike *The Mother*, *The Child* never made it to a museum. It's been passed from one private collector to the next for almost eight hundred years. It's acquired somewhat of a folkloric reputation and has become quite famous, even though it's seldom been seen by the public. *The Child* was declared to be a national historic treasure in 1997, and that's when it completely disappeared from the market. Whoever has it knows that when it surfaces, the government will likely appropriate it for the museum."

"And if *The Child* ended up outside of China?"

"Well, I imagine the Chinese would demand its return, but if it was in a country without relations with China, it would be quite valuable, almost priceless, in fact. Of course, you couldn't simply walk across the border with *The Child*. Almost everyone in China at least knows of the piece. Plus, the penalties for trying to smuggle antiquities outside the country are quite severe."

Jeez, what am I walking into?

Janice looked at me with a look that was hard to pin down. It was curiosity mixed with anticipation. "Laura, do you have any information on the location of *The Child*?"

"Who? Me? Nope, not at all."

~~~~

My meeting with Janice Lee didn't take as long as I had expected, which meant I didn't have to rush to get to the Tropical Paradise for my meeting with Tony and Max. It was a beautiful day, and I lowered the top to take full advantage of it. Instead of taking the highway, I drove up to Camelback Road and enjoyed the city as I made my way back to Scottsdale.

I had just passed Goldwater Boulevard when Gina called.

"Hey, Gina," I said when I answered.

"Laura, I have some news." Gina was using her cop voice; the same one Reno uses when he's doing something official.

I hope this isn't about Stig.

"Um, what is it?"

"They've found Stig's car. It was in the parking lot of Banner Desert Medical Center in Mesa."

"Was Stig in the hospital? That's like ten miles from where he lives."

"We checked, but Stig hasn't been there, and no one matching his description has been treated there since Wednesday night. Security noticed a flashy sports car with a license plate that read HAMMER4 in the parking lot. When it didn't move for a couple of days, they became concerned. They called the Mesa police, who called Stig's house to ask about the car. Carter said the car had been dropped off, and he sent someone down to pick it up."

"It sounds like Jeanette and Sterling briefed him on what to do in case the police called. They're still being careful not to tip off the authorities. But what about Stig?"

"There's no sign of him."

Damn.

"Okay," I said. "Thanks for letting me know."

~~~~~

As with most things at the Tropical Paradise, the Dreamland Cove Bistro sported a tropical island theme. It's one of the resort's casual restaurants that serves everything from breakfast to late-night desserts.

There's a full bar and a small stage where an acoustic singer or a group usually plays from about ten in the morning until late at night. The bistro is half inside and half outside the resort's main lobby.

During the hottest parts of the summer, the patio half goes largely unused even though a series of overhead misters are in place. Now that the summer heat had departed, the patio was again filled with tourists.

I headed through the hotel lobby to the hostess stand at the front of Dreamland Cove. Most of the tables were filled with people talking and laughing. I looked to the stage and a man in a Jamaican outfit was playing a steel drum on the stage.

The hostess led me through the restaurant to a separate area on the outside patio near a high lava-rock waterfall. The table was alone in an area that normally held another eight or ten tables.

Not only had the other tables been moved out, but several potted queen palms and honeysuckle bushes had been strategically placed around the remaining table, effectively screening the meeting from anyone who might be watching.

I was the first to arrive. Instead of sitting, I walked over to the waterfall, one of the many water features in and around the main lobby.

The water splashed noisily twelve or fifteen feet down a lava-rock wall into a blue water basin surrounded by banana trees, ferns, and sago palms. At least with the noise, we wouldn't have to worry about being overheard.

I felt someone come up behind me. I turned and was face to face with Max.

Without thinking, and without caring who was watching, I wrapped my arms around him and held his body tightly against mine. I stood there for several seconds before realizing he'd also put his arms around me.

I loosened my grip and looked up into his face. "I've missed you so much."

"I've missed you too," he said. "Maybe we should do something about it this time."

Before I could answer, I noticed movement beside us.

Johnny Scarpazzi had come into the space, pushing Tony towards the table.

Gabriella had also quietly come out to the patio and was standing in the corner, next to the lava-rock wall. Glancing around, three or four big guys in black polo shirts were now standing inconspicuously next to the restaurant's entrances and exits.

"Um, we should probably talk about this later," I said, stepping back from him.

"That's probably best," Max said as he led me to the table.

He held out my chair while I sat, and then took the chair on my left side while Tony slid into place on my right. A waitress appeared and handed me a menu.

She apparently already knew what Max and Tony were having. A few seconds later, a cocktail waitress came to the table with a scotch for both Tony and me while Max had an iced tea.

Feeling some pressure to order quickly, I got the club sandwich with fries. This was always my go-to choice when I'm with someone, and I don't want to risk making a mess on my blouse.

"It's good to see you again," Tony started. "If it's alright with you, let's get the business out of the way first, then we can enjoy our lunch. How was your meeting with Danielle?"

"Well," I said, "it went okay. She seemed pretty open with me about what the Black Death wanted. Nothing's changed with the heroin since the meeting with Carlos last month. They want to import the drug, and their only request is that you don't interfere as they consolidate their position. By the way, Sal told them you were the one who tipped off the police about the load of heroin back in March. It apparently caused a real stir in their group."

"We not only tipped off the police, Max and Gabriella blew up Carlos' pretty red Ferrari," Tony chuckled, as if reliving a pleasant memory. "I hadn't realized Sal had access to the information, but in an organization our size, such things were bound to get out eventually. Honestly, I'm glad he's out of the way. It was to our advantage being able to feed Carlos false information through Sal, but it was awkward being in the same room with a snitch."

"I let Danielle know about your moral opposition to heroin, and it seemed to reassure her."

"It's not only the morality of the drug," Tony said. "My main objection to bringing drugs up from Mexico is that it no longer makes sense from a business perspective. The authorities here don't spend a lot of time anymore looking for drugs, but they do often look for illegals. A truck or van coming up Interstate-17 might as well have a flashing red light on it begging to be searched, not once, but likely two or even three times between the border and Scottsdale. When you import drugs into Arizona, you have to expect a twenty to thirty percent loss off the top due to confiscation. I've found it to be more profitable to send merchandise down to Mexico. The authorities here never think twice about a truck headed south. All we need to do is drive the load over the border at one of the friendly crossings we've set up, and we're in the clear."

"Where things broke down last time was over the arms trafficking," Max said. "Did she clarify Sergio's position on that?"

"According to Danielle, they want to split the business. It's their position there's ample demand for both groups to succeed. She also talked about mutual cooperation in some cases. They apparently have an extensive list of clients, some of whom they can't fully supply. The people in Central America and Mexico sometimes have special requests, weapons the Black Death can't easily find on the streets in

Arizona. They believe, with your connections, you could fill up the trucks with whatever was required, and they could sell the merchandise to these specialized buyers."

Tony looked at Max. "It could be possible," Max said. "The tricky part is, we'd need to be paid upfront. Otherwise, all the risk would be on our side. In the end, the money would be paid directly to Sergio and his group from the buyer in Central America. If we didn't get our fee upfront, we'd need to rely on Sergio's goodwill to ensure we'd get our money. I can see such a system breaking down rather quickly."

"There is also the bigger picture to consider," Tony said. "We would need to guard against reducing the number of shipments we ourselves make, or we'd risk being seen as a smaller player. If Sergio is seen in Mexico as the supplier who can obtain the specialized products, we'll gradually lose our contacts."

"So, what should I tell Danielle the next time we meet?" I asked. "Will we be able to come to a decision on this?"

"The reason we asked you and Danielle to act as our go-betweens," Tony said, "is to more fully explore each other's positions without necessarily coming to a final decision. Sergio will not expect this to be finalized after only one meeting. It will likely need a series of meetings to decide on something we can both agree to."

A series of meetings? Shit, how long will I have to do this?

"Alright," I said. "Let me know when the next meeting is. We can figure out what to say then."

I then asked something that had been bugging me, but I was unsure how to ask it without saying too much. "Tony, is it okay if we're meeting in the open like this? Do you ever worry about who may be watching?"

"Not to worry," Tony said. "I know exactly who's

watching. The Scottsdale police have a team assigned here during the day and evening shift."

"Doesn't that worry you?"

"Not at all. They want to watch, so I make it as easy as possible for them. They always refuse food and alcohol, but I have one of the girls bring them coffee, and that they'll accept. Watching Max and me walk around the property and having meetings must be pretty dull work. In return, they don't make too much of a stink if Max or I disappear from time to time."

"That still seems a little weird."

"Why would it? We aren't at war with the police. It's all part of the dance we do to keep the peace. Honestly, it would worry me more if they stopped showing up. It would mean something was about to go down."

The waitress appeared with a stainless steel cart holding the food. "Now that our business is out of the way," Tony said, "let's have an enjoyable lunch."

~~~~

When I got back to my car, I called Sophie and asked if Lenny was in the office. I wanted to let him know about *The Child* and how it might be connected to everything.

She said he was there but would be on a conference call for at least another forty-five minutes. I asked about Gina, and Sophie said she'd probably be back in the office by four.

During lunch with Max and Tony, Sterling had texted twice, asking me to call him. So far, I had ignored both texts.

Concerned that he might go to the office to look for me, I drove to my apartment instead. I settled on the couch, and Marlowe came out from the bedroom and hopped up next to me. He curled into a ball and immediately fell asleep.

I opened my laptop and found out everything I could on

The Child. Now that I knew what I was looking for, I was able to identify several relevant sources. Unfortunately, almost all the sites were in Chinese, and even with Google Translate, I wasn't able to get a lot of new information.

From what I could piece together, Janice Lee at the Phoenix Art Museum had been correct about the history of the piece. Similar to Bigfoot, *The Child* was more of a Chinese urban legend than an established fact.

There was a fuzzy picture of it, reportedly from the late 1800s, and a much better black-and-white photo from the 1940s. The best picture was taken in the 1970s, but the website speculated that it could be a fake. I also saw several references to the fact that the Chinese government had declared it a national treasure and that if found, it should be turned in to the authorities.

I then went to the Chinese National Museum site and looked up what they had on *The Mother*. The information was much better here, and there was already an English version of the page.

The piece's history was clearly laid out, and several high-quality photos were included. The Mother was exactly as Janice had described: a wonderfully detailed green grasshopper sitting at the end of a long, smooth green leaf. Being from Arizona, the only leaf I could think of that resembled it was from a stalk of corn, but I supposed it was likely that China had different plants with similar leaves.

A link to the museum's gift shop from *The Mother's* information page inspired me to do some shopping. I was further inspired to put everything on Lenny's credit card.

~~~~

After another fifteen minutes of trying to organize my thoughts, I decided I might have better luck if I went to the office and talked everything over with Sophie and Gina. I got in my car, and as I drove, I mulled the assignment over in my mind.

Instead of heading directly to the office, I aimlessly drove through the city, looking for inspiration. This sometimes helps me see the bigger picture of how everything fits together.

I'd made it south over the Salt River on Scottsdale Road into Tempe when I got a call from Sophie. She sounded terrible.

"Turn on your radio to the news station," she said. "It's about Stig."

"What is it? You sound worried."

"Nope, you gotta hear this one for yourself. Then call me right back. I want to know what you think."

I looked at the clock and saw I had ten minutes until the top-of-the-hour news report. Since there wasn't enough time to get up to the office, I took Rio Salado Parkway to Tempe Beach Park and pulled into an open parking space near Tempe Town Lake. It seemed like a quiet place to sit and listen to what I assumed would be bad news.

I punched buttons on the radio until I pulled up KFYI, the local AM news-talk radio station. It was still five minutes to three, so first, I had to listen to the weather—*clear sky with a high of ninety-six degrees*—then the traffic, *back-up on the Loop-101 at Tatum* before the news came on. As soon as it started, I got a hard knot in my stomach.

Unconfirmed reports are circulating that a body pulled out of the Salt River, east of the Granite Reef Dam, is that of action movie star Stig Stevens. The popular actor came to Hollywood stardom back in the early nineties with his portrayal of Sargent Hancock in Guts 'n Glory and is widely known as The Hammer. Stevens has starred in such action movie classics as Hammer Fall, Hammer's Conquest, and Hammer Blast.

Stevens has been a longtime resident of Paradise Valley and has been prominent in the Scottsdale community for hosting multiple charity events each year. Police are releasing no details at this point, but we'll keep you informed of any further developments.

I turned off the radio and sat for several minutes. My mind was going in several directions at once. I reminded myself the story was unconfirmed, and they didn't say the body was definitely Stig. Until the identity of whomever they had found was better established, I wasn't going to give up hope.

I called Sophie back at work. "Well?" she asked.

"I don't know what to think," I said. "I'm having a hard time believing it. The news report didn't have a lot of detail about what happened, and they didn't say for sure it was actually Stig."

"Yeah, but why would they say the body was Stig's unless they had something to go on?"

"I don't know that either. We'll need to talk to Lenny. I don't know about Sterling and Jeanette, but I imagine Lenny'll want to contact the police to let them know what's been going on with Stig."

"Lenny took off a few minutes ago. He said he's going to learn if it's really Stig or not. We'll have to wait until we hear back."

I disconnected with Sophie and was about to pull out of the parking space to drive up to the office when Lenny called. From the background noises, he was in his car.

"I take it you've heard about the body they pulled out of the Salt River today. The location where the body was recovered is in the Tonto National Forest. We made some phone calls, and the U.S. Forest Service law enforcement division is handling it. I'm heading over to the district offices to see what I can learn. I need to find out how they made the preliminary ID on the body and learn if it's Stig."

"Is Jeanette or Sterling going with you?"

"No, the Hollywood press is already starting to gather, and Jeanette feels it's best if the members of Stig's inner circle aren't part of the news story. That may change if the body turns out to be Stig, but for now, they're going to lay low."

"How can I help?"

"Assume the body isn't Stig and keep digging into the disappearance. There's a lot about this we still aren't seeing. If Stig's still out there, he might need our help. If anyone from the press contacts you, let them know you have no comment. I'll let both you and Gina know as soon as I find out something definitive about the body."

~~~~

I got out of my car and walked down to the lake. My brain was numb, and I felt drained of all emotion. I aimlessly wandered through the park until I decided to sit on one of the benches overlooking the water.

Out on the lake, several small white boats with colorful sails billowed in the light breeze. Four teams of competitive rowers were out practicing on the water, their crews efficiently pulling the little boats across the lake with amazing speed. Mothers with strollers and noisy children walked by, everyone taking advantage of the great weather.

I slowly began to gather my thoughts. Lenny was right. If the body they'd pulled out of the Salt River wasn't Stig, it would mean he was still only missing. If that were the case, I still needed to do everything I could to help find him.

I tried to come up with an organized plan of how I was going to look for Stig, but I had nothing more to go on now than before I found out about the body in the river. Out of a sense of desperation, I knew what I had to do.

I'll probably regret this.

Chapter Nine

I pulled out the card Digga had given me and dialed the number. The phone rang several times before he answered.

"Hello," he said in his bright Australian accent. "Who's this?"

"Digga, it's Laura Black."

"Ah, Miss Black. How ya going? Changed your mind about helping me?"

"The radio says a body they pulled out of the Salt River today might be Stig. You seem to know what's going on. If I agree to partner up with you, will you tell me everything you know?"

"Right, I'll tell you both what I know and what I think. I suspect the bloke they pulled from the river wasn't him. I've heard *The Child* is still missing. Stig wouldn't be dead if there was a chance the jade could still be found. My offer to split the profits with you still stands, assuming we can find the bloody jade and I'm able to turn it over to my employer. The only bit of information I'll need to keep quiet about is who my employer actually is. I hope you'll understand my limitations."

"That's fine. My only requirement is for you to keep Cyril

away from me. I don't trust him, and I'm likely to shoot him again if he starts to bother me."

"On that, I don't blame you. I've wanted to shoot the little bleeder myself."

"Before I come over, there's something I need to know. Did you call Stig the night he disappeared?"

"You have access to his phone records? You're good. Yeah, I called him about half-eight that night and asked him to meet me at a café on Scottsdale Road. I told him I could explain things and let him know the danger he was in. I was hoping after he learned the facts, he might help me to find the jade so everyone would leave the country with no harm done."

"What happened?"

"I waited for three hours, but he never showed up."

"Alright, where can I meet you? Back at the motel? Honestly, I'd rather meet somewhere else if we could."

"Oh, I'm not staying at that bloody whore house. It was only a convenient place to meet so we could get acquainted. I'm actually staying at a rather lovely resort called the Scottsdale Blue Palms. Do you know where that is?"

"I know it. When can we meet?"

"Right. I'm out at the moment, but I'll be back tonight at about eight o'clock or so. I'll be in room twelve three thirty-two. I'll see to it Cyril isn't around."

"I'll be there."

~~~~

I sat on my bench overlooking the lake for about ten minutes. Lenny had told me to look for Stig, and I knew it was the right thing to do, but I wasn't sure where to look first. Sort of at random, I thought maybe if I looked around Stig's house, it would give me some new ideas.

I pulled out of Tempe Beach Park and drove up Scottsdale Road to McDonald Drive, then over to Yucca Road and Stig's. I punched in the code to the driveway gate and drove up to the big house.

None of Stig's sports cars were parked out front. I'd gotten used to seeing four or five of the colorful cars parked in the courtyard, and without them, the house looked a little depressing.

I rang the bell, and Carter answered the door. I asked if he'd heard from Stig. When he said, "No," I asked if I could come in and look around.

He seemed a little annoyed that I wanted to wander through the house, but once I was in, he rapidly composed himself. He asked me if I would like a drink, and when I turned him down, he told me to let him know if there was anything he could do for me.

"There is one other thing," I said. "Maybe Stig already asked you about this, but at the party last Sunday night, Stig had Jerry put a little green figurine on the table here in the entryway. Jerry then spread the word that anyone could have it. It turns out Stig wasn't supposed to give it away. Do you happen to know who has it? I'll need to talk with them about getting it back."

Carter told me he had no idea where the figurine was but would ask the other staff members. He then took off to perform his other duties, leaving me on my own.

I first went out to the patio, where the party's events took place. I could imagine the place alive with thirty people and a DJ, everyone dancing and laughing.

I then went into the big room with the pool. I looked over to the lava-rock wall and saw where Cyril and the man had fought.

I estimated where the guy had fallen into the pool and hit his head. As I looked at the spot, I got a little shiver of dread.

Next, I went into the music room. I looked over the bookshelves and saw the place where Stig had originally placed the box containing the jade. I've always been amazed at how much trouble something small and seemingly inconsequential like that could cause.

I then spent the next several minutes looking through Stig's bedroom, then going from room to room. I looked in offices, private libraries, bathrooms, the kitchen, and the formal dining room. Each room was beautiful and unique in its own way, but nothing in the house pointed me in a new direction.

I'd wandered back out to the patio and was spending a few minutes looking out over Scottsdale when my phone rang with Lenny's ringtone. With a sense of dread, I answered.

"The dead guy isn't Stig," Lenny said. "The Forest Service law enforcement division will be holding a joint press conference with the Maricopa County Sheriff's Office in about an hour. They'll explain the body had some papers on him that led to the preliminary ID, but the coroner has concluded it's not Stig Stevens."

"Are you sure it's not Stig?"

"I'm sure. I was at the coroner's office and saw the body for myself. The guy was about the same size and shape as Stig, but it wasn't him."

"Why did they think it was Stig? The news was rather vague on that."

"The dead guy was wearing a sports coat. Stig's wallet was in the pocket. Everyone's asking how that could have happened. The preliminary cause of death was a blow to the back of the head. The police are going on a theory that the dead guy in the river was involved in some sort of foul play with Stig. They want to talk with Stig to find out his side of the story. I had to tell them Stig is currently in seclusion. Unfortunately, I don't think that story will hold up for more than a day or two."

The dead guy in Stig's pool?

"Shit. Did they say who the dead guy was?"

"No, they still consider the information confidential. They'll first need to notify the next of kin. Once they feel it won't hinder the investigation, they'll issue a press release. I think the body is starting to match the description of the man Stig saw in his pool."

"I think I agree with you. It would make everything fit."

"Yes, but there's obviously a bigger picture we aren't seeing. You've been working on this all week. Do you know what's going on?"

"Maybe," I said. "I'll need to confirm a couple of leads before I can say for sure."

"Fine, do whatever you need to do. In theory, I owe Gina the weekend off, but feel free to get her involved any way you need. She's our pro when it comes to finding missing persons, and this one's heating up. She's in the office, and I'll fill her in. I'm less interested in the dead guy than I am that we find Stig. Keep that as your top priority."

Lenny hung up, and I called Sophie.

"Hey, I guess you heard the dead guy isn't Stig."

"Yeah, it's all I've heard since Lenny came back from the coroner's office. I'm glad, though. It would have creeped me out for years if the only Hollywood star I've ever met was murdered. That's the kind of thing that follows a person around for a while."

"I think the guy they pulled out of the river was the dead

185

guy in Stig's pool. Everything fits with the story Digga told me."

"Seriously? How'd he get from the pool to the river? It's a long way for a dead guy to walk."

"I don't know, but I'll try to find out. Do me a favor? Would you run a secret search on my Australian? He said his name is McKinsey, and he goes by Digger, or maybe it really is Digga. With the accent, I'm not sure."

"Do you know anything else about him? The more I can give the software, the better the search will be."

"Not really. His age is probably somewhere in the mid-to-late thirties. He has a big scar on his right forearm, but nothing else is obvious. He's about six-two and two hundred and ten pounds. He has reddish-blond hair and blue eyes."

"Okay, that isn't a lot of information, but I'll punch it in and see what comes up. You know, if you're thinking about partnering up with him, you should definitely bring him around the office sometime."

"I'll think about it. Are you still doing dinner with Gina and Danielle tonight?"

"Yup. Gina will be here in a few minutes. Hopefully, we'll head over there in about half an hour. Are you coming this time?"

I still don't think this is a good idea.

"I'll be there. Well, unless something happens with the assignment. I'll be at the office in about twenty minutes."

"Well, go ahead and park out back, but don't come in. If Lenny sees you, he'll probably give you some busy work to do. You know how he gets when things in an assignment are at a standstill. We'll meet you out there.

~~~~

I parked in my spot in the back alley. Sophie and Gina came out about five minutes later, and we all walked down to Dos Gringos.

Danielle was already there and had gotten us a table in our favorite location between the sidewalk and the street. A bowl of chips and another of salsa were waiting for us.

She must also have ordered everyone a margarita because four of them showed up as soon as we sat down. We each picked up a glass and clinked them together.

I was still uncomfortable being across the table from Danielle. She was the head of a vicious criminal organization and had once threatened to kill both Gina and Sophie. I'd promised at least to pretend we were good friends, but I wasn't sure how successfully I'd be able to pull it off.

I glanced around the restaurant and saw three of her bodyguards casually sitting near the entrances. All of them had a beer in their hands, but I noticed none of them were drinking.

I looked out at the street and saw two more in an SUV across from where we were sitting. As I thought about it, I picked up my margarita and drained about half of it in a single long gulp.

"Long week?" Danielle asked as I set my glass on the table. I was surprised that her concern seemed genuine.

"And it's not done yet," I said.

"Well, I hope it gets better. How's your week been?" Danielle asked Sophie. "Is there anything exciting going on down at the law office?"

"Plenty," Sophie said. "We got to meet Stig Stevens."

"The actor?"

"Yup. We got to go to his house and everything."

"I just heard on the radio that he's dead," Danielle said. "They pulled him out of a river or something."

"Oh, they're exaggerating the dead part," Sophie said. "They're going to have a press conference in about half an hour where they'll say the body in the river wasn't Stig but somebody else."

"Wow," Danielle said. "You really have had a busy week."

"And that's only the half of it," Sophie said. "We also got to meet Christine Johns."

"Christine from Paradise Park?" Danielle asked, her eyes wide with surprise.

"Yup. We drove up to Jerome with her. That's a little mountain town near Sedona."

"Why did you go up there?" Danielle asked.

Sophie opened her mouth to answer, but she caught Gina's look. "Oh, only part of an assignment Lenny has everyone working on."

From Sophie's tone, Danielle could tell she wasn't getting the full story. She looked between Gina and me. Gina shrugged her shoulders and gave her an innocent look.

"What about you?" Gina asked Danielle. "Anything exciting going on down at the truck company? We've heard it's run by some shady characters."

Danielle smiled and looked at me. "Well, if you want to know the truth…"

My eyes got big, and I had this crazy thought that she would start talking about what was really going on with her. I guess my thoughts showed on my face because both Gina and Sophie looked at me. I put on my best innocent look and shrugged my shoulders.

Danielle gave me her best innocent look back and smiled

again. "The truth is there isn't ever a lot that goes on there. Trucks come in, we unload them, then we load them, and then the trucks go out again. It's the same thing every day. Whoever runs the place pretty much keeps to themselves. I see men go in and out all day, but I've learned not to ask too many questions."

"That sounds like the secret to a happy life," Sophie said as she lifted her glass. "Here's to not asking too many questions."

We clinked our margaritas together, and everyone took a long sip. The waitress noticed we were almost dry and stopped by the table. We ordered another round along with dinners.

While we waited, I asked Danielle what she was doing for the weekend.

"I was thinking about looking for a dog. The place where I'm living allows cats and small dogs. I was thinking about going to the animal shelter and getting a Chihuahua. It would be great to have something cute and fuzzy to keep me company at night. There's a lady down the hall who has one, and she said she'd be glad to babysit during the day."

"I love those little dogs," Sophie said. "If you get one, bring it around the office sometime."

"Are you doing anything fun tonight?" Danielle asked Sophie.

"I think I have a date with Milo. I guess he got the night off, and he called me."

"You're seeing Milo again?" Gina asked. "I thought you dumped him last week."

"No, we're still seeing each other. Well, if he can keep quiet about getting serious anyway."

"What are you doing this weekend?" I asked Gina.

"I've been working non-stop for almost three weeks," Gina said. "Lenny promised me the weekend off, well, if the current assignment doesn't heat up. I'll be there if you need me."

"It would be great if you had a Saturday night off," Sophie said. "We could see if the cougars will be going out. That always turns out to be a big adventure."

"Well, um, you girls go ahead, but I won't be able to join you," Gina said. "If work doesn't get in the way, I have a date set up."

"That Brandon guy?" Sophie asked. "You went through with it? Well, I've already given you my advice for booty-call dates."

"Who's Brandon?" Danielle asked.

"He's a personal trainer Gina picked up at her gym," Sophie said. "Great body, lousy personality."

"Well, I do understand," Danielle said. "If you go to sleep horny, you've been too choosy."

We all laughed. Gina blushed, hung her head down, and covered her face with her hands. "It's true," she said, and we laughed harder.

~~~~

After dinner, the three of us walked back to the office, and everyone packed up for the night. I pulled out of my parking space and headed up to the Blue Palms.

As I drove, I thought about what I'd learned about Digga so far. His answer that he had called Stig to set up a meeting matched the information Jeanette had from Stig's phone.

Digga said he'd agreed to meet with Stig, but he never showed up. Of course, if Digga had been responsible for Stig's disappearance, he likely would have said the exact same thing. I was going to need to guard against putting too much trust in a criminal, at least until I could learn what his actual motives were.

~~~~

I pulled into the entrance for the Blue Palms. The main hotel lobby building was on a small hill near the entrance, but I knew there was a resort map in the main guest parking lot. I pulled the car over and looked up resort building twelve, which looked to be near the pro shop and the restaurants.

I parked in the parking lot near the Winchester Saloon and walked to a cluster of white four-story buildings surrounding one of the resort's larger tropical pools. Each building contained about a dozen guest rooms, each with an orange awning and a blue balcony.

I found building twelve, climbed a wide stairway to the third floor, and then knocked on the door to room three thirty-two. The door opened, and Digga was standing in front of me. Cyril was nowhere to be seen.

I walked in and looked around. It was a nice two-room suite with a beautiful view of the pool and the golf course beyond. As before, he was drinking a Kilt Lifter and said I should get one as well.

I figured it would be best if Digga felt comfortable and was able to tell the story his own way. I grabbed a beer and popped it open.

I then followed Digga out to the balcony and we each grabbed a chair. We both spent a few moments in silence, sipping our beers and looking at the tourists splashing in the pool.

As we sat, I glanced over to see what I could learn about Digga. From the way he conducted himself, he seemed to be ex-military.

I was starting to narrow down his age to somewhere around

thirty-eight or thirty-nine, but I could be off by several years. He obviously spent a lot of time outdoors. It would have been hard for him to get the crow's feet and sun freckles any other way.

I again saw the old scar on his right forearm and wondered how he got it. I got visions of Digga facing down a crocodile with a big hunting knife.

"What do you know about Stig?" I quietly asked.

"Like I said before, I don't know anything definite. However, I'm relieved the bloke they pulled out of the river wasn't him. It would have made our job that much harder. Plus, I rather like his movies. I'm hoping he has another *Hammer* film or two left in him."

"From what we've been hearing, it was the dead guy from Stig's pool."

"Right. I'd guessed it might have been him. From a distance, they looked identical. I don't know how he could have ended up in a river fifteen kilometers away, but the rest makes sense."

"So, tell me what you think. What's going on with this? Where's Stig?"

"Miss Black, as you may have already guessed, Cyril and I aren't the only team looking for the jade. Believe it or not, we're the nice ones. I'm a simple burglar who rents himself out for these high-profile jobs. I only want to find *The Child,* and then I'm gone. I'll collect my reward, and if you help, you'll get your share as well."

"And the others?"

"The others aren't nearly so gentle or polite. I suspect they have a local handler, but they were ultimately hired by a wealthy bloke out of China named Mr. Zhang. I've heard he helped finance the movie Stig just finished filming, mainly as a ruse to get the jade safely out of China. Apparently, something went wrong with the handoff once *The Child* got into California, and Stig ended up with it. I've heard Mr. Zhang has given orders to get *The Child* back at any cost. Nothing's off-limits, including murder and mayhem. I've also heard an internet billionaire here in the U.S. has already purchased the jade from our friend in China. Once it's recovered, the other team is supposed to deliver it to him in California."

"What do you know about this other team?"

"I've run across them a few times before. Each time, it was bad news. They're mercenaries led by an ex-army colonel named Wu. He's a ruthless bastard. I prefer to stay out of his way, and I suggest you do the same. They'll be on a search-and-destroy mission. I imagine they'll start with Stig, then they'll go through everyone important in his life."

"Are you saying they're responsible for his disappearance?"

"I suspect so. It's how they operate. I was able to obtain a detailed list with the names and addresses of his manager, publicist, accountant, studio handler, family, and several close friends. I suspect the other team will be able to gather a similar list. I also suspect they'll go down the names one by one to find what they want. Given your current relationship with Stig in all of this, I imagine you'll also be rather prominent in their investigation."

"So, how do you know all this?"

"Like I said, it's not my first time going up against them. I'm very familiar with their work. Bunch of wankers to tell the truth. They hold a grudge and have unlimited resources. Here's my piece of advice: If we're able to clear up this matter of *The Child*, you should probably lay low for a couple a days until Colonel Wu and his lot have cleared out for good."

~~~~

I got back to my car and put the top down. It was a beautiful night, and I wanted to enjoy it, especially after Digga's news.

I left the Blue Palms and took Scottsdale Road south. The lights of the city and the activity of the people on the street helped cheer me up.

I called Lenny and downloaded the basics of my meeting with Digga. I told him Digga suspected that Stig had been taken by a group of mercenaries led by someone named Colonel Wu to help them recover a piece of ancient Chinese jade called *The Child*.

I also told Lenny that Digga suspected the mercenaries would start to harass Stig's friends and associates. My suggestion was to go to the police, but Lenny wasn't so sure.

He told me to hold tight. He said he'd call Sterling and Jeanette to figure out what to do, then he'd call me back.

I disconnected and let out a long sigh. Since Jeanette and Sterling were there mainly to keep Stig's name out of the papers, I already knew what the outcome would be.

~~~~

I got back to my apartment about ten-thirty. I pulled out the list of Stig's friends and associates Jerry had given me earlier in the week. If Lenny decided not to go to the police, I'd need to warn everyone on the list about Colonel Wu.

I sat on the bed and tried to read a story on my Kindle while waiting to hear back from Lenny. By midnight, it was becoming obvious he wasn't going to call. I stayed up another fifteen minutes, then fell asleep.

~~~~

I woke up early and got dressed. Lenny hadn't called the night before, so I knew the police weren't going to become involved.

Since it had fallen to me, I needed to inform everyone to be cautious and take security precautions for the next few days. I knew Sterling and Jeanette were against any word of what was happening to Stig getting out, but I'd hate to think of any of Stig's friends being harassed or even harmed over a piece of jade.

I was sitting on the couch having coffee and toast, narrowing down the list of people to call first, when Sophie called. I answered, and she seemed excited.

"It's Saturday," I said. "You're calling me early."

"I couldn't wait. I came in to see what the secret software had on your Australian."

"Well?"

"I first had to sort through a bunch of people in order to find the right one. McKinsey is a relatively popular name, and Digger is a common nickname for someone with a military background. I had to conduct a secondary search based on the fact that he claimed to be a burglar. Telling me about the scar also helped."

"Well?"

"I think I've found the right one. The file had a picture from his days back in the Army. I've emailed it to you. Take a look and see if it's the right Digger McKinsey. I hope so. This one's cute."

My phone dinged, and I opened the file. Sure enough, there was a picture of Digga in an Army officer's uniform. He must have been in his mid-twenties at the time.

"Yup, you got the right one."

"The secret software only had one page on him. I guess the U.S. government doesn't spend a lot of time tracking

Australians."

"How long are you going to keep me waiting?"

"Okay, his real name is Daniel McKinsey. You were off on the age a little. He's actually forty-three. He spent several years in the Australian military and ended up as a captain in army intelligence. He was wounded while fighting with the coalition forces in the Middle East. The software doesn't have a lot of detail on what happened with that."

"Okay, what else?"

"Well, a couple of years after he was discharged, he was arrested for stealing some expensive art from the home of a wealthy businessman outside of London. The weird thing is, the Australian government asked he be returned to Australia, where they released him as part of some sort of clandestine government program."

"You're saying he's some sort of spy?"

"I don't think it's that exciting. It's more like he has a skill they need, and they use him whenever something comes up. Governments all over the region seem to use him whenever they've lost something and need to get it back. He's been caught several times over the last ten years, but some country will always ask that he be returned, and then he's released. There's a list of eight or ten countries he's thought to have worked with."

"So, you think a country is paying Digga to find *The Child*?"

"It wouldn't surprise me."

"Which country? Could it be the US?"

"The software doesn't have any record of him ever working for us, but it's always possible."

"Anything else?"

"That's it. Like I said, there wasn't much."

"Thanks for doing this. It'll help. How was your date with Milo last night?"

"It was okay. We went to dinner, then over to his place and watched a movie."

"Did he behave?"

"He didn't talk about getting serious or moving in together, if that's what you mean. I think he's finally got the message on that."

"What are you doing tonight? Still going out with the cougars?"

"I think so. I called Annie, and she said almost everyone was going out. I thought I'd give Christine a call and see if she'd like to come too. I know she'd fit in, and it would be great to have her in the group. Do you think you could come? It's always a lot of fun."

"Maybe, but I probably won't be able to. Until Stig shows up, I need to stay on that."

"What about Reno? Did you ever patch things up with him?"

"Honestly, I haven't had time to do anything with him. He seemed pretty ticked off at me, and I was giving him a few days to cool off. I'll probably give him a call later today to see if he's over it yet."

~~~~

I'd almost made it into the kitchen to get another cup of coffee when my phone rang. I picked it up, and I saw it was Jerry Phifer.

"It's Jerry," he said. "Look, they're saying the dead guy didn't drown but was probably murdered. I've already talked to Jeanette and Sterling, so I have a good idea of what they know and what's happening. I don't want this to get any worse. I want to talk to you about what really happened the other night. We can then get together with Lenny and figure out the best way to handle this."

"Where are you?"

"I'm at my house."

"Okay, give me the address, and I'll be right over."

~~~~

I drove to Jerry's, and it turned out to be a pleasant but modest house in South Scottsdale. It was only a few blocks from Navajo Elementary, where I had attended grade school. I was thinking I was in the wrong neighborhood, but Jerry's Tesla was parked in the attached carport.

I walked to the front door, but Jerry opened it before I had a chance to knock. He looked terrible and already had a drink in his hand.

I walked in and followed him into the kitchen. It was decorated in the 1980s. In fact, it looked so similar to the house I grew up in, I almost laughed.

"I like your house," I said. "I grew up a few blocks from here."

"I've always lived in this house. My parents died about twenty years ago, and it's been mine ever since."

I turned down his offer for a drink, and we both sat at the kitchen table. I knew Jerry had a story to tell, and I was going to need to let him tell it his own way.

"So," I asked, "what really happened after Stig went to bed the night of the party?"

Jerry lit up a cigarette and took several puffs. I didn't say anything, letting him tell his story his own way.

"It happened like I told you before, well, until I went into the bedroom to change. I hadn't even gotten out of my suit when Christine started moaning from the next bedroom. I gotta tell you, listening to Christine having sex really got me going. Maybe you won't understand, but like every other guy growing up, having sex with Christine Johns was always a fantasy of mine, and it's only gotten worse since I've gotten to know her. And I'll be damned; there I was, standing naked in a bedroom listening to Christine, not ten feet away, moaning, and screaming to be fucked harder. After ten or fifteen minutes of listening to that, I needed to go out and have another drink. I put on a robe, went out to the cabana bar on the outside patio, and made myself a stiff one."

"What happened then?"

"As I headed back inside, I saw Stig sitting in a chair next to the inside part of the pool. Only as I got closer, I realized it wasn't Stig but Frank Fender. You gotta understand, the only lights in the big room were coming up from the pool. I couldn't tell who it was until I was right next to him. I noticed he was wearing Stig's sport coat and drinking Stig's Patrón tequila straight out of the bottle."

"Frank Fender, that's the guy who tried to crash the party earlier?"

"That's right. He used to be Stig's stunt double. He was in the first ten or twelve movies Stig did. He did the early *Hammer* movies and a couple of the early science fiction ones. He'd tried to come into the house earlier, but he was drunk, so Luther and I told him to go home. I guess he must have come back sometime around two. The driveway gate was still open, and with everyone coming and going, it wouldn't have been hard for him to slip back in."

"What did he want?"

"That's what I asked. I sat down next to him and asked,

'Frank, what the hell are you doing here?' I mean, it was crazy having him in Stig's house like that."

"And what'd he say?"

"Well, he was pretty drunk. He was going on about how he wanted to talk to Stig about doing stunts in the new movie."

"Why wasn't he doing Stig's stunts anymore?"

"Well, it's like this: being a stunt double's very demanding. As Frank got into his forties, he started getting hurt. Seems he'd get injured in almost every movie, and the studio would need to scramble to find a replacement halfway through filming. Eventually, they found a guy half Frank's age, and the new guy's been doing Stig's stunts ever since. According to Frank, he had a verbal contract from Stig to do his stunts for as long as Stig did movies. He'd been suing the studio for the past couple of years to be allowed to do the stunts again."

"What did you do with Frank?"

"I didn't do anything. I sipped on my drink while he rambled on about how hard it had been being Stig's double."

"What'd he talk about?"

"I don't remember much of it. I was pretty drunk myself. Plus, the sounds of Christine having sex were still echoing down the hall. Honestly, I was paying more attention to her than I was to Frank. I remember he said the studio originally picked him, not because he was a good stuntman, but because he was exactly the same size as Stig."

I looked at Jerry, trying to make sense out of that.

"It's to save money on the wardrobe," Jerry said. "Frank and Stig always ended up sharing several outfits, so Frank needed to be the same size as Stig."

"You said Frank was wearing Stig's sports coat?"

"Yeah, Stig must have left his jacket on a chair next to the pool. Frank said he'd put on the jacket to prove he and Stig were still the same size."

"What happened after you both had a drink?"

"Frank took off. Well, at least I thought he did. I walked him to the front door, and he went out. It was about then that I realized I was too drunk to drive, so I went back to the bedroom and fell asleep on the bed. I would say I passed out right away, but the truth is, I probably spent another five or ten-minutes listening to Christine orgasm before I actually passed out. Crazy world, huh?"

"What happened then?"

"Well, I woke up with a bitch of a hangover. I went out to use Stig's Keurig and find some Advil, but on the way to the kitchen, I saw Frank floating in the damn pool. I assumed he snuck back in, fell in the pool, and drowned. I knew how drunk he'd been. I sort of went nuts thinking of the issues this was going to cause."

"What'd you do?"

"The house was quiet, so I assumed Stig was still asleep. I didn't realize at the time that Stig had already seen the body and had headed down to your law office to try and handle it on his own. I called up Luther and told him what happened. We both thought it would be best to move the body somewhere else so it wouldn't be found in Stig's pool. Luther lives close by, and he showed up in about ten minutes. We pulled Frank out of the pool and wrapped him in a bedspread Luther brought so he wouldn't drip all over the house. We drove the body up to the Granite Reef Dam and dumped him in the Salt River."

What the hell?

I stared at Jerry, and after a moment, he continued.

"Okay, so we probably shouldn't have done it, but we had

to act fast. I knew what a field day the press would have with the story. You don't understand how these things work. Something like this would turn him into a laughingstock and completely finish off his days on the A-list. Honestly, he only has a few good movies left in his career unless something drastically changes, and I want him to be able to do every one of those movies."

"You left the jacket on Frank?"

"Yeah, it was stupid, but I thought, what the hell, it's only a jacket. And to be honest, the thought of pulling a jacket off a dead guy was making my stomach turn over. I didn't know Stig had left his f'ing wallet in the f'ing pocket."

"But then you heard that Frank didn't drown but was murdered?"

"Yeah. It changed Frank from being a stupid fuck to a murder victim, and it's crossed my mind that whoever killed Frank was likely after Stig instead. Hell, I didn't know it wasn't Stig until I was right next to him, and I've known him for thirty years."

"We'll need to talk with Lenny about this. I don't know exactly how illegal moving a dead body is, but I'm guessing it'll need to be reported. Oh, one more thing. The other day you said you still had the key to Stig's box. The one that got stolen. Would I be able to get it?"

Jerry disappeared into his bedroom only to come out a minute later. He was holding a red silk ribbon with an ornate silver key dangling off the end.

"It's nice, huh?" he said. "This is only the key; you should see the box. Someone put some work into that. If you ask me, it was good enough to go into a museum. It's a shame someone swiped it."

~~~~

I was driving back to my apartment from Jerry's when a text from Jeanette popped up. Ten seconds later, Gina called. I pulled over to read the text and answer the phone.

"Laura," Gina said. "We've got a hit on Stig's phone."

"Jeanette texted a few seconds ago," I said. "She wants me to call."

"I just got off the phone with her. The phone's in the Lost Dutchman State Park. It's been on for almost five minutes and apparently hasn't moved."

"Lost Dutchman Park? Isn't that outside of Apache Junction?"

"Yes, it's across the highway from the Goldfield Ghost Town, the tourist village northeast of AJ on the Apache Trail Highway."

"Okay, I've been there. I know where it is. Who's closer?"

"I'm in Sun City West, and even if everything goes smoothly, it will take almost an hour to get there."

"I'll go then," I said. "I'm in South Scottsdale and could get there in about twenty minutes if I hurry. I'm assuming Sterling and Jeanette still want to keep the police out of this?"

"Until there's more evidence of a problem, they're still looking at this as an actor having an emotional outburst."

"Okay. I'll let you know what I find."

Chapter Ten

As I drove over to Lost Dutchman State Park, I called Jeanette and asked what information she had. She said the phone was still on and within about two hundred yards of the Treasure Loop trailhead parking lot.

I drove to the park and studied a large map posted near the main entrance. I found the Treasure Loop parking lot and drove to it.

I hadn't been here since I was a kid, and we'd had a family campout. It was a desert park set at the base of the east cliffs in the Superstition Mountains. Part of the park was set up for camping, while the rest was a series of scenic hiking trails.

Four cars and a white van were parked in the lot. I couldn't tell about the van, but the cars appeared to be empty.

I parked next to a Ford Taurus and walked up the trail for about two hundred yards without seeing anyone. Several large creosote bushes and mesquite trees surrounded both sides of the trail, which could possibly have hidden a body. I went off the trail and spent several minutes checking the places that weren't visible from either the trail or the parking lot without finding anything.

I called Jeanette to get an update. She said the phone was still turned on and was somewhere near the parking lot or possibly slightly to the south.

I walked back to the parking lot and walked due south until I came to a small building that looked like some sort of maintenance shed. Unfortunately, the shed had a large padlock on the door and was inaccessible.

I pounded on the door and called out to Stig without getting any sort of response. I then walked around the building and searched the area but found nothing.

Having a sudden inspiration, I pulled out my phone and called Stig's number. Almost directly behind me came the sound of a ringing telephone.

I followed the sound to a low rosemary bush about halfway between the shed and the parking lot. The phone was wedged into the middle of the bush, and I had to reach in and feel around before I could pull it out.

With a feeling of triumph, I held up the phone. It was then I realized I wasn't alone. Three large men had crept up, and one of them was pointing a stun gun at my chest.

"You're Laura Black?" the lead goon asked.

"Yes. What are you doing here, and where is Stig?"

They answered by firing the stun gun. My world became a haze of pain and loss of control. I dropped to the ground and was only dimly aware that the men had surrounded me.

I felt some new pain jab into my neck. There was a brief burning sensation in my head, and then the pain in my chest faded, as did the sounds of my screaming.

The world began to grow dim. I fought it as long as I could, but within a few seconds, the world went black.

~~~~~

When I came to, I was hurting in so many places it was hard to keep track. The stun gun darts had hit me on either side of my sternum, and I felt the burns from where the electrodes had gone in.

My neck hurt from where someone had roughly jabbed a syringe into it. My head ached with a sensation I could only peg as a bad hangover.

Whatever drug they had used to knock me out was fast-acting, but it wasn't easy on the system. The only pain I couldn't account for was on the ribs on the side of my chest.

It was in the same area I'd been shot the month before, and the bruise had only recently healed. Lifting up my shirt, I could see a new bruise forming in the shape of the toe of a boot.

I guess that at least one of them had decided to give me a quick kick before dragging me off to wherever I was. I shuddered as I thought about what else they might have done to me while I was unconscious.

Looking around, I was in a small room with unpainted cinder block walls, a metal roof, and a bare concrete floor. From the many stains on the walls and the floor, I assumed I was in some sort of manufacturing space.

There were some empty wooden boxes, and I made enough of a pile to climb up and look out a small window with a thick metal grating. The view was not helpful, as it only showed a generic alleyway and a cinder block building on the other side.

I saw several seagulls circling overhead. At a guess, I would say I was somewhere near the Salt River, either in South Scottsdale or maybe South Phoenix. From the angle of the sun, it was sometime in the late afternoon.

My head still pounded, but fortunately, I wasn't nauseous. I sat on the floor with my back against the wall for probably an hour. I couldn't tell closer than that because my phone and my purse weren't with me.

From outside the door, the sound of several men grew closer. They stopped in front of the door, I heard a bolt slide, and the door opened.

Three men came into my cell. One was Asian, one was black, and one was white. All three were solidly built and gave off a military vibe.

They wore black cargo pants and black T-shirts. From Digga's description of the group of mercenaries, I had to assume I'd found them.

Without a word, two men grabbed my arms, lifted me to my feet, and then walked me down the hall. The third man pulled out a stun gun and trailed behind, in case I caused trouble, I assumed.

We ended up in a large but shabby office. The walls had cheap wood paneling, and the carpet smelled of mildew.

In the center of the room was an older-style metal executive desk. It was painted green and had a chipped Formica top.

A middle-aged Asian man was seated behind the desk, filling in some paperwork with a pen. Like the others, he appeared to be a military person.

Behind him, on either side, were two large men standing at attention. One was white, and one was Asian. I was marched in front of the desk, and my arms were released.

"You're Laura Black?" the man asked without looking up.

There didn't seem any point in denying it, especially since I'd already admitted it, and they'd had time to go through my handbag and confirm my identity.

"Yes, I'm Laura Black. What do you want with me, and where's Stig?"

"My name is Colonel Wu," he said as he looked up. "Please do not insult me. We have Stig, and I suspect you already know what we want."

"You're looking for *The Child*," I said.

"That is correct. My employer arranged for Stig to take the piece out of China, and he has given me the honor of collecting it here in America."

"Why did you wait so long to start looking for it? Stig's had the box and the jade here for almost three weeks."

"Unfortunately, my employer initially chose to use local people to retrieve the object, and they failed. I have come to complete the task."

Digga? He's not local. Cyril? Not likely.

"We have questioned Stig several times. He told us you work for his solicitor and are also currently looking for *The Child*. We understand that you have full access to his house, his family, his friends, and his associates. Stig told us the piece was of no value to him. He claims the reason he doesn't have it is because he gave it away."

"That's my understanding, as well. No one involved knew anything about jade, and it was of little value to anyone other than as a keepsake of the trip to China."

"I'm not sure I believe you Americans are as stupid as that," Colonel Wu said. "But it is possible."

"Before two days ago, I'd never heard of *The Child*. Not many people in America are up on ancient Chinese jade."

"Again, it is possible. In any case, as of this moment, you are now working for me."

"You want me to volunteer to be on your team?"

"That is correct. You will find *The Child* and give it to me."

"Alright, if I'm on your team, tell me what you know. Where have you already looked for the sculpture?"

"After we obtained Stig Stevens, he gave us the codes to the gate on his driveway and the front door. I've had six men searching Stig's house every night since we took him three nights ago."

"You've had people crawling through Stig's every night?"

"That is correct. Stig was apparently telling the truth. We found no trace of it at his house. We have now learned all we can from him. We are releasing him into your custody. Stig has been warned not to go to the police, and I will also warn you. I would look on it as extremely disrespectful to me if the police should find any of my men and arrest them."

"You're letting Stig go?"

"Yes. Please describe your plans for locating *The Child*."

"Well, it should be fairly straightforward. Stig didn't want the jade, so he had it placed on a table at a party he was hosting. He spread the word that anyone could have it. After the party, it was gone. There were only about thirty people in total at the house that night, so in theory, all I have to do is go down the list one by one, and eventually, I'll find out who has it."

"That matches what I know. However, your task may not be as easy as you assume. If the person who has *The Child* realizes the value of what they have, they may not openly admit to having it. In fact, it may already be in the hands of an art dealer. Speed is of the essence in obtaining the piece."

"I've been looking for it, and now all you're doing is delaying me. If I'm on your team, are you going to back off and let me do my job, or are your people going to keep interfering?"

"You are only one small part of our undertaking. You may rest assured that we will not slow our independent efforts. It is inevitable that your efforts and ours will overlap."

"I figured. Well, tell your people to stay out of my way. If we continue to bump into each other, it will only slow things down."

"Agreed. My people will not interfere with your efforts as long as you are obtaining positive results."

"How can I contact you?"

The tall white goon next to Colonel Wu handed me a piece of paper. "You may write me at this email account," the colonel said. "It is monitored twenty-four hours a day. I will give you until five o'clock tomorrow afternoon to deliver *The Child* to me. If not, something, well, unpleasant will happen."

"You don't need to threaten. It won't make me look any harder."

"It has been my experience that people achieve greater things when they are properly motivated. Remember this, I will need your results by five o'clock tomorrow."

~~~~

I was escorted back to my cell and found Stig sitting on an upturned wooden crate. His clothes were filthy, and he looked like someone who'd had a rough couple of days.

"Ah, Laura," he said. "It looks like I dragged you into a real mess."

"Don't worry about that," I said. "How are you doing?"

"I feel terrible. I've been hit with a stun gun and drugged. I've had to answer a bunch of stupid questions about that little piece of jade I got back in China. I never wanted it in the first place. I only took it because Mr. Zhang, the big money guy, was handing out presents, and I was trying to be polite."

After five minutes, three new men showed up. One had two black bags in his hand, and I knew what was about to happen.

"They're going to put those bags on our heads," I said. "Don't fight them."

Stig started to protest, but I knew if we didn't voluntarily let them put the bags on our heads, they were going to have to knock us out again. I didn't want to add to my headache, plus I didn't want to be unconscious and vulnerable again to whatever sick urges the three men happened to have.

As expected, they put the bags on our heads and led us outside to what I assumed was the white van. We drove for about forty minutes before the vehicle came to the final stop.

If we had driven in a straight line, we could've been as far west as Goodyear. Of course, we also could have been in Apache Junction the entire time, and they'd decided to take the scenic route back to Lost Dutchman Park.

I heard the door to the van slide open, and the bag was removed from my head. My purse was pushed into my hands, and I was shoved out of the van.

Stig came out close behind me. The van took off, and we were back where I'd started—the trailhead parking lot in Lost Dutchman State Park.

I looked through my bag. Fortunately, I still had my keys, my wallet, my phone, and even my gun. I picked up the tiny pistol and could feel it was still loaded.

Although we had been incredibly lucky, I knew our dealings with Colonel Wu were far from over. I also knew I'd need to have the locks in my apartment re-keyed.

Knowing the men I was dealing with, it wouldn't surprise me if they had already used the keys and searched my place. They also, no doubt, had made copies of all the keys for future use.

"Get in the car," I said. "I'll drive us to your house. There was a story out yesterday that you were dead. Only it turned out to be the dead guy from your pool. You're supposed to be in seclusion, so they're likely to be reporters and photographers in front of your house."

"Do you have a coat or something I can use to cover up with?" Stig asked.

I went back to the trunk and found a blanket in a plastic storage bag. That and an emergency road kit were the only two things in the trunk.

"Will this work?" I asked as I pulled the blanket out of the bag.

"Perfect," he said.

I put the car in gear and shook my head.

"Don't worry about it," Stig said, "I've done it before. It's all part of being a movie star."

On the drive to Stig's, I called Gina. She had tried to call me a dozen times while I was being held.

Her voice was filled with relief when she found out I was alright. She said that after I didn't call, she had gone to Lost Dutchman Park and found my car.

She said she looked around the area for over two hours without finding me. I told her the basics of what had happened and that I was taking Stig back to his house.

She asked how she could help, and I told her to go out on her date and have a good time. She made me promise to call her if I needed any help.

~~~~

As we got near the driveway to the house, Stig bent over and flipped the blanket over his head. I smoothed it out, so he looked like nothing more than a pile of laundry.

Outside the gate were a half-dozen cars and several

photographers standing in loose groups. They perked up when they saw I was going up Stig's driveway, and a couple of them took pictures of me and my car.

Once in the house, Stig took off to get a shower and a change of clothes. I went out to the patio and called Lenny.

"I've got Stig. He's back at the house."

"Alright, keep him there. Good work on finding him. I'll call Sterling and Jeanette. We'll meet you at the house as soon as we can."

~~~~

Half an hour later, Stig made it back out to the patio. He looked much better as he made his way to the cabana bar to pour himself a drink.

The door from the house opened. Jeanette, Sterling, and Lenny came out and surrounded Stig, everyone talking at once.

Lenny wanted to take Stig to a hospital to have him checked out. Jeanette and Sterling wanted to ascertain the situation before doing anything as radical as making Stig's condition public.

Lenny suggested having a doctor come discreetly to the house to examine Stig. Jeanette and Sterling looked at each other and nodded in agreement.

The door to the house opened again, and Jerry came out. He came over and joined the group.

"Stig," Jerry said. "What happened? Where were you?"

"It's all a bit fuzzy. I got a call Wednesday night from a man. He seemed to know all about the dead guy in the pool. He said he was a friend and only wanted to help me clear up the situation."

"Tell me about the man," I said. "Was there anything

distinctive about his voice?"

"Yeah, um, I think he was Australian or from somewhere down there."

"What did he want?" Lenny asked.

"He wanted to meet at a coffee shop and tell me about everything that had happened. I made it down my driveway to the street, but there was a white van blocking the road. I got out to ask them to move when five men jumped out of the van and surrounded me. They all attacked at once. They used a stun gun on me, and then one of them shot me full of something. When I woke up, I was locked in a room somewhere."

"Did they hurt you?" Jeanette asked.

"What did they want to know?" Sterling asked. "What did you tell them?"

"I'm okay. They spent most of the time asking about the little jade sculpture I got from China a couple of weeks ago. It seems they were looking for it and were pretty pissed I didn't have it anymore. I let them know I'd given it away. They kept questioning me, and I kept giving them the same answers. I spent three nights there. This morning, they stopped asking questions. A couple of hours ago, Laura showed up and brought me home."

Sterling looked at me. "Well, what do you know about this?"

I was a little uncertain how much to tell. The fewer people who knew all the details, the easier my job locating *The Child* would be. I glanced at Lenny, and he gave a slight shake of his head, urging me to say as little as possible. That seemed to settle it.

"I really don't know anything," I said. "The people who took Stig turned on his phone in a park on the east side of The Valley. When I went there to look for Stig, they grabbed me. I had a bag on my head, and I don't know where we ended up. When I got there, they asked me about the jade figurine. I said I didn't know where it was. They told me to look for it, then told me to take Stig home."

Jeanette, Jerry, and Sterling began a long discussion with each other on possible outcomes if Stig gave a press conference or if he simply stayed at the house. Lenny pointed out the police would want to question Stig at some point about the dead guy who was wearing Stig's jacket.

Jeanette said they had been lucky, but if anything got out, it could still blow up. This went on for about half an hour. With the four of them still in their discussion group, I went over to where Stig was sitting.

"Thanks for getting me out of there today," he said. "I kept thinking that if this was a Hammer movie, I could come up with a way of overpowering the guards and escaping. It's not so easy in the real world."

"Don't worry about it," I said. "I'm glad you're alright."

"I assume you promised to help them find the jade?"

"They didn't give me much of a choice. It was pretty obvious neither one of us was getting out of there unless I volunteered to help them."

"Well, you know as much about the jade as I do. As far as I know, someone at the party took it. It could be anywhere now."

"I'll start looking again first thing tomorrow. I'm concerned that Colonel Wu and his goons might start to harass the people who were at the party."

"They didn't ask me any questions about who was there that night. From the way they talked, I assumed they already had that information. I have no idea where they got it."

"Starting tomorrow morning, I'd like you to call everyone who was at the party. We'll need to ask them if they have the figurine. We'll need to be tactful and let them know to be on the lookout for strangers."

"I'd hate to think of Colonel Wu going after any of my friends. I still have a copy of the list Jerry and I put together. It's around here somewhere. I'll find it and start calling first thing in the morning."

"Unless we tell everyone about the men who may be after them, no one will take a general security warning very seriously. Of course, we also don't want to start a panic. The best thing for us to do is to find the jade and get it to Colonel Wu as quickly as possible. He'll leave, and things can get back to normal."

~~~~

Sterling, Jerry, and Jeanette eventually finished up with Lenny. It was getting late, and they wanted to discuss things over with Stig in private.

They walked him back into the house, leaving me alone with Lenny. I walked over to where he was sitting at a table with a million-dollar view of Scottsdale.

"Why didn't you want me to tell everything to Sterling and Jeanette?"

"I'm not sure," he said. "Something about this isn't right. Jeanette and Sterling are refusing to go to the police. Even Jerry is against going to the police. This is after Stig was kidnapped, and the men who did it are still out there."

"Isn't that so there won't be any publicity?"

"Maybe, but this is starting to feel a little weird. Do I take it that Stig was released with the implied threat of more harm if you don't come up with their jade?"

"Yes, it was more than implied."

"Okay then, I'm going to urge Stig to actually go into seclusion for a few days. I don't want him anywhere accessible to these guys again. What about you? Should I pull you off this and give it to Gina? It's not that I don't trust you, but having a trained police investigator is why I hired Gina in the first place."

"No, let me keep it. I'll be okay and I have some ideas about how to find the jade."

"Alright then," Lenny said. "Let me know when you have some information."

~~~~

We stayed at Stig's until about ten-thirty. By then, everyone had given their opinion on what to do.

In the end, they decided to have Stig stay in the house and not to leave it until things blew over. I was worried about Colonel Wu and his men, but Lenny convinced Stig to hire an off-duty Scottsdale police officer to be stationed outside the house twenty-four hours a day.

I drove home and was asleep within minutes.

~~~~

I woke up early the following day, made a pot of coffee, and went back to the list. I was going to need to be organized in how I went about my search, or else I could spend days looking for the jade. Since Colonel Wu had only given me until five o'clock, I was going to need to act fast if I had any hope of succeeding.

Jerry didn't have it, so I crossed his name off the list. That left me with about twenty-eight people who could have taken it.

I realized I needed some help with prioritizing. Jerry said

he'd mostly talked with the women at the party about the jade.

Unfortunately, I had no idea if he told all the women or only some of them. I thumped my head that I hadn't asked Jerry about the list last night when I had him at Stig's house.

It was only a little after eight, early for a Sunday morning, but I picked up the phone and called Jerry.

"Hello?" he answered. It was pretty obvious he'd still been asleep.

"Sorry to wake you. Now that Stig's back, I need to find the jade sculpture you put on the table the night of the party. After you set it out, who did you tell about it?"

"Um, I really don't remember anyone specific. As the night went on, I mentioned it to whoever I happened to be talking with."

"Do you remember any of the names? It will help me prioritize the list of people I need to interview."

"Well, I told Vicky and Christine. They both collect stuff like that. Luther knew about it too. He likes little souvenir knickknacks. I also told several others. Honestly, I don't remember the names of most of the people who were there. The women who come to Stig's parties are mostly in their mid-forties to mid-fifties, and they all dress more or less the same. It leads to a lot of confusion about the names. Let me wake up and have a coffee. I'll go down the list and see if anything rings a bell."

Jerry disconnected, and I picked up the list. I took a green pen and circled Vicky Vaughn and Christine Johns.

These two would be straightforward since I already knew both of them and had been to their houses already. The only others I knew were Nails and Jackie Wade.

I could ask about Nails when I talked to Christine. From

what Jerry had said earlier, Jackie hadn't been at the party for more than an hour or two, but she was still worth looking into. That left me with twenty-four people who could have taken the jade with no clear priority as to who it could be.

I got dressed and filled my *Doctor Who* mug again. It was approaching nine, so everyone should be up by now.

I needed to choose between simply calling the people on the list and interviewing them in person. I decided that the only way to know for sure was to talk with everyone face to face.

Colonel Wu might be right. If someone took the jade and then found out what it was, they might not be eager to advertise the fact that they had it.

I first called Christine Johns. "Hi, Christine, it's Laura Black. I need to talk with you. It's about Stig and everything that's been happening."

"Sure, we all had quite a scare after what they had on the news on Friday. I'm glad he's alright. I'm headed out the door now, and I won't be back for a couple of hours. Would twelve-thirty work? We could meet at my house, unless you had something else in mind."

"Your house is perfect."

"Are you sure we can't do this over the phone?"

"It's better if we talk in person."

"Okay, see you at twelve-thirty."

I then called Vicky Vaughn. She answered right away, but she seemed to be breathing hard, and there was the sound of traffic in the background. "Hi, Vicky," I said. "Did I catch you at a bad time?"

"No, I'm good. I'm out for a morning run. I like to get out before it gets too hot. I can run and talk at the same time."

"Great. I'd like to come over and talk with you sometime today. It's about Stig and everything that's happened over the last few days."

"That would be great. We heard on Friday afternoon he was dead, and then on Friday night, he was alive again. Let me finish my run and take a shower. Meet me at my place at ten-thirty?"

"Ten-thirty sounds perfect. Thanks, Vicky."

I had just disconnected with Vicky when Jerry called. "Okay," he said, "I went down the list. Most of the names still aren't familiar, so I could have talked with any of them. I do specifically remember talking with Ellen Martinez. She's the wife of Eduardo Martinez, from the Scottsdale city council. I told her about the green figurine."

"That's great," I said. "Who else?"

"I spent a while talking with Jackie Wade. She owns the Saguaro Sky Resort. I also told Nancy Anderson about it. She's the wife of Judge Anderson from the Federal District Court. Any of them could have taken it. Plus, we were usually talking in a group, so anyone could have overheard me. Most of the people there wouldn't have cared about a piece of tourist junk, but some of them might have taken it to have a story about how it once belonged to Stig Stevens."

"Okay, thanks. That gives me three more people to look into first."

"Let me ask you about the jade thing. Stig isn't talking a lot about it, but I hear that's why he was kidnapped. It must be more valuable than we first thought it was. Is that why you're still so hot to find it?"

"It's not so much that it's valuable," I said. "The guys who took Stig only let him go because I promised to help find the sculpture for them. If I can't find it and give it to them, it's

220

likely they'll be back."

"Alright, that makes sense. Lenny was insistent that Stig barricade himself inside his house, and he's hired off-duty cops to sit outside in the courtyard and read the paper twenty-four hours a day for the next week."

"It seems like a prudent step."

"Um, what about Frank Fender, the dead guy we moved? Do you think all this has anything to do with that?" Jerry asked.

"Not directly. I think he was just in the wrong place at the wrong time."

"Yeah, well, that's Frank's life summed up in one sentence."

~~~~

I sat on my couch and called Ellen Martinez, Nancy Anderson, and Jackie Wade. These were the three names I'd gotten from Jerry and my next targets for interviews.

Ellen Martinez said she'd be home all day, and I set up a meeting at her house at two o'clock.

Nancy Anderson said she'd be out until the middle of the afternoon, so I set up an appointment with her at three.

Jackie Wade didn't answer, so I left her a voicemail.

~~~~

I went down to my car in the apartment lot. As always, I got a reassuring thrill when I started up the Mercedes, and the powerful engine thrummed under the hood.

It was another beautiful day, and I lowered the top to take advantage of it. I hopped on the Loop-101 and went north to Hayden, then up to Greyhawk and Vicky's place.

~~~~

Vicky Vaughn answered the door and led me into her kitchen. "I'm about to have a glass of organic passion fruit iced tea. Would you like one too?"

"That sounds wonderful," I said, suddenly thirsty.

Vicky dropped ice cubes into two tall glasses and poured tea from a pitcher in the refrigerator. She handed me a glass, and we walked into the living room.

As I remembered from the last time I'd been here, the living room had a shelf of carved animals, mainly horses. I could imagine how a carving of a grasshopper on a leaf might appeal to her.

"Friday was terrible," Vicky said as we sat on her couch. "I first heard about Stig when Vivian called me. Some reporters had shown up at her house and started asking for comments on a report about Stig being dead. She called me to see if I knew what was going on. I called around, but no one knew anything. The radio kept repeating the same report, a body had been pulled from the Salt River, and they thought it might be Stig. It wasn't until about seven that night when Jerry called and said it wasn't him."

"It was a scare for everyone," I said. "I talked to Stig last night, and he was pretty upset about the news report."

"I know. I talked with him about ten-thirty last night. He called to let me know he was alright."

"I'm here about something else," I said, trying to come up with something plausible on the spot. "Stig got a present after they finished filming in China a couple of weeks ago. It was a jade sculpture of a grasshopper on a leaf. Stig didn't want it, so he had Jerry put it on the table in the entrance hall. Jerry let everyone know they could have it, and someone took it. Um, it turns out Stig was supposed to turn it over to the studio. It's supposed to be displayed in the lobby, and the studio wants Stig to get it back. Did you happen to take it? Did you see anyone else who took it or who was maybe excited when Jerry told them about it?"

"Well, I remember Jerry talking about it. It sounded like something I might want since I collect animal carvings. But honestly, I completely forgot about it until you mentioned it. I don't know if Jerry told anyone else about it or not. I didn't look for it as I left that night. It still could have been there. Stig has so many pieces of art in his house. One more carving wouldn't have caught my eye."

As I left Vicky's, I drove the three blocks over to Jackie's house. I hated to show up unannounced, but I knew Jackie probably wouldn't mind. Unfortunately, when I knocked on her door, no one was home. I pulled out my phone and called, but again, no one answered.

The next stop on my list was Christine. I drove down Scottsdale Road to Jackrabbit and then west into Christine's neighborhood.

I parked in front of her house and got out. I was about halfway up her driveway when a voice called out from across the street.

"Hey, Laura. Is that you?"

I looked across the street to see Terry Lennox standing next to a line of rosemary bushes. He was holding a pair of hedge trimmers and had apparently been pruning.

He was wearing green cargo pants and a Cardinal's T-shirt. I wasn't used to seeing him dressed so casually, and for a second, I didn't recognize him.

"Hey, Terry," I yelled back as I drifted across the street to talk with him. "How've you been?"

Terry walked down to the sidewalk, still holding the hedge trimmers.

"I've been doing great," he said. I noticed his fake MTV-style New York accent was gone. He definitely sounded better.

"I like what you've done with the house."

"Yeah, well, I'd let it go before. You know, I never really thanked you for what you did for my dad and me. We were both pretty messed up for a while."

"I'm glad it's working out. How is your dad?"

"It's been hard for him. Dealing with those guys from Mexico pretty much wiped him out financially. Your boss helped him sort out everything with the police, so that never turned out to be a big deal. I've been helping as much as I can, and of all people, Jackie Wade's been helping too. She offered him a job a couple of months ago at the Saguaro Sky. At first, I thought Dad would be pissed, but he really appreciated it. I think he'll do okay."

"I'm glad to hear that. I also hear from Christine that the band is still going."

"Yeah, Dog Farts have never been more popular. We're booked solid three months out. Christine's been great. She's sung with us a couple of times, and that's boosted our name recognition with people beyond the Scottsdale club scene. I'm trying to convince her to be on a few tracks of our new release. If that doesn't boost sales, I don't know what will."

~~~~

I went back to Christine's, and when she answered the door, she was wearing a casual sundress. It still struck me as incredible that I could simply pop by and talk with Christine Johns.

We went back to her living room, and I turned down her offer for a drink.

"Okay," she said as we both sat on her couch. "So, how

can I help you? You said this had something to do with Stig."

"The other night at Stig's party, Jerry was going around telling everyone about a green sculpture he was trying to give away. It turns out Stig was supposed to keep it, and he's asked me to see who has it."

"That's it?" Christine asked. "I thought this had something to do with the dead body they pulled out of the river."

"Nope, nothing to do with the dead guy."

"I heard on the radio that the man used to work as Stig's movie stunt double. I guess that's why they reported at first it was Stig."

"It led to some confusion about who it was. But I was over at Stig's last night with Jerry and Jeanette, and he's doing alright. I hear he has a big movie premier coming up next weekend, and they're lying low until then."

"I'm glad everything's alright. Stig and I have been friends for a long time, and I'd hate to think of anything happening to him."

"Do you happen to know anything about the green sculpture?"

"I remember Jerry talking about it. But Nails and I were some of the last to leave. As I was heading out, I looked on the table and it wasn't there."

"Is it possible Nails may have taken it?"

"No. By the time we left, he wasn't doing so well, and I was helping him out. Honestly, I think I wore him out."

~~~~

I said my goodbyes to Christine, then went to Ellen Martinez's and Nancy Anderson's. Both women were friendly and wanted to help.

Both remembered Jerry talking about the jade sculpture, but neither admitted to taking it. Neither knew who had taken it, and both seemed sincere, which left me with nothing.

Chapter Eleven

I sat in my car in front of Nancy Anderson's house with a growing sense of frustration. Colonel Wu had threatened me with something unpleasant unless I came up with the sculpture by five. I wasn't looking forward to seeing what that might be.

It was approaching three thirty, which left me with less than an hour and a half to produce some results. Hopefully, if I had good visibility on obtaining the jade, he'd extend his timeline by a few hours.

I decided to take a chance on Luther. I knew he collected animal figurines, and I was running out of obvious people from the party list. I called and asked if I could come over to the house and see him.

"I'll be glad to see you, but I'm working out of the office today."

"On a Sunday?"

"I have a tax deadline coming up, and it's easier to do everything here. I'll be here until at least six tonight. Call me when you get to the door, and I'll let you in."

~~~~

I parked in the nearly empty lot and walked to Luther's

building.

Luther came out to the front and unlocked the office door. I walked in, and he led me into his inner office. I again noticed all the animal sculptures on his bookshelf.

Luther offered me a comfortable client chair in front of his desk while he settled himself in his black executive chair. He looked a little uneasy.

"Jerry says he told you about what we did with Frank Fender the other morning. I'm assuming you'd like to discuss that?"

"No, I'm not the police, and it no longer concerns my assignment. If something comes of it, I won't be the one who instigates it. I'm here about something else. The little jade sculpture Stig got from China."

Luther seemed surprised. "Stig told me he got something like that as a present. He said he liked the box it came in. What has it got to do with anything?"

"Stig had Jerry give it away the night of the party. I know he told several people about it, and now I'm trying to get it back. It's sort of indirectly the cause of a lot of what has been happening the past two weeks."

"Well, okay, I do remember Jerry talking about something like that. I didn't realize he was talking about the same figurine. But no, by the time I left Stig's house, I wasn't thinking about green sculptures. If it was still there, I didn't notice it. Actually, it surprised me that Jerry had time to talk with me at all. Whenever he's at one of Stig's parties, Jerry spends most of his time trying to convince aspiring actresses to take him on as their manager."

~~~~

We walked through the outer offices, and then Luther unlocked the door and let me out. As I stepped into the parking lot, I pulled out my phone and saw it was two minutes after five.

Colonel Wu had said something unpleasant would happen if I didn't give him *The Child* by now. I'd need to contact him and let him know of my progress.

Suddenly feeling uneasy, I looked around the parking lot to see if anyone was there. Fortunately, I'd purposely parked far enough away from anyone else so that no one would be able to creep up on me.

I was almost to my convertible when I heard a loud buzzing sound. It seemed to be coming from my car.

I took a couple of steps, then stopped and listened to my car buzz. I'd never heard a car make a sound like that before, and it didn't sound good. I caught a brief whiff of gasoline and suddenly understood what was going on.

Shit, no!

I took two slow steps forward when there was the distinctive *whoop* sound of a barbecue grill lighting, and the underside of my car was completely engulfed in flames.

My car!

Out of instinct, I took a few more steps toward the burning convertible. The fire was rapidly spreading, and the smell of gasoline was now even stronger.

It was a totally surreal experience as I stood helplessly in the parking lot and watched my car burn. I didn't want to watch it happening, but I couldn't seem to look away.

My body wanted desperately to do something, to stop what was happening, but I knew the car was already gone. I tried to think if there was anything vital in the car.

If I acted quickly, I could perhaps run in and have enough time to pull something out. Fortunately, the only things of value in the car were some of my old CDs. I hated to lose them, but I knew it could have been much worse.

Somebody, maybe Luther, must have called 911 because five minutes later, a fire truck rolled into the parking lot with its lights and siren going. By this time, the car was fully involved and was causing a thick column of black smoke to rise up over Scottsdale.

Close behind the fire truck was a Scottsdale police cruiser. My friend Chugger McIntyre got out of the car with a look of concern.

He scanned the scene, and his eyes locked onto me. The look he gave me was both recognition and annoyance.

"Is anyone in the car?" Chugger yelled out from across the parking lot.

"No," I yelled back. "It's empty."

The firefighters spilled from the truck and began to set up. One of them pulled out a hose from the side of the truck.

Chugger called out that the car was clear. The firefighters gave him a thumbs-up and trotted toward the car with a foamy spray already shooting out from the hose.

Shit. My beautiful car.

I saw Chugger talking into the microphone on his collar. Then he walked over to me. "What happened?" he asked.

"I'm not sure. It didn't explode or anything. It just sorta caught fire."

"Your car just caught on fire?" Chugger asked. "You do know cars typically don't spontaneously catch on fire, at least, not in September. That usually only happens in July and August."

"Um, I got it used. It must have had some bad wires or something."

"Uh huh," Chugger said in a tone that said he didn't quite believe me. As he talked to me, he kept giving me a weird look, almost like my burning car was disappointing him.

Chugger's partner, Arny, had also gotten out of the cruiser and was walking toward me with a clipboard. I knew I wasn't going to be able to talk my way out of filling out forms for the next hour or so. Arny was usually the more somber of the two partners, but today, he seemed more cheerful than usual.

I started filling out the first form while Chugger went down to talk to the firefighters.

"Hey, Arny," I asked. "Why is Chugger in a bad mood?"

Arny smiled at me. "Chugger had you pegged in the division pool for finding a dead body this month. I had you down for a fire. I just won a Yeti cooler."

"Oh, um, I guess that would explain it."

After I'd filled out the first set of forms, I called Sophie. When she answered, she was somewhere loud.

"Hey, Laura," she said. "What's up?"

"Um, I'm having a really shitty afternoon."

"Again? What happened this time? You weren't kidnapped again, were you?"

"My car."

"Oh no, not your new convertible. How bad is it?"

"Totaled. Someone set it on fire."

"Damn. Do you know who did it?"

"Yeah, I've got an idea. Colonel Wu, the guy who took Stig, told me he'd do something unpleasant if I didn't get *The Child* back to him by now. I'm pretty sure this is it."

"Where are you? I'll come get you."

~~~~

After an hour of filling out forms, my car had been extinguished and hooked up to a flatbed. I asked Chugger if someone could pull the plate. When they brought it over, it was partially burnt, but the validation sticker was still legible.

"I guess it's still legal," Chugger said as he handed it to me, "but you might want to head down to the DMV for a replacement. They'll tow the car to the impound lot. Since we don't know how the fire started, the fire marshal may want to inspect it for arson."

~~~~

Sophie picked me up and drove me back to my apartment building. In the corner of the parking lot was my Accord, still exactly where I had abandoned it over a month earlier.

I got out and glanced down at it. The driver's side was scraped and dented, with black paint mixed in with the factory brown.

The driver's side mirror was hanging down at an odd angle, held onto the car by some weathered duct tape. The rear quarter panel had a neat round bullet hole, and the trunk lid was open about an inch, held down by a faded red bungee cord.

I didn't need to look to know the front passenger fender had a large gash. Looking at the car pulled my mood further down than it already had been.

For some reason, I still had the key on my key ring. Sophie waited while I unlocked the doors and tossed the license plate in the back.

I sat in the familiar driver's seat, inserted the key, and it fired right up. Sitting in my old beat-up car after having something so beautiful filled me with a sadness that was hard to explain.

It wasn't as if someone had died, I told myself. It was only a car.

But I couldn't convince myself to cheer up or look at the bright side. I felt more like going upstairs for a good cry.

Shit.

I banged my head against the steering wheel a couple of times, shut off the engine, and got out. I opened the door to Sophie's car and sat down.

"Well," I said, "it looks like my car still runs."

"I'm thinking maybe I should get one of those next time I get a car," Sophie said. "They seem to be pretty indestructible. You've had it run into, shot at, the trunk was ripped open with a crowbar, and someone threw a hatchet into it. Even after all that, it still runs better than my car. You should think about calling the dealership. Maybe they'd want to put your car into a commercial or something."

"Thanks," I said, knowing she was trying to cheer me up. "I don't know how I'm going to tell Tony that I destroyed his car."

"Um, I'm guessing he probably already knows."

"How would he already know?"

"Didn't you say Max had a tracker put on your old car a few months ago?"

"Yeah, but I assumed he stopped following my movements after we got the diamonds back."

"Well, maybe. But if he didn't think twice about putting a tracker on your car back then, do you think he'd hesitate to have a tracker on Tony's car when you were getting it as a freebie?"

He better not have.

"Well, I hope he didn't. I'd feel creepy knowing my movements were being tracked. Even if Max thinks he's doing it in my best interest, I wouldn't want anyone snooping on me."

"Alright, you tell me how that works out," Sophie replied.

~~~~

Sophie took off, and I went up to my apartment. Before I did anything, I took out my gun and searched room by room, looking for anyone or anything out of place.

I then put on the security chain and pushed a chair against the door. I still hadn't had time to change my locks, and I didn't want any surprise visitors.

I had just sat on the couch when my phone rang. It was a local number, but I didn't recognize it. When I answered, it was Colonel Wu.

"Miss Black, it is past your assigned time to deliver the jade. You've learned what happens when people disobey me. I will give you one more day to deliver *The Child* to me. If I do not have it in my hand by five o'clock tomorrow afternoon, you will be personally abused by a man who will not care about your comfort or your emotional well-being."

"Look," I said in a voice that was louder and angrier than it probably should have been. "I'm looking for the jade as quickly as I know how. Blowing up my car and threatening me isn't going to help anything. All you're doing is slowing things down."

"Nevertheless, you will deliver *The Child* to me tomorrow, or you will be most unhappy. That I can promise."

The line clicked off, and I sat on my couch, trying to collect my thoughts on what to do next. Most of the obvious leads proved to be useless, and it looked like I'd be stuck going down the list one by one to find out where the jade had gone. I knew from experience it wasn't going to be a quick or easy process and would likely take several days to talk with everyone.

~~~~

Half an hour later, my phone rang with Reno's ringtone. I could guess what it was about, and I knew it was going to be trouble. My stomach was in a knot before I even hit the button to answer.

"Laura," Reno said, "we need to talk." The flat cop voice was back.

Shit.

"Sure, what's going on?"

"Even after we talked on Thursday, the lieutenant called me at home to say you met again with Bettencourt and DiCenzo on Friday. According to the team, you even gave Bettencourt a very friendly hug."

Shit.

"I told you I'm working on an investigation for Lenny about the Stig Stevens thing, and it led me back to DiCenzo's group."

Reno spoke with a flat, controlled voice, but I could tell he was upset again. "Laura, you can't be seen having a friendly meeting with the number one and number two criminals in the state. I thought you understood that."

"I was only having lunch and following up on the information they had on an investigation I'm working on. I think what you're saying is that *you* can't have a girlfriend who was seen having lunch with someone like that."

"No, I can't. I'm leading a team looking into drugs coming into the city, and I can't have you hanging out with the largest importer of heroin in Arizona, maybe the entire southwest."

"That's the Black Death. I told you before. Everyone

knows that."

"We know about the Black Death," Reno said. "It's our understanding they're a relatively minor distributor. I can almost guarantee they're not a major importer."

"Well, that's not what I've heard."

"Look," Reno said, "I've never said a word about your job, even when I see the bruises and scrapes all over your body. I didn't make a big deal when we went down to Rocky Point last month, and you had rope burns on both wrists. I understand that your job is physically demanding and carries some risks. I also know how independent you are. When we started dating, we were together almost every day or at least talked to each other on the phone. When we got back together, I couldn't understand at first how you could go for three or four days at a time without calling me. I thought maybe you were seeing other guys, or maybe you weren't that into me. I soon realized how independent you were. It's especially true when you're working on a project for Lenny. I know there are stretches of days or even weeks when you don't have the time to be with me."

"The first month we were dating was unique for me. I'd never been that close to anyone in my life, and you're right. It was out of character for me. I'm pretty independent. I know it caused problems back when I was married."

"Laura, I know who you are, and I can accept all that. What I can't ignore is having a girlfriend who's meeting with the heads of the largest crime family in Arizona. You're becoming a known associate of some very nasty people, and by doing so, you're placing yourself between the police and the criminals. You could be in serious danger. Not to mention, you're putting my career at risk. Bettencourt's group can now have a direct path to me through you. That opens me up to blackmail, and everyone in the department now knows it."

The knot in my stomach tightened. I knew what was about to happen but didn't see a way out. "So, what are you saying?"

"Are you going to keep seeing Bettencourt and DiCenzo?"

"I might have to. My job sometimes involves mixing with a lot of people, and some of them aren't completely legitimate. You've known that from the start. Talking with criminals isn't my first choice, but they often have information I can't get anywhere else. Is this going to be a problem?"

He sighed a sigh full of sadness and regret. "I figured as much. One of the reasons I love you is you're a bulldog when you're on one of these assignments for Lenny. But I can't have any association with you if there's a possibility you'll have contact with Bettencourt or his group."

"It might be unavoidable, at least for a while."

"Alright. I hope you know what you're doing. Please be careful. These aren't nice people you're dealing with. If you start to get in over your head, give me a call, but it'll need to be official. I hope you can understand."

"Um, sure," I said. "I understand."

"Take care of yourself."

The phone disconnected, and I sat there with a very hollow and empty feeling.

Shit.

~~~~

I woke up the next morning with a headache and a lousy disposition. I'd tossed and turned all night, going back and forth between Reno and Colonel Wu.

When I woke up for the last time, it had been four-fifteen, and I knew sleep was over for the night. By five o'clock, I'd gotten ready for my day.

I made a pot of coffee, then went back to the list. Jackie Wade was the first, as she was the last person Jerry remembered talking to directly about the jade.

If she didn't have it, I'd need to go down the list one by one until I found the right person. I'd also need to check back with Carter to see if he'd been able to get any information from the household staff.

With any luck, I'd find who had it by the five o'clock deadline. If not, I'd need to find a way to look for the figurine while avoiding Colonel Wu and his men.

~~~~

I left my apartment and took the stairs. All my senses were on alert for anything out of the ordinary. My purse was open, and my pistol was within easy reach.

Colonel Wu might not wait until five to have me attacked. In addition, Digger and Cyril were still out there and might want to come at me as well.

As I walked out to the parking lot and remembered my beautiful car no longer existed, a fresh wave of sadness and anger hit me. As I unlocked and sat in my old beat-up car, I once again questioned my choice of career.

~~~~

My first stop was the office. I wanted to let Sophie know what had happened.

I opened the rear security door, tossed everything but my coffee mug in my cubicle, and headed up front. I could tell Sophie had also just gotten to work.

She was still sipping her coffee and going over the California Surfline surfing report. As I sat next to her desk, she looked at me and got a crease between her eyes.

"You look terrible again today," she said. "Still bummed

about your car?"

"It's not only that. Reno and I broke up last night, and I didn't get a lot of sleep."

Sophie perked up. "Really? Well, it's about time. How'd he take the news? You were going to break up with him last month before the big shootout, and then you chickened out. Are you going to start seeing Max now?"

"It wasn't like that. Reno broke up with me."

"Really? What a jerk. How could he do that to you? What kind of breakup was it? Did he come out and say he's found someone better and he doesn't love you anymore? Or was it one of those ultimatum break ups, like *if you don't give me more blow-jobs, we're breaking up* sort of things? I hate ultimatum breakups."

"It was an ultimatum one, but not about blow-jobs. The police are running surveillance on both Max and Tony, and they know I've met with them twice this week. Reno said he can't see me if I'm going to have contact with either Max or Tony again."

"But if you agree to stop seeing them, Reno will be okay with dating you again?"

"I guess so. We didn't get that far. We only got to the break-up part."

"So, it was a *conditional* ultimatum break up? Those are the worst kind. The guy breaks up with you, but he acts like it's all your fault. Men are really pathetic sometimes. I remember the first time you and Reno broke up. That was the time you were supposed to go over to his house on Christmas to make him breakfast, and instead, you went to Italy and broke your leg. You didn't call him for a month, so he thought you'd dumped him, and he started seeing that kinky blonde bimbo, Cynthia, or something like that. Do you remember her? She's the one who liked having her toes sucked on, all of them crammed into his mouth at once. That woman was nasty. That was more of a *misunderstanding* break up."

"It's not like that this time. I think it's really over."

"So that leaves you free to start seeing Max?"

"I guess so, but it doesn't change the fact that Max probably won't see me, romantically anyway, especially now that the police are running surveillance on him."

"I imagine if you tried hard enough, you could find a way to be with Max without anyone else knowing about it. Although it would probably be best if you don't tell the world you're seeing him. Of course, whether you see him openly or in secret, Gina will probably give you a lecture."

"I don't know what will happen with Max."

"What am I going to lecture you about?" Gina said as she came in from the back.

"Laura broke up with Reno and is going to start dating Max," Sophie said.

"Oh," Gina said, looking at me. "I don't care. You're a big girl and can do whatever you want."

Sophie looked at Gina, and her mouth was hanging open.

"Hey, what's wrong with you?" Sophie asked. "You normally give her a lecture whenever she talks about dating Max. You say he's a criminal, and it will all end in prison and tears."

"Yeah," I said. "What gives?"

"I've had the nicest weekend," Gina said with a huge smile. "It turns out once Brandon shuts up and gets down to business, the man is definitely useful."

"Nice," Sophie said. "Did you take my advice and go to

his place?"

"Well, yes, the first night. The second night we stayed at my place."

"Second night?" Sophie asked. "Um, you know you aren't supposed to double-tap a guy on the same weekend. That's how a 'booty-call gone bad' relationship starts. You said you spent two nights together? Where'd he go on Sunday, during the day between dates?"

"He didn't go anywhere. We went to breakfast together, and then we spent the day shopping and walking through the art galleries downtown. It turns out we have similar taste in both music and art."

"Uh oh," Sophie said. "This doesn't sound good."

Gina looked at me. "Your old Honda's parked out back. Why aren't you driving your new car?"

"Someone set it on fire yesterday," Sophie said.

Gina raised an eyebrow and looked at me. "Seriously? Someone set your convertible on fire?"

"It looks like it," I said.

"I assume you weren't in it when the fire started."

"No, it was parked. They used some sort of remote timer or ignition device."

"Any idea who did it or why?"

"I'm pretty sure the people who took Stig did it. They're after the jade and are pissed that I'm not finding it for them fast enough."

"I assume the police are involved?"

"Right now, they're checking the car for arson. If they look hard enough, they'll probably find the device that set it off. But even with that, I doubt they'll have any more to go on than I do."

"Do you want to tell me what's going on?" Gina asked.

"I didn't want to tell you about it right before your date, but there's a group of foreign mercenaries in Arizona led by a man named Colonel Wu. They're the ones who kidnapped Stig Wednesday night. Jeanette and Sterling still don't want the police involved, and Stig agrees with them. The Colonel and his men only came into Arizona a few days ago, and they'll likely be gone as soon as the jade is recovered. They seem to be good at what they do, and I don't see them leaving a trail for the police to find them."

"Maybe so, but I suggest you cooperate with the police as fully as possible. You were lucky you weren't in the car when the device went off. Next time, you may not be as fortunate. Do you need my help?"

"Not yet. The next part of the search is pretty straightforward. Maybe later this afternoon or tonight. I'll let you know."

~~~~

I went back to my cubicle and called Jackie Wade again. This time, she answered, "Hi, Jackie. It's Laura."

"Laura, how have you been? I haven't seen you in a while. You'll need to go out with us again soon."

"Sure, I'd like that."

"Are you okay? You sound upset."

"Yeah, I'm okay. I'm actually working on an assignment, and I'm hoping you can help me."

"I'll be glad to. Do you want to discuss this over the phone or in person?"

"In person would be better. It has to do with Stig and what's been going on the past few days."

"Okay. I'm about to do my morning rounds, but I'll be free after that. If you stop by around ten, we can chat. You remember where my office at the Saguaro Sky is?"

"I'm sure I can find it. See you at ten."

I had about half an hour before I needed to leave, so I grabbed my phone and started down the list. I was able to reach six of the remaining women.

Four were available in the afternoon, and I made arrangements to meet with them before five o'clock. If Jackie turned out to be a dead end, I'd have a busy afternoon.

~~~~

I pulled into the Saguaro Sky Resort and parked in the guest lot. It was a five-minute walk to the offices at the main reception building, but it was a pleasant stroll, and it helped calm me down.

The landscaping and overall feel of the property evoked a relaxing tropical retreat. Jackie did a great job of keeping the resort one of the nicest in Arizona.

I walked into the main building and then made my way to the administrative offices on the mezzanine level. Jackie had apparently alerted her admin because she showed me to Jackie's office as soon as I got there.

"Laura," Jackie said as she came around her desk to hug me. "It's so good to see you."

"The resort looks great. You've done a wonderful job with it."

"Well, I never thought I'd run a place like this, but so far, I'm enjoying it. Plus, I have a great staff who makes the place run smoothly whether I'm here or not. Thank you again for everything you did for me. I really owe this all to you."

"Don't worry about it. I'm glad everything worked out."

"You said you're working on an assignment?"

"I'm working with Stig Stevens. It seems he received a small green figurine as a gift about three weeks ago after he finished filming his latest movie. Stig isn't into travel souvenirs, so he asked Jerry Phifer if he could find someone who'd want it. Jerry put it on a table in the entrance hall before the party last week, and he told everyone they could have it. Unfortunately, it turns out Stig wasn't supposed to give it away. Stig's asked me to help find out who has it and to see if I could get it back."

"You don't need to go any further," Jackie said. "I have it, and if Stig needs it, I'll be glad to give it back."

Yes!

Inwardly, I made mental *woo-hoo* noises, but outwardly, I did my best to remain calm.

"Jerry talked about it when I was at the party the other night," Jackie said. "I didn't stay long and spotted it on the table on the way out. I typically don't collect things like that, but it was big enough and unusual enough that I thought it would be a nice conversation piece here in the hotel."

The hotel? That doesn't sound good.

"It's here?" I asked. "Um, somewhere in the hotel?"

"I put it in the Kokopelli casita. It's one of our nicer stand-alone suites. The color scheme for the suite is dark wood and various shades of green. The little figurine seemed to go nicely on one of the bookshelves."

The Child is sitting on a bookshelf in a guest room at a hotel?

"Um, great. I'm glad you know where it is. Will we be able to go and get it?"

"Hold on, let me see if the suite is vacant." She picked up

244

her desk phone and called somebody. She asked about the Kokopelli casita and listened for the reply. When she hung up, I could see it was bad news.

"Well, the room's currently occupied, but the guests are scheduled for check-out today. They didn't ask for an extension, so they'll likely be out by noon."

I looked at a clock on the wall of Jackie's office, and it was only ten-thirty.

"If you'd like to hang out with me until the guests check out, we could go out together and get the sculpture. In the meantime, I'll buy you an early lunch. We're rolling out a new menu at the Courtyard Café, and I'm looking for opinions on it."

"Um, sure," I said, not exactly wanting lunch, but I'd need to do something until we could go up and get the jade. I was starting to feel a sense of desperation about finding *The Child*. If it wasn't where Jackie thought it was, my job finding it would become that much harder.

I only had about seven hours until the next deadline Colonel Wu had given me. I've been threatened before, but this time it seemed more personal.

Of course, now that I'd been alerted, I'd take precautions against having anyone come after me. Unfortunately, I was afraid this time I might have to do more than shoot someone in the foot.

Jackie called someone else and asked to be informed when the Kokopelli casita was vacant. She then led me down through the main lobby and out to a restaurant.

It was half in the lobby building and half out on an outdoor patio next to one of the resort's pools. We sat outside at a table with a beautiful view of the water and the surrounding tropical landscaping.

I got an iced tea and let Jackie order for both of us. I nervously sat and watched a group of kids playing Marco Polo while weaving in and out of the other guests in the pool.

Within about ten minutes, our lunches came out. Even in my anxious state, I could tell it was delicious, and I let Jackie know.

I checked the time on my phone every few minutes. I tried to eat but only got about three-fourths through before my tight stomach told me I'd had enough.

Jackie noticed what I was doing and became concerned. "Are you alright? If the figurine's something you need right away, I can call the room and see if it would be okay if we came up for a minute."

"Would you mind?" I asked. "I know it's an imposition, but that little green sculpture has caused me a lot of grief. The sooner I have it in my hands, the better I'll feel."

Jackie looked at me with some worry as she picked up her phone and called a number. As soon as she started talking, she perked up.

"It's vacant? Perfect. I need to go out and check something. I'll let you know when it's ready for housekeeping."

She hung up and looked at me. "They were about to call me. The guests have checked out, and the suite's clear for us."

Yes!

I felt a sense of relief as we walked out to the side of the building to a row of purple golf carts. We walked to the end of the row, where an especially large cart was waiting.

When we got in, Jackie pulled a key from a stretchy band on her wrist and inserted it into the cart. She then backed up and drove us through the resort.

The Kokopelli casita appeared to be a separate little house

in the middle of what looked like a tropical oasis next to one of the pools. It had a large patio and upstairs balcony that both faced the water.

If you tried, even a little bit, you could imagine you were in a private home on a beautiful tropical island. Jackie parked the golf cart in the private carport next to the casita, and we went to the back entrance.

She pulled a card from her pocket and held it next to the lock. There was a soft metallic sound, and she opened the door.

I was expecting the inside to be as beautiful as the outside. Instead, the place was trashed.

It wasn't anything destructive, but there were piles of garbage everywhere: crushed beer cans, empty liquor bottles, empty pizza boxes, wadded-up towels, pillows, diapers, small plastic pool toys, and even a deflated beach ball.

"Yuck," I said. "Is it always this bad when the guests check out?"

"Not usually, but you'd be surprised how badly people will mess up a room while they're on vacation."

"Where's the figurine?" I asked. Now that we were in the room, I wanted to get the jade and leave as quickly as possible.

"I put it over here," Jackie said as she walked to a set of built-in bookshelves in the living room. She looked, but as she turned, I could see by her expression that it wasn't there.

Shit why does my life suck so much?

"It's not here," Jackie said.

My heart sank. I'd been so close to getting the jade, and now it looked like I'd be back to square one.

"Well, let's look around," I said. "But, if we can't find it, would I be able to get the contact information for the people who stayed here?"

Jackie's look showed that she wasn't eager to share personal information about her guests. "Um, sure," she said. I'll need to check the records. The figurine's been in the room since last Monday, so there were probably other guests who also stayed here. I assume you'll need their names, too."

"Yes, but let's search here first. Maybe we'll get lucky."

Already feeling deflated, I went into the kitchen and started sorting through a pile of pizza boxes and empty cardboard beer cases. The smell of stale beer and day-old pizza was adding to my tight stomach. Jackie had gone upstairs, and I heard her sorting through the bedrooms.

I searched the entire kitchen, with the exception of the garbage cans. They were overflowing, and I wanted to wait until the end to paw through the used diapers, food remnants, and beer-soaked paper towels.

I then went up to help Jackie. She'd finished the bedrooms and gone into the bathroom. We both went through a pile of wet towels in a corner.

When nothing was found, we went back downstairs and started on the living room. Jackie pulled cushions off the couch, and I went over to a pile of pillows, sheets, and plastic toys in the corner.

It seemed like some kid had turned the corner into their private fort, with pillows for walls and a sheet for a roof. I pulled off the sheet to reveal a pile of plastic pool toys and a blue beach bucket.

I bent over and turned the bucket upside down. Something green slid out and landed on the carpet.

Oh my God.

My breathing stopped as I picked up the little green

sculpture. As everyone had told me, it was a smooth green leaf with a carved grasshopper perched on one end. The grasshopper was so delicately carved I was amazed it hadn't broken while being used as a child's toy.

Jackie came and stood next to me. "Hey, you found it. Great." I could hear the relief in her voice.

"Yes," I said, emotions thick in my voice. "Thank you so much. You really have no idea how much this will help me."

Jackie called the head of housekeeping and said the Kokopelli casita was ready, but she might want to send over some extra help to straighten up the mess. She then drove me back to the reception building.

"Thanks for your help," I said. "This assignment has turned out to be a lot more complicated than I thought it'd be."

"I'm glad you found it. Tell Stig hello when you see him. Hey, I hope you'll come out with us soon. We always enjoy having you around. Sophie said that Christine Johns might come out with us sometime."

"Thanks," I said. "I'll be glad to as soon as I can schedule a night off."

Jackie went back inside, and I headed out to guest parking.

Chapter Twelve

Now that I had *The Child*, I needed to figure out what to do with it. The obvious choice was to simply call Colonel Wu and have him pick it up.

In theory, it would stop his group from harassing me further. Of course, Digga and Cyril were still hunting for the jade, and I'd likely be placing myself in jeopardy with them if I gave it away to the Colonel.

I thought about handing it over to the authorities. They could give it to the Chinese government, and that would solve part of the problem. Unfortunately, if I did that, I'd have both the Colonel and Digger after me.

I drove back to the office. I was hoping I could discuss the problem with Sophie and Gina, well, assuming either of them was there. I parked in my spot under the carport and went through the rear security door.

With a feeling of triumph, I walked up to the front, ready to tell Sophie about the jade sculpture. When I got there, she had a weird look on her face.

"Sophie?" I asked. "What's wrong?"

"Um, Reno stopped by. You just missed him."

"Reno? Why would he come here?"

"He brought, um, the box."

"What box? You mean Stig's box? How could he have found that?" Then it hit me. "Oh shit, *that* box."

"Yup, the last nail in the breakup coffin," Sophie said. "He cleaned out his house and put everything of yours in a box. Funny, he didn't even wait a full day to bring it over. Most guys wait a week or two. They'll use the box as an excuse to plead their case one more time."

"Reno was always very efficient. Where is it?"

"I put it next to your cube. You also got an express box. It's on your desk. The paperwork says it came from China. It has all sorts of Chinese labels and writing on it."

"Um, thanks." Thinking about the box from Reno made me feel like crying or maybe hitting something. I couldn't decide which would be more helpful.

"Are you going to be okay?" Sophie asked. "We could go out tonight, get drunk, and then take home some college boys who are barely old enough to shave. You could borrow one of my paddles and take out your frustrations by spanking some college boy's ass. You know, if you spank him hard enough, he might start to cry. I like it when they cry."

"Yuck, why would I want to do that? No, I'll be alright. But it'll be a few days until I'll be able to open Reno's box. It's no problem getting my clothes back, but what if he put our pictures in it? What if he put the presents I've given to him in there?"

"I hate it when they do that. It's like you never existed. The worst part is when they put all of the birthday and Valentine's cards you've given them in the box. Something about seeing a stack of your cards that all say, 'I love you' is a big gut punch."

After hearing about the box from Reno, I suddenly wanted to be alone. I went back to my cubicle and sat. I felt like my world was crumbling around me.

I was under the credible threat of personal harm by a group of foreign mercenaries. There was also the implied threat to my safety by a big Australian and his wacko-American sidekick. Plus, I'd lost both my boyfriend and my new car in the space of less than a day.

Shit.

I spent several minutes thinking about career options. I'd worked for a couple of years as a bartender at Greasewood Flat. I liked doing that, although at the time, I'd hated the hours.

I'd gone into investigating because it had sounded exciting, and the hours had promised to be better. Unfortunately, I now knew the hours were worse, and I was getting tired of the exciting things that were happening to me as a result of my career.

After ten or fifteen minutes of daydreaming about being wealthy and living in a house on a hill in Hawaii, I pulled myself back to reality. I still needed to figure out what to do with the jade.

Should I give it to Colonel Wu? It pissed me off to think I'd be helping him after he'd kidnapped me and destroyed my beautiful car. But he'd promised to do worse if I didn't give *The Child* to him, and I believed him.

Digga also wanted the jade. I didn't get creepy vibes from him, but with Digga came Cyril, and that guy pissed me off. True, Digga had promised to pay me for the jade, but those types of promises tended to be forgotten as quickly as they were made.

Everyone associated with the figurine had threatened me, or worse. I then thought of several clever schemes where I would involve the police, and everyone would be rounded up and thrown in jail. I could then turn the jade over to the authorities and have them sort out where it should end up, probably with the Chinese.

After several minutes of trying to be clever, I decided it was probably best to simply hand *The Child* over to Colonel Wu and be done with it. I'd need to lay low for a while until Digga cleared out, but getting rid of the jade quickly seemed like the safest way to go.

While I was mapping out my strategy, Sterling called. This time, I answered. "Hey, Sterling."

"Where have you been?" he asked. "I've been calling all day."

"I told you, when I'm investigating, I turn the sound off on my phone."

"I'd like to help you find the jade. I don't want anything else to happen to Stig."

"It's not going to be a problem. I've got *The Child.* I'm about to turn it over to the people who are looking for it. They'll leave, and everything will be good."

"You've got it with you? Really? Where are you?"

"I'm at the office, but I won't be here long. I need to stop by my place to change, and I have to make a phone call. Then, I'll be off to make the handover. In a couple of hours, all this will be over. I'll call you later with all the details."

Before I left, I called the women I had talked with earlier in the day and told them everything had been resolved. While making my calls, I saw the express box from China that Sophie had put on my desk.

A few minutes with a letter opener, and I had it open. Seeing what was inside made me laugh. I then organized everything and went out the back door.

~~~~

As I drove to my apartment, I made a plan. First, I'd call Colonel Wu and arrange the handover. I'd ask for a meeting somewhere public, preferably with a large crowd.

After the jade was safely transferred, I'd call Digga and tell him I'd found the jade but had already turned it over to the Colonel to avoid personal harm.

He'd be pissed, but hopefully, he'd go after the Colonel rather than come after me. Cyril was a local boy so he might be more trouble as the days went by, but I couldn't think of a better way.

Now that things were in motion, I began to relax. With things coming together, I started to feel good about everything.

The handoff would be tense, but I didn't get the sense that Colonel Wu would go back on his word not to harm me. Once he had the jade, he'd want to be gone as soon as possible.

If everything went well, this whole mess would be over by dinner. Of course, if I were wrong about Colonel Wu or Digga's reaction to what I'd done, it could cost me my life.

~~~~

I made it to my apartment house and pulled into the space where I'd been parking my convertible. When thinking about my beautiful car and how it was destroyed, I felt a fresh wave of anger. I spent several seconds again trying to come up with a clever way to have Digga, Cyril, and Colonel Wu rounded up and carted off to jail.

As I got out of the car, I looked up in time to see Cyril coming around the corner of the SUV, his big revolver pointed at me. I couldn't help but see he was limping. He probably still had a bandage over his gunshot wound.

Shit.

I opened my bag to get my gun, but it was now buried underneath everything that had accumulated during the day. Since I already had the jade, I'd assumed I wouldn't need to use my gun.

"Get your hand out of your purse," Cyril said as he walked toward me. "If you try to pull your gun out, I'll shoot you. This is a .45 Magnum with hollow point bullets, so I don't think it'll matter where I hit you. You'll feel it."

"Um," I said. "Does Digga know you're here?"

"Screw Digger," Cyril said. "He's just one more asshole. I've had to take matters into my own hands. Give me your purse."

I carefully handed it over to him, hoping he wouldn't accidentally shoot me as he took my bag. He held it with one hand while the other trained the big gun on me.

"Your purse is heavy," he sneered. "Still have your fucking gun in it, huh? Well, too bad you won't be able to use it to shoot me today." He then opened my car door and tossed the purse in the back seat.

He looked down at the keys in my hand and then over at my Honda. "Nice car," he sneered. "What happened to the fancy convertible you had?"

"I got rid of it," I said. "This one's more reliable, and it gets better mileage."

"Whatever. You're going to drive us to a house I have in south-central Phoenix. If you try anything cute, I'll shoot you. In fact, I hope you do try something. I've been looking forward to shooting you to make up for what you did to me."

We both got into my car, and I started it up. As I did, I saw Sterling's car pull into the lot. I could see he recognized me and that I was with someone. He had a confused look on his face, but as I pulled out of the lot, he followed.

Cyril directed me to go down Scottsdale Road to the Loop-202. From there, we went west to Interstate 10.

As we drove, Sterling was almost directly on my back bumper the entire way. He obviously had never trailed a car before, and I was hoping Cyril didn't think to look behind us. Fortunately, Cyril was too intent on watching me to make sure I wasn't deviating from his directions.

When we pulled off the interstate, I glanced in the mirror to see that Sterling had his phone to his ear. I was hoping he was calling Gina or even Lenny.

My situation was starting to get a little out of hand, and I could use the assistance. Even the police would be welcome at this point, although I guessed Sterling would still be dead set against involving them, if only to protect Stig.

We eventually ended up at an abandoned house at Eleventh Street and Mohave, near Sky Harbor Airport and only a couple of blocks from Carolina's Mexican restaurant. As we got closer to the house, the look on Cyril's face slowly went from a sneer to a sick and lustful smile. I got the feeling shooting me wasn't the only thing on his mind.

Cyril had me park on the street, then directed me to walk up the cracked driveway to the front of the beat-up house. I could see the yellow Property Condemned sticker on the front door.

Apparently, this house was one of many the airport had purchased as part of its expansion plans. It likely would be torn down within a month or two, and Cyril was only using it as a temporary hideout.

I pushed open the front door. It gave without a lot of effort since it had apparently already been kicked in a time or two, with pieces of the lock scattered across the living room floor.

The house was nothing but a hollowed-out shell. The furniture, the fixtures, and any copper that could be pulled from the walls had already been ripped out and removed. Nothing remained except for some crumpled beer cans and an empty whisky bottle on the filthy floor.

Cyril directed me to a room that was once the kitchen with an attached dining room. Shadows of paint on the walls and dirt patterns on the linoleum floor told where the cabinets had once been.

The only intact things in the room were two wooden chairs and a small dining room table. The table had an overflowing ashtray and a half-dozen crushed beer cans on it.

Both the table and chairs seemed relatively new. I guessed Cyril had brought them here for his use while the house still stood.

"Sit," Cyril directed as he pointed to one of the chairs.

I couldn't think of anything else to do, so I sat. Cyril pulled out about ten feet of bright pink nylon string from his pocket. The string was thin, but I knew it would be strong enough to keep me securely tied to the chair.

"Tie one end to your wrist," he said. "Make it a slip knot so I can cinch it up tight. If you fuck around with the knot, I'll shoot you in the foot, right where you shot me. Except, with *these* bullets, it will take half your foot with it."

Under Cyril's watchful eye, I tied one end of the string to my wrist, making a slip knot as he instructed. He then had me put both hands behind the chair as he came around. I thought about throwing my free elbow into his face to maybe catch him off guard, but when he came around, I felt the barrel of the gun being pressed against the back of my head.

Using his free hand, Cyril tied my first hand to the chair.

He then removed the gun from the back of my head and finished the job.

He made sure to put slip knots on both wrists, so the more I pulled, the tighter the string bit into my skin. Both hands were already going numb, and I knew I couldn't struggle my way out of the chair.

He then pulled another length of string from his pocket and tied my left ankle to the chair. For some reason, he didn't seem to care about my right foot.

Damn, this isn't good.

Cyril pulled the other chair about three feet away and sat facing me.

"Now, tell me where *The Child* is. I know you have it, and I want it."

As Cyril talked, I desperately thought about my situation. Sterling knew where I was and had already called for help.

All I needed to do was stall for time and wait until it arrived. I only hoped Cyril was gullible enough to go along with it.

"Um, yes. I have it, but I've hidden it. Why is Digga having you do this to me?"

"Digger? I already told you. He's one more asshole, just like all the other assholes I've worked for lately."

As Cyril talked, he casually held the big revolver in one hand, occasionally waving it to make a point. "Digger McKinsey is some sort of international spy who's only interested in getting the jade so he can collect a paycheck from his government. Colonel Wu's man offered me twice what I'll get by working with him."

"If you're not happy about working with Digga, why did you agree to do it?"

"Because I was told to. I'm not sure why Digger's government contacted my boss. I guess they thought we could help him get in and out of the country more easily. Plus, they said they needed someone local. I've grown up here, and I know all there is to know about Phoenix and Scottsdale. Now, if you're through with the questions, tell me where the jade is."

"You know," I said. "You can't get away with this. My car has a tracker on it, and I'm sure the police are already on their way. If I were you, I'd take off while I could."

Cyril looked at me like I was an idiot. "You're bluffing, and even if you're not, we'll be out of here soon enough. I'm going to give you one more chance to tell me where *The Child* is before the fireworks start."

He then took the big revolver and pulled back the hammer with his thumb. As it went back, there was a series of clicks, and the cylinder containing the bullets rotated into position so that a fresh bullet was now directly under the firing pin. He carefully aimed the gun at my left foot, the one securely tied to the chair.

"You see," he said, "the thing about shooting you in the foot is you can't die of your wound. If I'm ever caught, I can only be charged with assault with a deadly weapon and battery. You, on the other hand, will walk in a boot for the rest of your life. Plus, I imagine the pain from the gunshot and the many surgeries will be a constant reminder of what a nosy bitch you are. You shot me in the foot. Now I'll shoot you in the foot. There's a nice symmetry to this, don't you think?"

"Wait," I said. "Can't we talk about this?"

"No, last chance." He moved the barrel of the gun until it was less than six inches from the center of my left shoe. "Tell me now or lose a foot. You decide."

"Okay, okay," I said. "It's in my car. You could have had

it back at my apartment."

Cyril thought about it for a second, then lifted the gun and released the hammer. "Alright, I'll go out and search your car. If it's there, I'll call the Colonel, and we'll make the exchange. What happens to you then will be up to him. If it's not there, you'll lose your foot. Nothing you say will stop that if you've lied to me."

Cyril stuck the pistol in the waistband of his pants and walked out of the kitchen and into the living room. I immediately heard a loud commotion and assumed Sterling had finally decided to help.

The commotion turned into what sounded like men in a fight. It didn't last long. I heard something heavy falling on the floor, and then the house became quiet again. Ten seconds later, footsteps sounded in the other room, coming closer.

I was hoping it would be Sterling, but I was afraid it would be Cyril. If so, I hoped he would still be only interested in the jade and not in exacting revenge on me.

Instead, Digga walked in, holding my bag. He had a broad smile and a large red mark on the side of his face.

Cyril was nowhere to be seen. He sat my bag on the table, reached into his pocket, and pulled out a large knife.

He flicked his wrist, and the long blade snapped into position. Digga slowly walked to my chair and looked down at me.

My eyes were focused on the sunlight from the windows shining off the blade of the huge knife. It looked very sharp, and my heart sped up as I was unsure what the big Australian's intentions were.

Without saying a word, Digga slowly circled the chair until he was behind me. I tried to turn my head but was unable to see what he was doing.

My heart was pounding with dread, but then I felt the knife cutting the rope holding my hands together. He then sliced through the string, holding my foot to the chair.

"It's best we be off," Digga said as I stood, and he handed me my bag. "It's likely the Colonel already knows you're here with *The Child,* and I don't fancy being around when he shows up."

"What happened?"

"Cyril's been acting squirrely the past couple of days, and he was too quiet today. He took off at about ten this morning. At first, I was happy not to have the little bleeder around. But by about half-one, I thought maybe he was up to something."

"How did you know to find me here?"

"This is Cyril's safe house. I figured he'd be here after I couldn't find him. I wasn't expecting to find you here as well, but when I saw your car parked outside it wasn't hard to figure out what Cyril was up to."

"Did you see another man out there? Sterling followed me here, but I haven't seen him."

We both heard a noise in the outer room. Digga turned toward the doorway and raised the knife. I was expecting Colonel Wu and his men. Instead, Sterling was standing there, and Cyril's big gun was in his hands.

"I suspected you'd be giving the jade to Digger McKinsey," Sterling said to me. "I see I was right not to trust you. I've already called Colonel Wu. He should be here in a few minutes. In the meantime, nobody moves, except you'll need to toss that big knife against the far wall. Who are you anyway? Crocodile Dundee?"

Digga began to take a slow step toward Sterling. Sterling responded by firing off a shot in the general direction of Digga. In the closed space of the room, the large caliber gun sounded like a cannon going off.

"Stay where you are," Sterling said. "I have no reason to harm you, but if you try anything, I'll shoot you in the center of your chest. This gun will blow a hole big enough to see through. Now then, the knife?"

Digga casually flicked his wrist, and the knife flew against the far wall of the kitchen. The blade went in about two inches, then vibrated for a second before stopping.

"Sterling," I said. "Why are you doing this? Why are you helping Colonel Wu?"

Sterling shook his head and sighed. "You really want to know? Well, it's simple, I've devoted the last thirty years of my life to making sure Stig was a success and the studio made a lot of money. I haven't been able to have a family or even keep a steady girlfriend because I've been on call twenty-four hours a day, seven days a week. Now that Stig's career is winding down, I asked for another up-and-coming star to mentor and manage. I'm good at what I do, and you'd think it would be a no-brainer, but the head of the studio has been putting me off for months. Every time I ask him about it, he wants to discuss it at a 'more appropriate time.' Three months ago, he let me know Stig was still too valuable to assign me to anyone else. He tried to spin it that it was in my best interests only to represent Stig, but I knew it was only his way of easing me out. As Stig's career goes from two blockbusters a year down to minor supporting roles, I know I'll be out of a job."

"But why do all of this?" I asked. "What does any of this have to do with Stig?"

"While we were shooting *Hammer's Revenge* in China, I was approached by a very wealthy businessman named Mr. Zhang. It seems he had access to a valuable artifact, and he needed my help in getting it out of the country and selling it over here. In exchange, he would pay me enough money to start my retirement. I arranged for Stig to receive *The Child* as a going-away present. No one knew anything about ancient jade, and everyone assumed it was only a tourist trinket. We then packed it up with the props we'd used for filming. I knew the authorities would never think that something as valuable as *The Child* would be stashed away with the movie props and the other bits of tourist junk we'd picked up. My plan was to retrieve the box when the equipment was delivered back to the studio and safely through customs. Unfortunately, when I went to get the box, it wasn't there. I spent several days looking through the equipment and props that came back from China. I then found out one of the crew had pulled it out as soon as the shipment arrived and had given it to Stig."

"But if you knew Stig had it, why didn't you simply fly out here and get it from him?"

"I would have, only Stig hates me and won't ever have me in his house."

"Stig hates you?"

"Is hate too strong a word for you? Fine, he *dislikes* me very much. You see, I was originally assigned to Stig by the studio back when he was starting out. We've always worked together well enough, but we really don't get along on a personal level. He doesn't invite me to his house, and we never socialize. When I found out *The Child* was at Stig's house, I arranged for him to be out all day at a charity event. I then broke into his house and tried to find the box with the jade. Unfortunately, one of the household staff heard me, and I had to take off before I could find either the box or the jade. I don't think anyone got a good look at me, or they didn't recognize me if they did. After that, I spent a lot of time on the phone with the people in China. They decided to send over Colonel Wu and his team.

"What about Digga?"

"Digger? Until this week, I'd never heard of him. I have no idea how he fits into this."

From outside the house, we heard the sounds of two or three cars pulling up. The car doors opened, and there was a babble of voices and commands. In less than a minute, seven or eight grim-looking mercenaries had poured into the kitchen. They were dressed in black fatigues, and they all seemed eager for a fight.

Two of the men grabbed me, one on either side, and three took control of Digga. I think he would have been glad to get into a fight with the men, but both a mercenary and Sterling had a pistol trained on him. The mercenary's pistol had a long black silencer on it.

In addition, another man with a stun gun had positioned himself behind us. I still remembered how it felt to be hit with one, and I didn't want it to happen again. Based on the noises coming from the living room, another couple of men had been posted out there as well.

We heard footsteps come from the living room, and then Colonel Wu walked into the kitchen. Like the others, he was dressed in black fatigues. Unlike his men, the Colonel wore a blood-red beret. He stood silent for a moment as if appraising the situation.

"Captain McKinsey," the Colonel said. "I thought it likely you'd show up before this was over. My contacts back home said you'd been sent to recover *The Child* as well. When we recruited Cyril, he mentioned you were in the country and had already attempted to recover the jade by breaking into Stig Steven's house. When that failed, you turned to Miss Black as an accomplice."

"Colonel Wu," Digga said. "We keep meeting. When was the last time, Taipei? I'm starting to think you like to follow me around."

"Miss Black," the Colonel said, ignoring Digga's taunt. "I must confess, I'm disappointed to find you here as well. You had a clear understanding of our exclusive arrangement regarding *The Child*. You were to bring it to me as soon as you recovered it. You've already had a demonstration of what happens when you disappoint me. I was hoping to avoid another unpleasant situation, but I'm starting to think you're actively working against me."

"I was going to bring it to you," I said. "Unfortunately, Cyril out there kidnapped me and had me drive here. Digga's only here to rescue me. I was about to call you."

"I doubt that's entirely true," Colonel Wu said. "However, some of what you say may be plausible. Captain McKinsey has a long history of having women do things that are against their best interests."

The Colonel walked over to Sterling and took the big revolver from him. He made a sign, and the men holding my arms straightened me up and tightened their grasp on my arms.

Colonel Wu then casually walked over to where I stood, pointed the gun at my head, and used his thumb to pull back the hammer. As with the last time, there were several clicks, the cylinder rotated, and a fresh bullet was again in position to explode out of the gun.

"What happened before is unimportant," the Colonel said. "Now is all I'm concerned with. I understand you possess the jade. Where is it?"

My mind started racing, and I sort of froze. I was still hoping to find some advantage in the situation, but all I could see was the black opening in the barrel of the big revolver. From where I was, it looked to be roughly the size of a train tunnel.

Okay, stay calm. You'd planned on giving the jade to

Colonel Wu anyway.

I was about to tell him where it was when Digga spoke. "Colonel, it's out in the car. You and your men walked right past it. I can get it and bring it in."

Wait, how could Digga know that?

Colonel Wu cocked his head to the side, and I could tell he was thinking intensely. I suspected he was less apprehensive about the jade being outside in a car.

He was likely more troubled that Digga was laying some sort of trap. I was concerned the Colonel might forget he had his finger on the trigger of a .45 Magnum that was currently pointed at my forehead.

After thinking for almost a minute, Colonel Wu seemed to come to a decision. He raised the pistol so it no longer pointed at me and released the hammer.

"Four men," the Colonel said. "One on either side, one directly behind, and one five steps back. Get the jade, then return. Keep it tight. If Captain McKinsey flinches or hesitates, shoot to kill."

The two big mercenaries led Digga out of the room, and the man with the silencer trailed behind. There was the sound of the front door opening and then closing.

I had an uncomfortable thought of Digga escaping and leaving me alone with Colonel Wu. Based on everything that had happened before, I knew it wouldn't be pleasant.

Much to my relief, three minutes later, Digga came back into the room holding an ornate wooden box. Although I'd never seen it before, I instantly knew what it was.

Digga carefully set the box on the table next to my purse and stepped back. Colonel Wu motioned to a man who tried to open the box. It was tightly locked, and there didn't seem to be an easy way to force it open.

"You will now open the box," Colonel Wu said to Digga, a touch of exasperation in his voice. "You have deceived me before, and it would not surprise me if this is not another of your tricks."

He pointed to the man with the silencer, then to Digga. "If you attempt a trick, you will be dead before you hit the floor."

I was about to say I had the key in my purse and there was no need to destroy the beautiful box when Digga reached into his pocket and pulled out the ornate silver key on the red silk ribbon. He held it up, and it swung back and forth in an almost hypnotic motion.

What the hell?

I couldn't figure out how he'd gotten the key. After Jerry had given it to me the other day, I'd put it in the front pocket of my purse. It should still be there. Digga must have pinched it while he had my bag.

Colonel Wu looked at the key for a moment, then changed his mind about having Digga open the box. Instead, he motioned to one of his soldiers.

The man took the key, clumsily inserted it into the lock, and turned it. There was a gentle metallic sound, and the box was unlocked.

Colonel Wu stood next to the box, and everyone in the room watched as the lid slowly came up. The interior of the box was lined in red silk with a cutout that appeared to be custom-made for *The Child*. Unfortunately, the box was empty.

"You attempt to deceive me?" Colonel Wu asked Digga angrily. His face had started to go red, and he was breathing hard. "You think me a fool?"

"No, I'm not deceiving you," Digga said. *"The Child* is

here. Matter of fact, Laura Black has it." Digga then pointed to my bag, still on the table, "It's in her purse."

Shit, no. Don't do this.

"No, you've got it wrong," I said as I took a step backward. The men holding my arms pulled me forward again.

Colonel Wu glanced at me and raised two fingers on one hand. The two men walked me to where he stood.

"You have *The Child*?" he asked.

"No," I said as I tried to struggle against the men.

"It's in her bag," Digga said. "I saw it a few minutes ago. It's wrapped up in a blue silk scarf."

"You will give it to me," Colonel Wu calmly said.

One of the goons released my arm, and I was able to flip open my bag. I reached in and pulled out my blue scarf, along with the object it was wrapped around. I then handed it to Colonel Wu.

He carefully unwrapped the scarf to reveal a smooth green carving, about eleven inches long, in the shape of a leaf. A detailed grasshopper was sitting on one end.

"Ah," Colonel Wu said. He smiled, and his eyes were filled with wonder. "So much trouble over such a small item. When you look at it, it appears to be rather common, no?"

He then took the sculpture and placed it in the box. It was a snug fit.

The Colonel hesitated between pushing too hard on the figurine and having it not exactly fit the cutout. Finally, he seemed satisfied.

He closed the lid and locked the box with the silver key. He then stood up and placed the key in his front pocket.

Colonel Wu looked at Digga. "Captain McKinsey, I'm

glad you've acted honorably. It was very wise of you to do this in a civilized manner. Unfortunately, it appears you've lost our little competition. I now have *The Child,* and you do not. I will release you to await your fate in returning home with empty hands. I know whose interests you represent, and I do not think they will easily tolerate your failure. Your shame will make it rather hard for you to find employment in the future, I think."

The Colonel then looked at me. "You did well to recover the jade, but your initial lack of effort resulted in the loss of your car. Be thankful that's all you lost. Many others have not been so fortunate when dealing with me. You are also free to go."

Sterling stepped forward. "What about me? I called you when I found out she had the jade. If it weren't for me, McKinsey would have it and be heading out of the country by now."

"Yes," Colonel Wu said. "You have done well. Come, you've earned the honor of being present when we hand *The Child* over to our buyer. It will be a day that brings honor to us all."

Colonel Wu made a signal to his men. They quickly gathered their things and left the house. Several cars started up, then faded as they sped down the street. Within a minute, I was standing alone in the quiet kitchen with Digga.

We walked into the front room, where Cyril was still sprawled out on the floor. If it weren't for his breathing, I would've assumed he was dead.

"I was in here listening to you two having a conversation in the kitchen when Cyril walked in on me. I had to knock him out as soon as he came into the room. I was afraid he'd do something foolish with that big gun of his. I should have hidden it so Sterling couldn't have found it. That was rather stupid of me. Cyril's a wanker, truth be told, but I really didn't think he'd turn on us like that."

"What are we going to do with him? We can't just leave him here."

"After we've cleared out," Digga said. "I'll call an ambulance to have them come and check him, but I think he'll be alright. Maybe the police would be interested in him as well."

"Thanks for rescuing me," I said. "I wasn't sure what Cyril was going to do to me, but I suspect it wouldn't have been nice. I owe you one."

"Before we finish our business, there are a few things I'd like to discuss with you. I'm going to need to write a long report on this. Is there somewhere we can go that's more pleasant than here?"

"Sure," I said. The other day, I was at Tempe Beach Park, and it was nice. Let's go there. It's public and has a large crowd. We both should be okay there."

"Sounds perfect, lead on."

~~~~

I drove down the Loop-202 with Digga trailing close behind me in his rental car. I got off on Priest, and we made our way over to the park. There were plenty of free spaces, and we each found a spot.

I led Digga through the main walkway, past play areas filled with noisy children, and then down to the water. After a very long and eventful day, the sun was nearing the horizon. The few clouds in the west had started to take on an iridescent yellow glow.

There were several boats on the lake, enjoying the last few minutes of sunlight before coming in for the night. There was a warm breeze coming off the desert, and it was nice.

We both stood there for several minutes, taking in the view. I was happy the assignment with Stig and the jade was over, and I could feel the tension starting to drain from my body.

"That was quite an adventure," Digga said. "But all in all, we came away very lucky. As you might have gathered, I've had my little run-ins with the good Colonel before."

"I don't think he likes you."

"No," Digga said with a smile, "but he doesn't really *dislike* me either. He could have had me killed several times before but never has. I think, in a strange way, he appreciates someone who'll keep him on his toes. Maybe I'm wrong, and the next time I see him, it won't work out so well, but I guess we'll see."

"You said you wanted to talk something over?"

"Right. It's about that little trick we just played on Colonel Wu."

"Um, so you know what the Colonel actually has in the wooden box?"

"You mean that he doesn't have anything but a pretty piece of green plastic?"

"Yes, how did you know I had a copy of *The Mother* in my purse?"

"When I saw your car on the street, I looked in it before I went into the house. I found your bag and took the opportunity to go through it. Sort of an occupational habit, I'm afraid. I found the key to the box and was happy enough with that. Then I found the sculpture. At first, I was thrilled you'd found *The Child*, but I quickly realized I was only holding a glass copy of *The Mother*. I took my thumbnail and scraped off the 'Made in China' sticker, then re-wrapped it in your scarf. I thought it might come in handy in case we ran into Colonel Wu. It was very clever of you to carry a copy of *The Mother*. I wish I'd thought of it. Wherever did you get it?"

"They sell them online at the Art Museum in Beijing. I found it the other day while I was doing research on *The Child*. I had it express shipped from China, and I only got it today."

"Well, good on you for that."

"Thanks."

Digga started laughing. It wasn't loud, but coming from the big Australian, it seemed a little out of place.

"What?" I asked.

"Sometime tomorrow, there's going to be a formal handoff between Colonel Wu and that internet billionaire bloke out in California. I was thinking about how much I'd like to be there to see the look on the Colonel's face when they tell him what he's delivered as *The Child* is actually nothing more than a cheap plastic replica of *The Mother*. I imagine Sterling won't be so thrilled to be there then."

"Um, maybe you should avoid the Colonel for a few months, just in case."

"I'll keep it in mind. And now, since I'm assuming you really do have *The Child*, I'd like to have it. Well, that's assuming we're still partners in this. Once I get it, I'll be gone."

I thought about it for a second. Perhaps it would be foolish to simply hand over the jade to Digga, but it somehow seemed like the right thing to do.

I led him back to my car, unhooked the bungee cord holding my trunk shut, and lifted the lid. Inside my trunk were a lot of boxes and things I'd been meaning to throw away. I moved an old sweater and lifted out a shoebox. Inside was a faded Arizona Diamondbacks T-shirt wrapped around something hard. I carefully unwrapped the shirt to reveal a green figurine, about ten inches long, in the shape of a leaf. The now familiar grasshopper was perched on one end. It was slightly smaller than the plastic replica I'd bought from the museum store and had given to Colonel Wu.

"Well, here you go," I said as I handed it to Digga. "It's caused everyone a lot of trouble, and I'm happy to get rid of it."

Digga held up the ancient sculpture and slowly moved it back and forth. Even in the fading sunlight, the translucent imperial jade appeared to shine with an inner glow. It was really quite lovely.

"Would you mind holding it for one more minute?" he asked, giving *The Child* back to me. He then went to his car and came back with a sturdy stainless-steel briefcase. He sat it on the hood of my car and opened it to reveal a red satin interior with a padded cutout for the jade. I placed it inside, and it was a perfect fit. Digga slowly closed the case and locked it.

"Right then," he said. "I'm off."

He reached into his pocket and pulled out a business card with only an email address printed on it. "I don't check it every day, but I do check it. If you ever have anything that goes along with my particular line of work, toss me a note. Maybe we can partner up again."

"I'd like that. Maybe we will."

He held out his big hand and I shook it. Digga then got into his car and headed west.

His car briefly merged with the setting sun before disappearing down the road. I stood in the parking lot for several minutes after he left and watched the children play.

~~~

I sat in my car and made some phone calls. Within a few

minutes, Stig, Jerry, Jeanette, Lenny, Gina, and Sophie all knew the trouble was over. I also let them know about Sterling. Funny enough, nobody seemed all that surprised.

I put down the phone and realized I hadn't eaten all day. All I wanted to do was to get some Thai takeout and go home to Marlowe.

Chapter Thirteen

I slept until almost nine the next morning and only woke up when Sophie called and interrupted an erotic dream.

"Hey," she said. "Why are you still asleep? Are you coming in today?"

"Not this morning. I'm staying in and catching up on my bills. I should probably also go to the store. There's nothing here but coffee and olives."

"Good idea. Lenny won't care if you're here or not. He said he wants a report from you, but it really won't matter. He's already worked up the billing for me to send to Stig. He's put you down as working eighteen to twenty hours a day on this."

"It sometimes feels like it. I'll probably stop by later this afternoon. If Gina's around, maybe we can all do dinner."

~~~~

I'd gotten dressed and was on my third cup of coffee when the theme to *The Godfather* started playing on my phone. As always, I got a brief surge of adrenaline as I answered.

"Hi, Tony," I said when I answered. "How are you feeling today?"

"Laura Black, it's good to hear your voice. I'm doing well. I have another physical therapy session this afternoon, and I seem to be making good progress toward walking again. I was informed about what happened to your car. I hear it happened in relation to a case you were working on for Lenny. Max tells me you didn't require assistance, but I wanted to call and personally let you know that help is always available if you require it."

"Thanks, Tony, but the situation resolved itself, and I'm okay. I'm so sorry about what happened to your beautiful car. It was wonderful to drive something so nice."

"Don't trouble yourself over it. It was only a car. It served me well, and I'm glad you also got to enjoy it, if only briefly. However, I did want to talk with you about another matter. We had a meeting with Sergio and his group yesterday. It was purposefully informal, almost a social gathering, you could say. Based on the work you performed, both sides were able to state their positions clearly. I think we now have a good basis for moving forward."

"You had a meeting with the Black Death? Did everything go okay?"

"The meeting went well; both sides seem able to move past the events of two months ago. However, I did notice one unusual thing. We are dealing with a man named Sergio, but I see how he looks at his assistant, Danielle. She's the same person whom you have been negotiating with. Twice, I noticed he glanced at her way before deciding on an issue. It was subtle, and I don't think he was even aware of doing so. When I think back to our final meeting with Carlos the Butcher, I seem to recall he also glanced at Danielle. I thought nothing of it at the time, but now I'm not sure. I'm starting to believe she has more influence over the Black Death than is let on."

Shit, that's not good.

"Um, how can I help?"

"Laura Black, it appears I'm going to need your services a bit longer. We're going to need to clarify our positions further before any final decisions can be made. In addition, you seem to get along well with Danielle. I need you to find out everything you can about her background, perhaps even socialize with her. Why does Sergio look to her for approval? I need to know what hold she has over the group."

How do I get myself into these positions?

"Okay, Tony, let me know when the next meeting is."

Damn.

~~~~

For the next couple of hours, I kept myself busy catching up on all the things I'd been ignoring while I was working on the assignment. At about two o'clock, the Eurythmics song *Would I Lie to You?* began to play from my phone.

Damn, what now?

"Hi, Laura," Danielle said when I answered. "I'd like to get together with you sometime soon. This isn't about the negotiations, but I do need to talk with you."

"I'm not doing anything this afternoon. Would you like to meet now?"

"Great, I'll meet you at The Huddle Room. It's a sports bar in the strip mall at Scottsdale Road and McKellips. At this time of day, it'll be quiet enough to talk without being overheard."

~~~~

I drove over to the sports bar, and, as Danielle had assumed, it was empty. The only other people in the place were a bored-looking bartender and a couple of day drinkers who were comfortably seated at the bar.

We took a table against the back wall. I noticed Danielle didn't have her bodyguards with her, which struck me as unusual and a bit troubling.

"Thanks for coming," Danielle said.

"Tony said he had a meeting with you."

"Yes, I proposed it as a way to move past the bad memories from two months ago. I think it helped."

"So, things are getting better between the two groups?"

"I wish I could say they were, but Escobar still wants to take a hard line with Tony. He's pretty upset about what happened to Carlos, and he doesn't forgive easily. He thinks Tony's group is what's stopping us from expanding, not only in Arizona but throughout the entire desert southwest."

"What do you think?" I asked.

"I think refusing to come to an agreement will only result in a confrontation with high losses on both sides. It's easy for Escobar to give ultimatums when he's twelve hundred miles away, but I know what a war would mean to everyone involved here. I want to work to make sure we can live together peacefully if it's at all possible."

"I don't think either Tony or Max wants a full-scale conflict. They see this as a business. As long as they see some benefit coming out of it, they'll likely want to come to some sort of agreement."

Danielle looked at me. I could see she had several emotions running through her mind at once. "Laura, I know you don't like me. It's a shame because I like you and consider you to be a friend. It's funny, but you, Sophie, and Gina are the three people I'm closest to in Arizona. I wouldn't want to see anything happen to any of you."

"You still think there's going to be trouble?"

"The truth is, Escobar wants to send up two hundred men to wipe out Tony and his entire organization. He wouldn't care if your country needed to send in the army to stop the killings. He wants to turn Scottsdale into the cartel's next war zone. If I'm going to prevent this, I'll need Max and Tony to work with me. You're close to both of them. I'll need you to let me know everything that's going on behind the scenes, at least in terms of the negotiations. What will they accept, and what do they consider out of the question? I'll need you to help them accept a reasonable offer, even if their first instinct is to hesitate. If you can do that, maybe we can prevent the war."

Shit, how do I get myself in the middle of these things?

"Nobody wants to get into an all-out fight," I said. "I'll do what I can."

I saw relief wash across Danielle's face. "Thank you," she said. "Maybe this actually has a chance of working out."

She then smiled as she seemed to remember something. "Before I forget, I have something for you."

Danielle looked around the bar to make sure no one was watching, then reached into her purse and pulled out a gun. At first, I thought she was going to shoot me, but she instead held it out for me to take. My heart sped up further as I recognized what it was.

"This was confiscated from you the day of the meeting with Tony," Danielle said. "I know how attached a girl can get to her gun, so I thought you'd want it back."

As she gave me back my Baby Glock, a flood of emotions swept over me. Although I could tell it was unloaded, there was a real sense of relief as I felt the weight of the gun in my hand.

Ever since the goon had taken it away from me, I'd been carrying my old .25 caliber semi-automatic pistol, what Reno always called my little 'get off me' gun. Although I was comfortable with my old pistol, it never seemed to offer much in the way of personal protection compared to the nine-millimeter Glock.

I remembered the night Reno had given me the gun. It had been Christmas Eve, almost two years ago. He gave me the gun and said it was so small it was nicknamed the "Baby Glock."

I joked about this being our first baby. Instead of laughing, Reno asked me to move in with him. I've often wondered how different the last two years of my life would have been if I'd simply said "yes."

"Laura?" Danielle asked. "Are you alright?"

"Yeah, I'm doing okay." I looked down at the gun in my hand. "Thanks for returning this. You're right. I'm very attached to it, and I've missed not having it. I got it from an, um, ex-boyfriend, and it has a lot of memories associated with it."

Ex-boyfriend? Somebody that I used to know? Is that all Reno is to me now?

"I like it too," Danielle said. "Most of the more powerful handguns are too big for a woman to hold in her hand comfortably. Your gun has a nice feel to it. I'm thinking about getting one for myself."

"Well, it's always been reliable for me. I'd stick with the standard magazine. I tried one of the higher-capacity magazines once, and it wouldn't fit in my purse."

"Thanks," Danielle said. "I'll keep that in mind."

~~~~~

I drove up to the office. It was getting to be later in the afternoon, and I was starting to get hungry. Lenny's parking space was empty, but Sophie and Gina were there.

I went in through the rear security door and then went up

to reception. Sophie was at her desk, and Gina was in one of the wingback chairs.

"Hey Laura," Gina said. "I'm glad you're here too. I was about to tell Sophie, but I spent the last half hour talking to the detective in charge of the case. We went to the academy together, and he was more than happy to talk about what happened as long as I didn't spread it around."

"I won't say a word," I said.

Sophie made the motions of locking her lips and then throwing away the key.

"Well," Gina said, "it seems Frank Fender had a good amount of DNA under his fingernails from when he was fighting with Cyril. It also seems that when Frank hit Cyril, some additional DNA became embedded in one of Frank's rings. The size and shape of the ring matched up with the recent wound on Cyril's face. They knew the DNA belonged to Cyril because it was already on file from two stints he'd had at the state prison in Florence. It was an open-and-shut case. The only piece of the puzzle the police were missing was Cyril himself. Apparently, they got an anonymous tip last night that led them to where he was hiding. The tip came in on a disposable phone, and the detective said the tipster had a heavy Australian accent."

"Lucky break for them," Sophie said. "Did they ever find out who called in the tip?"

"No, it looks like Digga got cleanly away."

Somehow, that made me happy. Yes, Digga was a criminal, but he didn't seem like the bad guy here.

"From what the detective said, Cyril tried to spin a complicated story about Stig Stevens, Australian spies, ancient jade, Chinese mercenaries, and Laura, even you. He was doing his best to implicate everyone he could on this."

Shit.

"Well, that's not good," Sophie said.

"Fortunately, for us anyway, this will be Cyril's third strike. After talking with Lenny earlier this afternoon, it looks like the Assistant District Attorney will make a deal with Cyril. If he pleads guilty to negligent homicide, they'll recommend a sentence of only three to five years. If he tries to go to court under his current charge of second-degree murder, he'll be looking at a sentence of up to twenty-nine years. If he takes the deal, then no one will need to testify in court to anything."

"What about Jerry and Luther?" I asked. "They moved a dead body and dumped it into the Salt River."

"As far as I know, the police aren't going to pursue that," Gina said. "Moving a body without intent to cover up a crime is only a misdemeanor. The murder was solved, and the police aren't going to worry too much about the details. Apparently, Stig does a lot of charity events for both the City of Scottsdale and the Scottsdale Police. It gives him a certain level of, um, deference in things like this."

~~~~

I got back to my apartment about eight o'clock that night. As I was waiting for the elevator, Grandma Peckham came in from the parking lot. Walking next to her was Grandpa Bob.

They were both laughing about something that had apparently happened at dinner. I held the elevator open for them, and we all rode up together. I saw Grandpa Bob was carrying a sack with the neck of a wine bottle poking out.

We walked down the hall together, and I said, "Good night," before they disappeared into Grandma's apartment.

As I sat on my couch, I was happy Grandma had sorted out her love life. I wished I could do the same. Reno had dumped me, and Max wouldn't see me. I tried not to think about it, but it was hard not to.

Unfortunately, I could already hear Grandma and Grandpa Bob talking and laughing through the thin apartment walls. I knew what would be happening soon, and I was hoping it wouldn't keep me up all night.

~~~

On Wednesday morning, we heard the news that Sterling had been arrested for trying to sell Chinese antiquities to an FBI undercover agent in California. There was no mention of Colonel Wu or an internet billionaire, so we had to assume they set Sterling up as the fall guy so they could get away cleanly.

In a way, I felt vaguely sorry for him.

~~~

That afternoon, Stig asked if I could stop by his place. I got there about two in the afternoon and was led out to the back patio.

Stig was sitting under the shade of a brightly-colored umbrella next to the pool. He was reading something on his tablet but sat it down when I came out.

He got up and gave me a friendly hug, then asked me if I'd like a drink. Since Stig already had a drink on the table and I wasn't actively working on anything, I said, "Sure, scotch, one ice cube."

Stig made the drink at his cabana bar then we both sat under the umbrella and looked out over Scottsdale. From up on the side of the mountain, the city below looked peaceful and calm.

"I was reading about Sterling," he said. "It's crazy. I've worked with him for twenty-five years, and I've never known him to do anything close to this. According to Lenny, he and a businessman from China planned the whole thing. I suppose it was a good strategy. Giving me the jade in the open, then having us smuggle it out of the country. No one suspected anything unusual about it. If one of the studio property guys hadn't pulled the box out of the shipment and sent it to me directly, everything would have gone smoothly, and no one would have ever known about it."

"It's funny how these things happen sometimes," I said.

"I'd like to thank you for everything you did for me," Stig said. "I'd never been kidnapped before, and it was a little disconcerting. I'm glad you were able to find me and bring me back. I'm still amazed about my little green sculpture and all the fighting over it. I guess I should look at things more closely before I give them away. It's a shame about the box, though. I really liked it. Maybe I should call the FBI and see if I can get it back after Sterling's trial is over. I hope things somehow work out for him. We were never exactly friends, but he did know how to organize a schedule. The studio assigned me someone new. I'm heading out to LA tomorrow, and I'm supposed to meet her then."

"Good luck with this one. Hopefully, she's not a crook. I was meaning to talk with you about something else. I think you should consider upgrading your home security. Colonel Wu apparently had people crawling all over your house while you were kidnapped."

"I know. I heard them talking about searching my house while they were holding me. I've already started looking for contractors to set up a state-of-the-art security system. It's something I should have done years ago."

"That sounds like a good start."

~~~~

By Thursday, things had pretty much returned to normal. Lenny had court for the rest of the week, and we were in one of those lulls where both Gina and I had some time off. It was nice.

Sophie was feeling lonely, so she asked Gina and me to come in so we could all walk down the street for lunch. When I got in, Gina wasn't there yet, but Sophie seemed excited.

"You got a letter," she said. "They delivered it about two hours ago." She opened the top drawer of her desk and pulled out an express envelope.

I looked at the envelope, and the markings on it seemed to be Asian. I'm not an expert, but I would have guessed Chinese.

"Well, are you going to open it? I've been waiting for you all morning. If you'd been any longer, I might have had to 'accidentally' open it by mistake."

"Alright, hold on."

I opened the envelope and took out a letter. There also appeared to be something else in the envelope.

Dear Laura,

Thanks for your recent help. I'm sorry I couldn't have been more open with you, but I'm actually working for a very large government agency, and they prefer to keep a rather low profile. I'm happy to report that the item we went out of our way to recover is now with the proper authorities and will soon be on permanent display next to its mother. Don't worry about our Colonel friend. I heard he tried to pass off his counterfeit item as genuine, and there was quite a row over it. If he ever has the nerve to show his face again, it'll be me he'll be interested in talking to about the incident. It'll add some spice to my otherwise dull life. As per our agreement, please find a check for fifteen thousand dollars U.S.

Cheers,

D. McKinsey

I pulled out the check and showed it to Sophie.

"Holy crap," she said. "That's a cashier's check for fifteen thousand dollars."

"Yup," I said. "It looks like the three of us will actually get a bonus from this assignment."

"Damn, I know I could sure use an extra five thousand. I put a few extra pairs of shoes on a credit card last month, not to mention a couple of dresses for going out with the Cougars. You know, you could use yours for a down payment on a new car and get rid of that old junker."

"Maybe," I said. "Or maybe I'll pay off a few bills and put the rest in the bank. You never know what the future will bring."

~~~~

Gina arrived ten minutes later, and we informed her about the check. She was hesitant to accept money from someone she considered a criminal, but when we told her that Digga was probably working for the Chinese government and *The Child* was going to the National Museum, she seemed to soften.

The phone on Sophie's desk rang. She answered, then got a strange look on her face. She looked back and forth between Gina and me as she told the caller that everyone was here. Gina became concerned as Sophie hit the button for the speakerphone.

"Can you hear me?" Jeanette asked. "Are Gina and Laura there?"

"We're here," Gina said.

"Great," Jeanette said over the speakerphone. "It's been a crazy week. First, Stig was dead, then he was alive, then his studio handler was arrested for smuggling. I feared we'd crap the bed on this, but the buzz about *Obscura 2* is off the charts. We're having the world premier Saturday night in Hollywood at the Chinese Theatre, and it's suddenly the hottest ticket in town. Everyone who's ever worked with Stig has called for a ticket. We've gotten confirmation from a dozen A-list celebrities who'll come out. The red carpet on this is going to be the event of the season."

"Why is everyone so eager to go to a movie premiere?" Sophie asked.

"It's a basic law of publicity," Jeanette said. "Fame attracts fame. Stig wants all of you to be a part of it. I know I'm only giving you two days' notice, but he's asked the studio to reserve seats for the three of you. We'll send a limo to the airport to pick you up. It will also take you to the after-party, and we'll even put you up in a nice hotel for the night."

Sophie started to squeal and clap her hands. Even Gina broke out in a smile. "Thanks," we all said at once to Jeanette.

"I'll have them email you the flight and hotel information. You'll get everything tomorrow morning."

"We'll see you Saturday," Gina said.

Jeanette disconnected, and we went to lunch, discussing the trip and what we would wear. Fortunately, since we went out so often with the cougars, all of us had outfits that would work well for Hollywood. Sophie said she was going to wear Raquel Welch's necklace again, and Gina said this would be a good time to wear her diamond earrings.

"You know," Sophie said, "for a freaking lawyer, Jeanette's not so bad."

~~~~~

After lunch, Gina took off to pick up a few things for the trip. Sophie and I had walked up to reception to discuss the weekend when the theme to *The Love Boat* started playing on my phone.

Sophie laughed and said I could talk to him out in

reception. I shook my head and instead started walking to the back before hitting the Accept button.

"Hey," I said.

"I hope I'm not disturbing you," Max said.

"No, I'm good. I'm in that 'in-between assignments' time when I really don't have to be doing anything."

"Good. I wanted to thank you for all of your help over the past couple of weeks. I know it was a busy time for you, but Tony and I both appreciate it."

"Why didn't you tell me your name was Bettencourt?"

Max started laughing. "It's not a secret. I thought you knew. My family is involved in numerous activities all over the world. They're into retail, chemicals, and mining, mostly diamonds and gold in Africa."

"Nice family you have."

"Unfortunately, I'm not close to that side of the family. If I were, I'd probably have my own island in the Mediterranean, like the rest of them do. Is there anything else you want to know about me?"

I had a sudden flash of inspiration, and it scared the bejesus out of me. But I also knew it was finally the right time.

Take a deep breath and just do it.

"Yes," I said. "There *is* something else. Um, look, we've been dancing around this for almost a year. I want you, and I think you want me, too. I know we'd need to keep our involvement secret, but I want to see you. I mean, see you romantically."

The phone went quiet. I could tell Max was still there, but he wasn't talking.

Damn.

"Max?"

Shit.

"Laura," he said, "I think that's a wonderful idea. I won't even ask what happened to change your mind. You're right, of course, we'd need to keep our involvement secret, but between the both of us, I think we can figure out how to do that."

"Um, before we go any further, there are some things you'll need to know about me. I'm pretty independent. I can't stand to have a guy who hovers around me all the time or who needs to know where I am and what I'm doing every minute. It's not that I don't need you. It's more that I don't need you to be physically next to me every minute. It's a bit much for some guys, especially the touchy-feely type."

Max started laughing.

"What?" I asked.

"I was about to tell you the same thing. With my position in the company, there'll be times when I won't be able to see you or even call you on the phone, perhaps for days at a time. I was going to ask if that would be a problem for you."

"Okay, looks like we dodged a bullet there."

"Can I assume you're no longer dating the detective?"

"Yes, we ended it a few days ago. I'm officially an unattached woman again."

Why does it still hurt when I think of Reno?

"So," he said, "you're a single woman out lookin' for a man, huh? What are we going to do about it?"

"I think you know exactly what we're going to do about it. The only questions are when and where."

"I think I could rearrange a few things and be free for the weekend. What about you? I have access to a place overlooking the Pacific near San Diego. It's not exactly the tropical beach we've talked about, but it might do for a start."

The weekend? Am I ready for that? It seems kinda fast.

"Well, I sort of have a commitment for the weekend, but I'm pretty sure I can get out of it. Okay, let's do it."

~~~~

I walked back up to reception, where Sophie was looking at me.

"Well?" she asked. "What did Max want?"

"I won't be able to go with you and Gina to Hollywood."

"Why not? What's wrong?"

"Um, nothing's wrong. I'm spending the weekend with Max."

"You're serious? Holy crap. When did this happen? I mean, it's about time, but when did this happen? Just now?"

"Yup, just now. He asked me to spend the weekend with him at his place on the beach in San Diego."

"Nice, but what about your ticket to the premiere?"

"Why don't we see if Christine's free? Jeanette might have asked her already, but if not, she'd probably love to go, plus Jeanette would appreciate the extra publicity Christine would bring."

"That's a great idea. If she can't do it, I bet Vicky Vaughn would go. You said she still has a crush on Stig."

"That's a good idea. Stig's friends with both of them, and either one would probably enjoy it."

"Okay then. I'll make the calls. I'll miss having you there, but I suppose Gina and I can handle going to a Hollywood premiere and after-party with Christine Johns."

She started laughing. "At least we'll have a story to one-up the cougars with next time we go out."

~~~~

By five o'clock, I was back at my apartment. My suitcase was open on the bed, and I was trying to decide what to pack.

It had been over a year since I'd been on a romantic first date, and I didn't have anything to wear. I searched through my drawers and eventually came up with three sets of bras and panties that sort of matched.

I then went to the back of my underwear drawer and pulled out a couple of negligées that I hadn't worn for a couple of years.

I was trying to decide between a red peek-a-boo and a black merry-widow when my phone rang with Reno's ringtone. It was weird hearing it since I'd assumed he'd never call again. I hit the button and answered.

"Hello?"

"Hey, I wanted to see how you were doing. I know you were working on the Stig Stevens thing. From what I hear on the news, it seems to have worked out alright."

"Yeah, everything worked out okay. As it turns out, Stig got some free publicity for his new movie, and the Chinese government got back a cultural treasure."

"Now that the assignment has ended, are you going to stop meeting with Bettencourt and DiCenzo?"

Shit why is he asking this now?

"Well, I might not be able to—at least not yet. I've ended up working on something else. They have information on the new assignment, and they're willing to share it with me. I'll probably still need to talk with them, at least occasionally."

I heard Reno sigh, a surprisingly sad sigh. "Alright, but be careful. They aren't nice people. My offer of help is always there, but it will still need to be official."

"Thanks, I appreciate it. I really do."

"Goodbye, Laura."

"Um, goodbye."

I disconnected and looked down at the phone for several seconds. It left me with a weird and hollow feeling.

~~~~

I went to bed early but was too excited to sleep. I felt like a kid on Christmas Eve.

As I thought about it, it wasn't so much the idea of spending the weekend with Max at the beach. It was something more fundamental.

I got the feeling I'd closed one chapter in my life and was about to start on the next one. The feeling was a little scary, but at the same time, it was rather hopeful.

Chapter Fourteen

At four o'clock the next afternoon, I walked out to the parking lot and threw my suitcase in the back of my old piece-of-shit car. I'd attached the partially burnt license plate, and seeing it brought a wave of anger and sadness.

When I got to Sky Harbor Airport, Max had a ticket waiting for me at the counter. I went through security and made it to the gate as they were starting to board the plane. Everything went smoothly, and the short flight landed in San Diego in less than an hour.

~~~~

As I got off the plane and walked out of the terminal, Johnny Scarpazzi met me. He took my bag and walked me to the parking lot, where a black SUV was parked.

He put my bag in the back, then turned to me. He started to speak, then stopped. His face turned a little red, and I could tell he was having a hard time putting his thoughts into words.

"Look," he finally said, "I know we've talked about this before, but I'd like to thank you again for everything you did for me two months ago. You probably know more about my personal life than anyone in the organization, including Tony.

As far as anyone knows, Mistress is my girlfriend. Everyone's happy with that explanation, and I appreciate the part you played in that. I also appreciate that you haven't said anything about my place up in Strawberry. I think of it as my personal refuge. You and Mistress are the only ones who know about it."

How is it that I keep finding out secrets from gangsters?

Johnny seemed a little embarrassed. "Anyway, I do appreciate everything you've done for Mistress and me. I was in a tight jam, and you helped get me out. I owe you a favor. If there's anything I can ever do for you, name it."

Shit, not another favor.

"Thanks, Johnny. But you and Suzi are both friends of mine, and I was happy I could help. I'm glad it worked out."

Johnny nodded his head and opened my door. I got in the back seat and buckled the seatbelt.

~~~~

We drove from the airport to a private resort on a hill overlooking the ocean. As Johnny opened my door, I felt a warm and humid breeze coming up from the beach. It felt great. Johnny pulled out my bag from the back, and, over his protests, I took it from him.

Gabriella was waiting in the parking lot, and she stepped up to meet us. Johnny walked back to his vehicle while Gabriella led the way through the resort.

As always, she carried a large black bag over her shoulder. But this bag was a little larger and looked to be better made than the one she had at the shootout with Carlos.

Looking closer, I had to smile. Gabriella was now using a Ferrucci Spy Bag to tote her Uzi and hand grenades.

"How are you doing?" I asked. "The last time we talked,

you'd taken a few rounds to your vest and had a couple of cracked ribs."

"It's no problem," she said. "I'm okay." As she talked, I realized that she and Stig had the same Eastern European accent.

I could never tell what it was. Perhaps it was Russian or Ukrainian? This made me wonder more than ever about her background.

"You got a new bag?" I asked.

"My other bag was shot when we fight with Carlos. I needed new one, and I remember the bag we were searching for when we had the diamonds and the Consortium. You said it was a Ferrucci Spy Bag, so I got one. It's very nice. More room than my last one."

Gabriella led me down a winding sidewalk through a beautiful tropical oasis. Along the way, we passed three big guys wearing sports coats.

As we approached a two-story casita, Gabriella took out a key card, rapped twice on the door, and used the key card to open it. She then took up a position in an alcove next to the door.

When I looked at her, she seemed a little sad. I again wondered if she had a relationship with Max that went beyond bodyguard. If so, how would she handle Max and me seeing each other?

"Gabriella, are you alright with me being here?"

"I'm okay. I'm glad you and Max are together. He's been cranky for months because you no want to see him. He's been better since you now say you see him."

"I was asking because you seem a little down."

"Oh, it's okay." She looked around to make sure no one

could hear.

"I'm a little sad tonight because this location is very secure. No men will come tonight to bother you or Max."

As she talked, she unzipped her bag and softly stroked her Uzi. I don't think she was aware she was doing it.

That's a little weird.

"But two months ago, you got to shoot Carlos."

Gabriella's face flushed bright red, and she tightly grabbed onto the Uzi. Her body shook, and she gave out a small, lusty moan.

"Ohhh yes," she said, her eyes bright and her breathing suddenly becoming erratic. "Carlos the Butcher was very bad man. He caused many problems for Tony and Max. He shot and almost killed Tony. I wanted to kill him for very long time. Shooting Carlos was good. He died painful death, and I think of it very often."

Yikes.

I walked into the bungalow, and Gabriella closed the door behind me. From a short hallway, I walked into the living room, where a huge, curved picture window overlooked the beach and the Pacific Ocean.

Half a dozen candles lit the room. A silver champagne bucket next to a leather couch contained a corked bottle with a white linen towel wrapped around the neck.

The song *Feelin' Love* by Paula Cole was softly playing from speakers mounted into the walls. I went to the big picture window and looked out at the ocean.

From our hilltop location, I could see a hundred yards of beach in either direction. The sun had gone down, and the western sky was orange and red. Lights had started to come on all over the resort.

I heard a sound and turned. Max was walking down the stairs from an upstairs loft.

He was wearing black pants and a loose, white, long-sleeved shirt. My heart was pounding as I realized this was really happening and not one of my made-up fantasies.

Max stopped in the middle of the room and held his arms out. I walked to him and pressed myself against his chest. As his arms wrapped around me, the world started to go into a slow-motion blur.

Yes, this is really happening.

"Well," Max said in his deep and steady voice. "It's been a long time since that day we first kissed in Lenny's office. Are you sure you're ready for this?"

"I'm ready," I said. "Are you?"

He answered by bending down and kissing me. It started out softly, with our lips barely touching but rapidly built into a kiss that was deep and urgent.

I felt a fresh wave of excitement and knew this was going to be a very memorable weekend.

Yes!

As a special bonus,

please enjoy the first chapter of:

Scottsdale Shuffle,

the sixth book in the

Laura Black Scottsdale Mystery Series.

Scottsdale Shuffle

Chapter One

Most people love October in Scottsdale. The brutal summer temperatures have started to fade into memory and the paradise weather Scottsdale is known for returns. While most of the country is bracing for the first snows of winter, October temperatures in Scottsdale are still comfortably in the eighties and nineties.

October is also the unofficial start of Snowbird Season and I'm not thrilled when it rolls around each year. I think of the summer heat as a protective shield, keeping out the hordes of winter visitors in their huge cars and RV's.

I know traffic will get bad, I'll have to get to the movies an extra fifteen minutes early to get a good seat, and any decent restaurant in the city will again require a reservation. Prices across The Valley will again go up, in some cases, two or three times what they were.

I think I prefer summer.

~~~~

It was Monday afternoon. I was sitting in my car doing surveillance on a cheating spouse when my phone rang with Rihanna's song *S & M*.

"Hey, Laura," Sophie said when I answered. "Hate to do this, but Lenny wants you to come in for a meeting."

"What's it about?"

"I think he wants to give you and Gina an assignment."

"But I already have an assignment."

"Well, I guess now you've got two. You know how this works. It's feast or famine. Now that everybody's coming back into town, it's going to start getting busy again."

"Fine, when does he want us there?"

"Right away. Gina's already here, so we're waiting on you."

"It's not another cheating spouse, is it? I'm starting to lose faith in humanity."

"I don't think so. Lenny had the client in this morning, and she's here again now for the follow-up meeting. She doesn't look like the jealous wife type."

"What *does* she look like?"

"Indiana Jones."

"Seriously? Okay, I'll be there in fifteen minutes. I've always wanted to meet Indiana Jones."

~~~~

"Gold?" Sophie asked. "Really? How much gold are we talking about?"

"Don't know," Gina responded. "But she said she found a nugget of solid gold the size of her finger."

I'd walked up to the front reception area in time to listen to Sophie and Gina in the middle of a discussion.

"Did she happen to say if there was more than only the one big nugget?" Sophie asked.

"Well," Gina said, "she didn't directly come out and say it, but she certainly implied there could be."

"That's good enough for me," Sophie said. "When are we going up to get it?"

"We're going up to get nuggets of gold?" I asked. "Really? Where are we going to get them?"

"The Lost Dutchman Mine," Sophie said.

"What?" I asked. "You mean the mythical mine in the Superstition Mountains that's supposed to be loaded with gold? Everyone knows it doesn't exist. People have been looking for it for hundreds of years."

"Well," Sophie said, "the woman who's in with Lenny says she's found it."

I gave Sophie my best skeptical look, making it look even more skeptical by raising an eyebrow.

"Fine," Sophie said, "If you don't believe me, ask Gina. She was in the office this morning when the client told Lenny she'd found it."

I turned my skeptical look toward Gina.

"Well, yes, she did say she'd found a cave, and there was at least one big piece of solid gold in it. She wants to know if she can officially place a claim on it so that she can legally take possession of the gold. Look, I'm as skeptical as you are about this. I've been hearing about the Lost Dutchman Mine all my life, and it seems every few years somebody new says they've found it."

"Well, Lenny wants you both to meet with the client when he's done talking to her," Sophie said, glancing over at the closed door to Lenny's office. "She's still in there, listening while Lenny tells her how much this all will cost. Maybe she'll tell us about the gold mine, too."

"Okay," Gina said. "I'll be back at my cube. Let me know when Lenny's ready for us."

Gina took off to the back, and I flopped down on one of the wing chairs next to Sophie's desk.

"Did you say you're working on a cheating spouse today?" Sophie asked. "Is this the aerobics instructor one? I'm still behind on my paperwork. What's the story?"

"The wife thinks he's having an affair with his aerobics instructor. She's found some suggestive notes and emails, not enough for proof, but enough to make her suspect. He also never wants to have sex with her on the days he goes to the gym."

"I didn't know anyone still did aerobics. Didn't that fade out about the time we were in high school? Besides, a married guy not wanting sex with his wife doesn't seem like such a big deal. From what I've heard, most married guys only want sex once or twice a week anyway."

"According to the wife, this guy's been a steady five or six times a week since they got married. Over the past couple of months, it's down to twice a week and never on a Monday, Wednesday, or a Friday. The wife put two and two together and figured out her husband is having sex with the aerobics instructor on the days he goes to her classes."

"Well?"

"Well, I followed him to the gym, and I had someone from the membership department walk me around while he was in class. And I guess you're right. They're called fitness instructors now, and the class he's taking is called Guerrilla Bootcamp or something like that. But to me, it looked a lot like an aerobics class. After that, I sat in the lobby until class was over, and he left."

"Did he have sex with her?"

"I don't see how he could have. The class must have had fifteen or twenty people in it. Everyone left the classroom at the same time and went into the locker rooms. My guy was dressed and left the club within about fifteen or twenty minutes."

"Did they get together after he came out? Maybe they snuck over to her place or something?"

"That's what I was thinking, too, but he got in his car and drove straight to his office. I was still in his office parking lot when you called me. It's possible they're meeting after work somewhere, but then they could meet any day of the week. Why is it only Mondays, Wednesdays, and Fridays he isn't interested in his wife? I'm thinking maybe I'll need to spend all day Wednesday following him around."

"You've been quiet about Max the past few days. Did you two get a chance to go out over the weekend?"

"No," I said, still feeling grumpy about it. "We made plans for Saturday, but he had to cancel. Something happened at work."

"So, what's going on with you two? You dated Reno for almost a year, and that whole thing crapped out. I guess that's what happens when you let Gina set you up with a cop. Then you finally hooked up with Max for a weekend, and now it's been a whole lot of nothing."

"I don't know. We spent the entire weekend together in San Diego last month. But now I'm lucky if I see him once a week. When we do get together, it's usually only a quick dinner over at the Tropical Paradise. Tony isn't coming back anytime soon, and Max's workload keeps growing. He gets to work every day by eight, and he's at the office most nights until ten or eleven."

"You mean you haven't been, um, together with him, except for the one weekend?"

"Well, I wouldn't say that. There are advantages to meeting in a hotel, even if it's only for a quick dinner. Lots of nice rooms at your disposal."

"You're such a bad girl. I imagine being head of the local mafia is a lot of work. Why doesn't Max hire some people and delegate that stuff, like all those rich CEOs do? You never see Mark Zuckerberg sitting behind a desk with piles of reports to sort through. He has staff to do that."

"When I asked Max about letting someone else take on part of the workload, he said he didn't want to make a lot of major staffing moves that Tony would need to switch around when he comes back. Mostly, I think it's because Max is very detail-oriented, and I don't think he wants to have anyone else making decisions. It's a big company, and it's keeping him busy."

"Yeah, but too busy for you?"

"I'm hoping it'll get better after Tony comes back."

"How's he doing? He went from being the boss of the largest crime family in Arizona to being shot and in rehab."

"He's doing great, considering Carlos the Butcher almost killed him. He's out of the wheelchair part of the time and starting to walk with a cane. He's still slow, but he's getting better every time I see him."

"Was he pissed when he found out you blew up his car?"

Thinking about my beautiful convertible brought instant feelings of sadness and anger. "I didn't blow up his car. Colonel Wu did. Tony said not to worry about it. These things happen."

"You know, at this rate, you could have stayed with Reno and still have gone out with Max on the side."

"I couldn't do that. I felt guilty when I kissed Max. I wasn't going to try to juggle two boyfriends. I don't know how you do it. You've dated Milo for nine months, and you've been with

Snake since the summer."

"It's not hard, all you have to do is tell them up front you aren't going to be exclusive. Most guys take it as a challenge to make me so happy I won't want to be with anyone else."

"Is that still working?"

"Pretty much. Saturday, I was with Milo. We drove over to the Boyce Thompson Arboretum, out by Globe."

"How was it? I haven't been there since my fifth-grade class took a field trip."

"It was nice. I'd like to go back sometime. Milo seemed to know all about the history of the place, and he knew the names of most of the trees there. For a hired henchman, he keeps surprising me."

"What about Snake? Have you been spending time with him too?"

"He had a game in Glendale yesterday. Snake was able to get me a ticket, so I went. If he could have gotten two tickets, I would have asked you to come along, too. But since he's only the third-string quarterback, the number of free seats he gets is kinda limited."

"How was the game? Did he get to play?"

"Well, the Cardinals won, but Snake didn't play. He's only been in for three plays all year. The starting quarterback took a hit in the first quarter and left the game. If he'd gotten a concussion, it would have maybe given Snake a chance to go in for at least a few plays if the second-string quarterback also went down. Unfortunately, the starter wasn't severely injured and was back in by the third quarter."

"That's a shame."

"Yeah, but Snake and I went out after the game so that part was nice."

"How was it being at the game with all of the football wives?"

"It kinda sucked. It was sorta like being with the cougars, but these women aren't so nice. There's a pecking order based on how much money their husbands got in their last contract. All the wives of the big-money players formed a group. Then there was a group of the wives of the guys who were starting but don't make as much."

"That doesn't sound so great."

"It wasn't. I ended up with the wife of the backup kicker. He's only been in for one play this year, so Snake has him beat. Unfortunately, she's from South Africa, and I hardly understood a word she said the entire game."

The door to Lenny's office opened. He stuck his head out and looked at us. "Where's Gina?"

"She's in the back," I said.

"Well, go get her and come in. Sophie, you'd better come in too and take notes, in case there are any more names. I always get lost after three or four names in a new case."

~~~~

We gathered Gina and went into Lenny's office. The client had a drink in her hand, and she stood while Lenny made introductions.

She was pretty much as Sophie had described her. She was tall, athletic, and outdoorsy-looking, and her age was somewhere between the late thirties and early forties.

She was wearing dusty brown boots, light brown cargo pants, a khaki shirt with big front pockets, and a brown leather vest. I'm not sure if she was going for the Indiana Jones look or not, but she had it nailed.

"Professor Parker," Lenny said, "you've already met Gina.

This is Laura, who's another one of our investigators, and Sophia, who's our paralegal. Ladies, this is Professor Parker from the archeology department at Arizona State. We'll be helping her work out some issues around a discovery she's made in the Superstition Mountains."

The woman held out her hand, and we shook.

"It's Mindy," she said, "and I'm only an Assistant Professor. It's sort of an honorary title they give to postdocs if they continue to hang out at the university after they get their Ph.D.'s."

I got a chance to look at her while she was talking. Her reddish-blonde hair was parted down the middle and hung to her shoulders. She was using her ears to keep it from falling into her face.

The only makeup she wore was around her eyes, which were partially hidden behind a pair of big black glasses. She had a lot of sun freckles on her face, something I've seen a lot growing up in Arizona.

She seemed a little out of sorts at being in an attorney's office. A lot of clients seem to feel nervous as they start off on a legal process. I think it's one of the reasons Lenny always gives them drinks. We all sat in front of Lenny's desk, and he began to fill us in.

"Dr. Parker seems to have made a rather important archeological discovery in the Superstition Mountains. She's come to us to help her obtain a legal claim to it."

"Did you really find the Lost Dutchman Mine?" Sophie asked.

"Well, maybe," Mindy said. "But if it isn't the actual Lost Dutchman, it's probably close enough not to make a difference."

"Professor," Lenny said, "I'm sorry, but I'm originally

from New Jersey. I've heard of the mine, but I don't know a lot about it. Could you give us the short version?"

"Well, the Spanish have been exploring the area since 1540. That's when a Spanish explorer named Coronado led an expedition of two thousand men along the Arizona-New Mexico border to search for Cíbola, a land with seven cities of gold. If we skip forward a couple of centuries, the first hard evidence of the mine's existence was in 1748 when the Superstition Mountains were given to a Mexican cattle baron, Don Miguel Peralta of Sonora. The land reportedly not only contained a rich gold mine but several silver mines as well. The last official mention of the mine was in 1847, when a descendant of Don Miguel Peralta led an expedition into Arizona. After taking as much gold as could be carried, the group reportedly concealed the entrance to the mine and then began to make their way back to Mexico. The group was attacked, supposedly by the Apache. Most of the group members were killed, and the gold was scattered. The area where they were killed is now referred to as the Massacre Grounds."

"I hiked the Massacre Grounds trail with a group back in college," Gina said. "We only got as far as the waterfall. Then, no one wanted to go any further. I didn't know it had anything to do with the Lost Dutchman mine."

"Ever since the massacre," Mindy continued, "several people claim to have found the location of the mine. The last credible tale was in the 1870's. Jacob Waltz was a German prospector who was apparently shown the location of the mine by an Apache woman he was dating. He spent the next several years coming down from the mountains with large solid nuggets and high-grade gold ore, but he died without telling anyone the mine's location. Locals began calling it the Deutsch-man's Mine, Deutsch meaning German. Of course, over the years, it simply became the Lost Dutchman's Mine."

"How many times have you been there?" Lenny asked.

"Twice, so far. When I originally found the cave, it was late in the day, and I didn't have more than about twenty minutes to look around. Last week, I spent several hours in the cave, performing mineral surveys and gathering samples. This is an example of what I've managed to find so far. I would assume there's more."

She reached into her pocket and pulled out a shiny piece of gold, about twice as wide as my thumb and as long as my index finger. She held it out, and I took it.

It was surprisingly heavy for something that wasn't very big. I passed it to Gina, who carefully examined it, then gave it to Sophie.

I could see the look of excitement on her face as she felt how heavy it was. After holding it for about ten seconds, Sophie reluctantly placed it on Lenny's desk.

"How valuable is something like that?" Gina asked.

"The piece is a little over ten troy ounces," Mindy said. "In terms of the gold itself, it's about thirteen thousand dollars. But the value to a museum of having a nugget pulled from the Lost Dutchman Mine would likely make it much higher. ASU has an archeology museum, and I can envision a themed exhibit with twenty or thirty items in it."

There was a brief stillness in the office as everyone looked down at the lump of solid gold. It was strange, but hearing about the gold mine and holding the nugget in my hand seemed to awaken something in me that spoke of adventure and the possibility of sudden wealth.

"Ordinarily," Lenny said, breaking the silence, "obtaining a mineral claim would be a straightforward process. But since the area you're describing has been taken out of public use, we'll need to acquire a treasure-trove permit from the U.S.

Forest Service. That will allow you to dig in the wilderness area. However, those aren't granted without verifiable evidence for what will be recovered. In other words, you basically must show them what you're planning on digging up before they'll consider granting you permission to do so. Even with the permit, anything taken out of the wilderness area would likely remain property of the government."

"It's funny," Mindy said. "I've spent years tracking down the mine, and it turns out the most difficult part will be the paperwork."

"Have you told anyone else about this discovery?" Lenny asked.

"I've started a petition through the university for an archeological site to be established, so my thesis advisor, Professor Babcock, and the department chairman know about it. Fortunately, setting up a dig site is pretty common, and I was a little vague about what I hoped to find there. Since the university is a state agency, they have a lot of authority when it comes to permitting, even in a wilderness area. I've only told a few close colleagues what I've found, but honestly, everyone in the department knows I've spent years hunting around the Superstitions for treasures, particularly for one called the Lost Sister."

"What's that?" Lenny asked.

"It's one of seven gold statues stolen from a temple in southern Mexico back in the 1520s. I've been doing research where I hope to show that the Lost Sister is the source of the original curse legend of the Superstition Mountains. But it's a long story and may not have anything to do with what I've found in the cave."

"It would be best if you don't mention this to anyone else until we can establish some legal rights to it," Lenny said. "As part of gathering the verifiable evidence for the permit, it would be helpful if we went up to confirm what you've found. We can then provide an independent validation of your story. The contract we've both already signed contains a non-disclosure clause, so anything we learn from you must be held strictly confidential."

"Alright," Mindy said. "Why don't we meet early tomorrow morning? That way, we can get up to the cave before it gets too hot. The first part of the hike is an easy public trail, but the last part is steep and rocky. I'd suggest we leave here by five-thirty."

Lenny looked at Gina. "Tomorrow will be tough," she said. "I'm booked until at least three o'clock, maybe four."

Lenny then looked at me, and I nodded my head. "I shouldn't have any activity on the aerobics instructor until Wednesday. That leaves tomorrow free. Of course, for something like this, I could probably use some extra help." I looked over at Sophie, raising both of my eyebrows this time. When Lenny didn't object, Sophie perked up.

"Well, I'm up for it," she said. "I've never been inside a mythical gold mine before."

"Great," Mindy said. She then started counting items on her fingers. "Bring some sturdy hiking boots, a broad-brim hat, a bicycle helmet, a day-pack, and a couple of big water bottles for each of you. Stop by a sporting goods store and get a light you can clip onto your helmet. Oh, and bring some leather gloves. It will make the hike easier, and when we get up to the cave, we're going to need to move some rocks."

~~~~

Sophie and I drove to the Walmart at Pima and Chaparral. We went down the list and picked up the bicycle helmets, gloves, hats, water bottles, and clip-on lights.

I already had a daypack, but Sophie got a new one. I also

remembered to get a fresh bottle of sunscreen and a small first aid kit. We then made sure to put everything on Lenny's credit card.

"I love gearing up for an adventure," Sophie said. "I'm not sure about the helmets, though. They sort of give off a creepy danger vibe."

"I'm thinking more about the hike tomorrow," I said. "It's been years since I've crawled around on the mountains. I'll need to dig out my old hiking boots."

"Thanks for reminding me. I'll need to stop by somewhere tonight and get some boots to hike in. I don't think Professor Mindy will be impressed if I show up in my old cross trainers."

~~~~

I dropped Sophie off at the office and then headed back towards my apartment. I stopped by a Filiberto's drive-through and got a carne asada burrito and a bag of warm tortilla chips. The grilled steak filled my car with a wonderful aroma, and I munched on the bag of chips the entire way home.

I walked into my apartment and placed the sack on the coffee table in front of my couch when my phone rang with the old Eurythmics song *Would I Lie to You?* It took me a moment to place the ringtone.

I then remembered it was Danielle's. My stomach tightened, and I suddenly wasn't hungry anymore.

I debated whether I should answer it or not. She'd likely want to set up another in a series of meetings where she and I would be negotiating the terms of an agreement between the Black Death and Tony's organization.

Now that work was starting to get busy again, I really didn't have time for another meeting. Unfortunately, Danielle was the secret head of the Black Death.

I couldn't stop the bad news, and delaying always made it

worse. I hit the accept button.

"Laura," Danielle said, "I really need your help. I need somewhere I can hide for a couple of days where no one can find me. I know this is a terrible imposition, but can I stay at your place?"

What?

"How can you even ask something like that? Don't you remember how you left me to die in a torture chamber at the hands of that sick fuck Raul? Why do you think I'd want to help you?"

"I know we have some history, but you're the only person in Arizona I can trust with this. I found out this afternoon that Sergio's trying to kill me."

As she was talking, I realized her voice was shaking, and it sounded like she was crying.

"Okay," I said. "Start at the beginning."

"Sergio thinks I want to remove him as head of the group. I found out he's going to have me killed and make it look like Tough Tony did it. Sergio not only wants to consolidate his power in the Black Death, but he also wants to use my execution as a pretext to wipe out Tony, Max, and their entire organization."

I'm so going to regret this.

"Where can I meet you?" I asked.

"I'm in the parking lot at Tempe Beach Park."

It figures.

"Okay, I know where you are. Stay there, and I'll be down in twenty minutes."

Despite my twisting stomach, I still took three or four bites of the burrito before wrapping it up and popping it into the fridge.

~~~~

When I pulled into Tempe Beach Park, I found Danielle's white Camaro convertible, but she wasn't in it. I parked and walked down toward the lake.

The sun was sitting low in the west, reminding me of the last time I was here, saying goodbye to Digga. I found Danielle on a stone bench underneath a mesquite tree, overlooking the water.

Three teams of rowers were practicing, and she watched them glide across the lake. Next to her on the bench was a big black bag.

It reminded me a lot of Gabriella's bag and I imagine Danielle had a similar arsenal in hers. I walked over to the bench and sat next to her.

"I'm sorry," she quietly said. "Maybe I shouldn't have called you. I know you hate me, and I understand why. But I didn't know who else I could turn to. Sophie doesn't know who I really am, and I don't want to get her involved in the Black Death."

"I don't hate you," I said. "But you did hurt me, and I was almost killed because of you. I thought we were friends, and then everything happened."

Danielle looked up. Her eyes were red, and she looked terrible. She was about to speak when I held up my hand and stopped her.

"You can stay at my place," I said. "I'm not sure why, but we seem to be stuck with each other. I don't want to see anything happen to you."

Danielle didn't say anything, but tears began to roll down her face. Overcome with an emotion I couldn't describe, I held out my arms, and Danielle fell against me, sobbing.

~~~~

At my suggestion, Danielle dropped her car off in long-term parking at Sky Harbor. She hadn't had dinner yet, so we stopped off at Carolina's Mexican.

Even though I still had most of a burrito in the fridge at home, I got a shredded beef burrito, enchilada-style, with green chili sauce. I then dumped several cups of their wonderful salsa over the top of it.

Neither Danielle nor I said a lot as we ate.

~~~~

After dinner, I drove back to my place. We took the elevator to the third floor and then walked down the hall to my apartment.

I was pulling the keys out of my bag when Grandma Peckham's door opened, and she stuck her head out.

"Well, Laura," she said. "I thought I heard you coming down the hall."

Grandma stopped short when she saw Danielle standing next to me. She looked at Danielle, then at me, and then back at Danielle.

"Laura, I didn't think you had a sister," Grandma said, sounding confused.

"Oh, no, I don't," I said. "This is Danielle. She's, um, my cousin from New Mexico. I haven't seen her in years, and she'll be here for a few days."

"It's good to meet you," Grandma said. "I'm Mary Peckham, but everyone here calls me Grandma. I've been Laura's neighbor since she moved in. We seem to share a cat, and Laura's been helping me with dating advice. Speaking of that, I really need your help with this one. Grandpa Bob proposed to me last night."

"Wow," I said. "That's good news, right?"

"Well, I'm not sure. I really don't want to give up my independence, but I also don't know if I want to live alone for the rest of my life."

"Did you give him an answer?"

"Not yet. I told him I'd need to sleep on it. We're going out on Sunday to meet his kids, so that gives me a few days to decide."

~~~~

I opened the door to my apartment and showed Danielle around. I had some extra sheets, so we made the couch into a bed. I'd often slept on the couch, so I knew it should be comfortable for her.

I went to my junk drawer and pulled out the spare apartment key. As soon as I gave it to Danielle, I knew I'd need to rekey the lock as soon as she moved out.

"I need to be at the office by five-thirty tomorrow morning, so I'll be up early. I'll do my best not to wake you, but I'm not used to having anyone in the apartment. I'm not sure when I'll be back tomorrow night. There isn't a lot of food, so you'll probably have to go out and get something. There's a market two blocks to the north and a bunch of fast-food places on Scottsdale Road. They might already be looking for you, so pay with cash. They might be able to trace your credit cards."

"Um, cash?" Danielle stammered.

"No cash?"

"After I found out about Sergio's plans to murder me today, I just left. I have a few dollars in my purse, but that's it. I have money in my bank account, but if you think they could trace the transaction, I shouldn't use my card anywhere around here."

318

I dug into my purse and pulled out forty dollars. "This should keep you going until tomorrow night. When I get home, we can drive somewhere and hit up an ATM."

As Danielle flipped through channels on the TV, I spent a few minutes pulling labels off the water bottles, the clip-on light, and the bike helmet. I then filled and tossed both water bottles in the freezer.

I said goodnight and went into the bedroom. I closed the door and felt annoyed that it didn't have a lock.

I tried to think of a better hiding place for my jewelry other than the box at the top of the closet, but there was nowhere that would be safe if Danielle decided to ransack my room. I briefly considered putting something heavy against the door for the night, but in the end, I left it alone.

~~~~

I crawled into bed and started to get comfortable when my phone rang with the theme to *The Love Boat*.

"Hey, you," I said to Max when I answered. "I wasn't sure if you'd be able to call tonight. How's your week starting?"

"It's been busy," he said. As always, hearing his deep and powerful voice both relaxed and excited me. "It's after ten, and I'm only now starting to pack up for the night."

"I'm sure Tony appreciates what you're doing."

"He does, but you know how much I'm looking forward to him returning to work. These long hours are starting to wear me down. What's been going on today with you?"

"Well, nothing so far on the cheating spouse, but I'm hoping for a breakthrough on Wednesday. It also looks like I've got a new assignment. This one involves a gold mine."

"Really? We should trade jobs for a day or two. All I'm doing tonight is reviewing financial statements."

"I'll take the gold mine. When can we see each other? I'm still disappointed the weekend didn't work out."

"So am I. Right now, it looks like Wednesday for dinner is a possibility. What do you think?"

"I think dinner would be a good start for the evening. Think there'll be time for anything other than dinner? Don't forget, we're a couple now, even if you're only my secret boyfriend. That comes with certain, um, responsibilities on your part."

"I can't wait to fulfill my responsibilities. We need to plan an actual weekend. It's already been a month since we were in San Diego. This weekend doesn't look good, but what about the next?"

"Well, you know my schedule, but yes, let's plan on it. Do you have anywhere in mind?"

"No, but I'm currently in charge of some of the best resorts in Arizona. I'm sure I can find us a room someplace."

About the Author

Halfway through a successful career in technical writing, marketing, and sales, along with having four beautiful children, author B A Trimmer veered into fiction. Combining a love of the desert derived from many years of living in Arizona with an appreciation of the modern romantic detective story, the Scottsdale Series was born.

Comments and questions are always welcome.

E-mail the author at LauraBlackScottsdale@gmail.com

Follow at www.facebook.com/ScottsdaleSeries/

www.ingramcontent.com/pod-product-compliance
Lightning Source LLC
Chambersburg PA
CBHW021446240626
47153CB00001B/317

* 9 781951 052065 *